Last Temptation

Last Temptation

MICHELLE STIMPSON

KENSINGTON PUBLISHING CORP.
www.kensingtonbooks.com

DAFINA BOOKS are published by

Kensington Publishing Corp.
119 West 40th Street
New York, NY 10018

All Kensington titles, imprints, and distributed lines are available at special quantity discounts for bulk purchases for sales promotion, premiums, fund-raising, educational, or institutional use.

Special book excerpts or customized printings can also be created to fit specific needs. For details, write or phone the office of the Kensington Special Sales Manager: Kensington Publishing Corp., 119 West 40th Street, New York, NY 10018. Attn. Special Sales Department. Phone: 1-800-221-2647.

Dafina and the Dafina logo Reg. U.S. Pat. & TM Off.

ISBN-13: 978-0-7582-4686-8
ISBN-10: 0-7582-4686-2

First Kensington Trade Paperback Printing: November 2010

10 9 8 7 6 5 4 3 2

Printed in the United States of America

For all my sisters in Christ. We are so loved!

ACKNOWLEDGMENTS

Thank You, Father, for the gift of writing. When it seemed I didn't have anyone or anything else for a while there, writing became my gift from You. Everything that comes from You is so good!

Special thanks to the book clubs who have supported me by reading my books and spreading the word. What would authors do without book clubs?

Special thanks to Lena Nelson-Dooley and the crew of writers who meet at her house weekly—especially the southwest crew: Jane, Kellie, Lynne, and Janice. Your literary eyes and loving hearts are greatly appreciated. To all those friends who read my work and tear it up, thanks so much. I'd rather be torn up by you guys than by the critics any day!

Much love to my Anointed Authors on Tour Sisters: Kendra Norman-Bellamy, Tia McCollors, Vanessa Miller, Shewanda Riley, Dr. Vivi Monroe-Congress, and Norma Jarrett-York. Slowly but surely, our dreams are coming true. It's so nice to have you all—writers understand writers, you know? And to all the other writers and aspiring writers who pour into me and allow me to reciprocate—let's keep sowing and reaping!

Thanks for the support from my church—Oak Cliff Bible Fellowship, the bookstore (Terri and Brenda), and the church's book club (thanks, Garretta).

Sara Camilli, my agent, you're just plain old good people.

And thanks to Selena James at Kensington for seeing the promise of this book and many more.

To my family. It's so nice to turn off my computer at the end of my work day and just "be" with you three. Stevie, Steven, and Kalen—thanks for surrounding me with so much love.

Chapter 1

Quinn's proposal was not a big surprise. Actually, it was one of those "it's about time" moments. We'd been dating exclusively for almost eighteen months, and those karats were long overdue, in my book. I believe in taking my time, but my body doesn't. Any Christian woman can be celibate when she's single, but throw a six-foot-tall, chocolate brown brother with a sharp goatee *and* a good job in the mix . . . hmph, a sister is liable to get all shook up. Yes, Quinn was a wonderful man who loved the Lord, loved me, and treated my eight-year-old son, Eric, like his own. The faith was there, the love was there, the Lord was there. But I won't lie—my flesh was so weak for Quinn I thought I was gonna have to go on eBay and find me a chastity belt.

So when he finally popped the question by calling me out and proposing onstage after the local college's production of *A Raisin in the Sun* (which he directed), I breathed a sigh of relief. Finally, the wait was over.

Don't get me wrong: The single life was good while it lasted. There's nothing like being able to do what you want to do, when you want to do it, how you want to do it. But that gets old after a while—thirty-four years, in my case. I suppose if my best friend, LaShondra, were still single, it wouldn't be so bad. And if Deniessa, my friend and former coworker, hadn't married that good and throwed-off Jamal last year, I would at least have someone to watch *The Best Man* with. Well, now it was my turn to join the ranks of married women and start the next chapter in my life. *Thank you, Lord.*

The first person I called with notice of my nuptials was LaShondra. She and I had been through thick and thin, good and bad, even black and white since she ran off and married a white man. Let me take that back. She didn't "run off," but her husband *is* white, and I was not expecting my girl to cross that line. I ain't hatin', though. Stelson is good people. He took some getting used to, but I'm over it now.

I hooked my cell phone up to the Bluetooth and selected her name from the radio display. "Hey, girl," I squealed when she answered the phone, "we've got a wedding on the way!"

LaShondra screamed, "He finally did it?"

"Yes, girl," I said with a big exhale. "We're looking at the first Saturday in July."

"Congratulations! Ooh—we've got, what, six months to pull this off—in July?" I knew LaShondra was already planning things out in her head. "You told your momma yet? You called the church yet?"

"No, I called you first, girl. You know I have to get your blessing."

"Pulleeze." She laughed. "Quinn is a good man. I've always liked him. He's a Christian, he treats you well, he's good with Eric. What's there to discuss?"

I sighed. "I guess I just had to ask you for the record, so if something goes wrong I can be like 'You da one who tole me to marry him!'"

"Don't even talk like that, Peaches. What God has joined together, let no man—or Peaches—put asunder. This is God's doing and you know it. Who else could match you up with the one man in the world who could get past your mouth and your attitude to find the real you?"

"I do not have an attitude!" I screamed. The woman in the next car gave me a confused look. I ignored her.

"Is this Patricia Miller I'm talking to? Oh, wait, I'm sorry. This must be the new and improved Patricia *Robertson*. My bad."

We both laughed at her enunciation of my soon-to-be last name. We ended the conversation with plans to meet Saturday and discuss the happy, snappy wedding. My second call was to my mother, who almost started speaking in tongues. "Oh, my baby! Finally! The Lord blessed you with a husband and Eric with a father!"

"Momma, Eric has a father," I reminded her. Raphael wouldn't win any Father-of-the-Year awards, but he'd been spending more time with our son and he was finally caught up on child support. I had to give him some kind of credit even though I suspected his fiancée, Cheryl, had shamed him into doing right by his child.

Next, I called Deniessa. I expected her to be ecstatic, but her response was more dramatic than anything. She busted out crying. I mean, boo-hooing. "Oh, Peaches, I just hope your marriage is a million times better than mine. I want the best for you, girl. Somebody gotta be happy, you know?"

Okay, what am I supposed to say to that—better you sad than me? "Girl, what's *really* going on? Why are you trippin'?"

She pulled in a nasty, snot-filled sniff that almost made me disconnect her from my phone. "Go blow your nose!"

"I'm sorry," she apologized. "Marriage is so overrated. People don't understand—I feel like I'm doing hard time here."

I imagine it *is* hard when you're married to a fool. *Lord, don't let me say that.* I was tired of dealing with Deniessa's drama, but I couldn't say so. After all, I was the main one cheering her down the aisle. Matter of fact, I was cheering everybody down the aisle, hoping to keep the line moving so it would be my turn soon.

I searched my mind for one of those good old standby Christian clichés to soothe her pain. All I could come up with was, "Prayer changes things." I said it in an old, deep, soulful tone—like Sofia in *The Color Purple* would say it—for effect.

Deniessa didn't buy it. "Not if the person you're praying for is an absolute idiot."

I was not in the mood to go down that road with her. It always led back around to point A: She married someone she had been living with for three years. The only reason he even asked her to marry him was because she gave him an ultimatum. I can't blame Jamal—he knew which side his bread was buttered on. He had to do *something,* because it gets cold out there on them streets, I hear.

"Girl, I'll be praying for you. How about me, you, and LaShondra get together this weekend and do one of our girls' movie nights?" I offered. I knew it was a long shot—those two had all but kicked girls' nights to the curb since they jumped the broom.

She sniffed again. "I don't know. I have to see. Jamal is using my car right now."

"Is he working a night shift?" I asked.

"No. He still hasn't found anything yet. But he might need the car Saturday night. I just have to ask."

The words flew straight from my brain out of my mouth before I could catch them. "How you gotta ask to use your own car if he ain't got no job?" I could have bopped myself on the head for fueling the hot mess already flaming in their marriage.

"You tell me." She could only laugh at herself.

I shook my head. "I gotta go, girl. Forgive me for adding my two cents to y'all's business. Let me know if you want to come Saturday night. I'll come pick you up if you need me to. I'm sure LaShondra won't mind taking you home."

"Thank you," she said. "I'll let you know."

I ended the call with Deniessa but continued the conversation with myself and my Father. "Lord, if I *ever* let Quinn use me like that, just take me on home to glory."

I talked myself all the way to Raphael's house to pick up Eric. By the time I got there, I had strengthened my resolve not to lose myself in my husband like I had seen so many married women do in my last, say, fifteen years of marrying off friends and relatives. It's like something clicks in their heads and they lose all sense of identity, all sense of independence, sometimes all sense *period.*

I had to give it to my girl LaShondra—she kept moving up in the school district and trying to get where she wanted to be even after she got married. She kept her house; she rents it out. The only thing she didn't keep, which surprised me, was her last name.

"It's not like Smith is a distinctive last name," she had said.

"Neither is Brown! But Smith-Brown—now *that* sounds important."

"Sounds like a law firm," she had said, giggling.

"Like I said—important. LaShondra Smith-Brown. She don't play. She will sue your behind any day." I'd acted it out as though on a low-budget commercial. She had laughed at me in one of those condescending you-wouldn't-understand-because-you're-not-married laughs. I just rolled my eyes at her. Nonetheless, she dropped the Smith and went straight to Brown. Something I sure wasn't about to do, no matter how plain-Jane Miller is for a last name.

Still building my mental list of marital dos and don'ts, I rang Raphael's doorbell and waited patiently for either Raphael or Cheryl to answer the door of their one-story home in one of the older, more crime-ridden areas of Dallas. I had some reservations about letting Eric spend the weekend with his father in this neighborhood, but once somebody got mugged in broad daylight right outside my condo, I said, whatever.

Besides, I figured Eric could use a little "hood" in his life. There's nothing like a good game of baseball in the hood with first base a shoe, second base somebody's car, third base a fire hydrant, and home plate a flattened plastic milk jug to prove that you can be happy with next to nothing.

Raphael opened the door and Eric squeezed past his father's frame to give me a tight hug. "Hey, son," I said as I rubbed my hand across his head. Apparently, Raphael had taken him to get a haircut—without being asked! That was one for the record books.

"Uh." Raphael rudely burped. "Is that a ring on your finger?"

"Yes, it is." I beamed, making note of the mixed expression on Raphael's face. I couldn't tell if he was about to congratulate me or say something sarcastic, so I gave Eric orders to get in the car.

"I'm getting married in July to Quinn. You met him at Eric's school awards ceremony," I reminded him.

Raphael nodded. "Yeah, I remember him. July? Why so soon?" He crossed his arms, looking down from his towering stance. If I could get up on a stool, I might be able to prove he was balding. The hard years of drinking and womanizing had caused him to age quickly. Still, he was good-looking, and I truly hoped that our son would grow up to be as handsome as his father.

"Because we're in love," I replied. "And we're not getting any younger."

Then came his true concern. "You're not planning to take my son away from me, are you?"

I rolled my eyes in disbelief. "You know me better than that."

He let his defenses fall to his side along with his arms. Something in me said, *awww . . . he loves our son.* I almost felt sorry for the poor chap, bless his sorry heart. But it had taken me eight long years, several hours on hold for the attorney general's office, and countless prayers to get Raphael right where I wanted him and Eric needed him. This was *my* victory, not Raphael's.

"Well, congratulations," he muttered.

"Thank you."

And loud silence transpired. I gave Raphael a quick smile before saying, "Good-bye."

His lips said, "Good-bye," but I could tell that he wanted to say something more. Finally, he stepped outside of his house, closed the door behind him, and said softly, "Quinn is a lucky man."

You could have bought me for a quarter.

Raphael turned and went back into the house.

"Thank you?" I whispered after he was long gone.

I drove home halfway listening to my son talk about his weekend and halfway wondering what on earth had gotten into one Mr. Raphael Sadiq Lewis. Well, I suppose I *was* looking extra nice in my form-fitting skinny jeans and my red, stretchy, button-down blouse. And I had just gotten my short do shampooed and flat ironed, not to mention my freshly waxed eyebrows. I wasn't much for makeup, because my skin turned into a pimple factory with most foundations. My deep brown skin tone held its own and fell into a nice glow after five. It was well after five, so I knew I had to be looking good.

Too bad for Raphael. He could have had anything he wanted from me, once upon a time.

Chapter 2

I couldn't go anywhere in the building Monday without people congratulating me on the engagement. I must have gotten fifty e-mails from people: Best wishes! God bless your union! All kinds of mess from people who barely spoke to me at work. Who knew that getting engaged would suddenly make me a celebrity at Northcomp?

By ten o'clock I had to call LaShondra and ask a favor. "Could you please call Stelson and ask him what is the big deal with white people and engagements?"

"It's not a *white* thing, Peaches. They're just happy for you."

"No, no, no. This is a white thing, I'm telling you. Black folk don't get this excited over an engagement. I'm thirty-four and I've already got a child. I ain't no Cinderella."

"Hmmm." LaShondra thought out loud. "Have they been asking to see the ring?"

"Some of them have, but not too many."

"Have they asked to see his picture? You know, when Stelson and I were engaged, people always wanted to see his picture to confirm I was marrying a white man," she recalled.

"Let me assure you, nobody here thinks I would marry a white man," I replied in straight, loud monotone.

"Anyway!"

That's when I saw it. After wading through the numerous e-mail messages from employees whose names barely rang bells, I finally found the e-mail message from our company's CEO, George Hampton, which explained everything. I read it out loud to LaShondra. "Due to recent spikes in the price of gasoline, a sharp decline in sales, and a less-than-desirable review of productivity, we have determined that Northcomp must make cutbacks in order to remain a viable competitor for the technological dollar. The personnel office, led by Patricia Miller, in conjunction with our consultants, The Yancey Group, will be working to review assignments, job descriptions, and productivity goals. We anticipate these reviews will result in early retirement offers and reduced demand for human resources. We understand these changes present a difficult but necessary transition for Northcomp, and we look forward to solutions that are least disruptive for our company and our employees."

"Wow," LaShondra said. "You've got a tough job ahead of you."

"This is crazy!" I hollered.

"What's the problem?" LaShondra asked. I had to forgive her nonprofit-world ignorance. Since she was a principal in a public school, her politics were different from mine.

"That man just sent out an e-mail saying that Patricia Miller is going to be firing folks!"

"That's not what he said, Peaches."

"He might as well have. Don't you see, LaShondra? He's trying to make me out to be the executioner. He's trying to paint me as the bad guy!"

"The consultants will have input," she tried to reason.

I huffed one good time. "The consultants will be good and gone after the smoke clears. Half these consultant folks don't know what they're doing. They don't know our company—they're just paid to agree with me. This is a corporate nightmare!"

There was a gentle tap on my door, and a woman I remembered vaguely from a past interview stuck her head into my office. "Hold on, LaShondra," I said as I acknowledged this unplanned visitor.

"I just wanted to say congratulations—"

"I'm busy right now." I shooed her out with my hand. I just couldn't take the fakeness anymore. The woman's face was suddenly painted with disappointment as she ducked back and closed the door. My blinds were open enough for me to see her stand outside my door for a moment and collect herself. Was she . . . crying? Yes, she was breaking female corporate rule number one: Do NOT cry at work.

"LaShondra," I whispered, "this lady is crying outside of my office."

"What? Why?"

"She's crying because I wouldn't let her come in here and give me her bogus congratulations."

LaShondra fussed, "Maybe she really meant it."

"I'm gonna hang up the phone now, LaShondra. I'll call you later."

"Later, alligator. And stop being so mean."

I buzzed my secretary, Theresa, and told her not to let anyone else in my office without official business. Next, I called George and let him know that I felt, what did I say? "Awkward" about the wording in his e-mail.

George tried to act like he didn't understand my concern. "Patricia, I don't think the message will come across the way you've interpreted it." Yeah, right. Hampton informed me that if we could convince several of the senior employees to take early retirement, we would probably only have to release hourly employees who had been with the company less than two years. "Honestly, this is really more a precautionary measure than anything else."

I still didn't appreciate him making it seem like I was the mad black woman running around with the ax while he was the innocent CEO who couldn't be blamed for anyone's demise. Why couldn't he just blame it on the economy like every other company? No, he had to go put a name and a face on it.

My third call was to the Yancey people to see when they planned to come look over my shoulder while I figured out this whole mess. I was on hold so long with their answering service, I swear—there is only one Yancey. There is no group. It's just one old man who probably plays golf with Hampton on Saturday mornings who agreed to put his name on a few forms so that Hampton could go before the board pushing his own recommendations backed by this nitwit, nonexistent Yancey Group.

Okay, my attitude was bad that morning. Really bad. So when Quinn called and said he wanted to talk to me over lunch, I was not feeling him. "Baby, I really have a lot going on here today."

"I really need to talk to you," he reiterated. I heard a twang of sincerity in his voice, so I agreed to meet him at the Chili's nearest Northcomp. No matter what he had to say, I didn't have much time to hear it. I needed to get back to work and begin reviewing employees' files as soon as possible.

My man was so sexy in dark colors. He almost made me forget about all my troubles when he walked into the restaurant wearing black slacks and a deep indigo polo shirt pressed to a tee. I motioned for Quinn to join me at a small booth and took a moment to appreciate his confident strut. As an experienced man-watcher, I caught the glances of several women in the restaurant as they watched him, too.

He kissed me on the cheek before sitting down across from me. "You look beautiful."

"Thanks, babe. I saw an old lady in red checking you out," I teased him.

He smiled. "Can't do nothin' for her."

"I know that's right." I laughed. I took a glance at my watch and asked, "So what's up?"

He fidgeted for a moment, which was not really in his character. His gaze drifted to the ceramic tiles covering our table. I knew better than to think he'd had second thoughts about his proposal, so I assured him, "Whatever it is, we'll get through it."

"You think we can get through it in Philadelphia?" he blurted out.

I squinted my eyes and cocked my head to the side like what-you-talkin'-'bout-Willis?

He continued. "I just got the opportunity of a lifetime, Peaches. They want me to transfer to Philadelphia and head up the marketing department for the northeast region."

Quinn was all smiles. I was all shocked.

"What do you think, baby? You're always complaining about the Texas heat. Plus, Philly is only a few hours from New York. I could really get into the theaters there, baby."

"Everything is baby, I see," I snapped at him, raising an eyebrow.

"Peaches, I've worked long and hard for this, and I'm really looking forward to starting this new life with you. Just so happens we'll be doing it in Philadelphia, that's all. Oh, and did I mention the raise puts me in a new tax bracket!"

"Have you looked at the cost of living in Philadelphia versus Dallas?" I really didn't mean to burst his bubble, but how dare he just spring this on me.

"Even with the cost of living increase, it's more than worth it." He tried his best to make the proposition appealing.

Philadelphia, Lord? "I don't know, Quinn." I took a sip of the water that seemed to have suddenly appeared. I was so taken aback, I don't even remember a waiter approaching our table. "I can't just up and move to Philadelphia with you."

"You're making it sound like we just met. I'm your fiancé, Peaches, soon to be your husband. This is a great opportunity for me, you, and Eric. You wouldn't have to work right away. You could take a few years off. Have the baby right away if you want to," he suggested.

Where did that come from? We'd discussed having children and I was all for it, once we had settled into our marriage, which I figured would be a good three or four years down the line. Quinn was trying to switch up everything at the last minute. "I don't want to be no stay-at-home mom," I retorted. "I like working." Never mind the fact that my job was not the happiest place right now.

Quinn started saying something else about me taking some time off, maybe going back to school, but I wasn't hearing him. My mind was thinking about Eric now. About Raphael. I had all but promised Raphael I wouldn't try to take his son away. Philadelphia was definitely *away*. "I can't go, Quinn."

The vein in Quinn's forehead thickened as he ground his teeth and looked down at the menu. I knew that look all too well. I laughed slightly. "You've already committed to this, haven't you."

He looked up from the menu for a moment, then back down.

That was all I needed to see. "How can you just unilaterally make a decision about *my* life?"

"It's *our* lives," he stressed. "I've prayed about it and I believe it's the right move for us."

The waiter returned to our table and took our orders. My appetite was gone, but I needed to eat a salad, so I did what was best. Quinn ordered a lunch portion of chicken and pasta. He must have lost most of his appetite, too. I stewed over my anger as we waited for our food to arrive. When our plates were set in front of us, Quinn held out his hands, gesturing for prayer. I looked him upside his head and rolled my eyes to a close.

"Lord, we thank You for this food we're about to receive. Thank You for bringing this wonderful woman into my life. Father, guide us in making decisions that glorify You in this marriage and this family. In Jesus's name we pray, amen."

"Amen." The prayer had caused my anger to subside a notch. In my heart, I wanted to do the right thing—whatever that was. "Quinn, I'm not against this promotion for you. And I'm not against moving to Philadelphia, per se. I've worked hard for my position at Northcomp, too, you know." And I still had thirteen thousand dollars worth of student loans for that MBA to show it.

"And what about Eric? He's really starting to establish a relationship with his father now."

"I'm not trying to come between Eric and Raphael and I'm not trying to undermine your career. Eric is old enough to fly back to Dallas once a month for his weekend with Raphael, and there are plenty of job opportunities in Philadelphia. Doesn't Northcomp have an office there, too?" Apparently, he really had given this a great deal of thought.

"What about my family? My friends? My church?" I rattled off my secondary list of objections.

"Your family and friends will always be here for you. And there are churches in Philadelphia. We won't be the first couple to move after getting married. People do it all the time. I moved throughout most of my childhood because my dad was military," he reminded me.

"Okay, I am not a . . . a globetrotter like you. I can't—"

"I can't live my life without you." He stopped my heart with those words.

Suddenly, I wasn't sitting across from some man who was trying to run me. I was sitting across from the love of my life. The man who had erased all my doubts and fears about falling in love. The man who had accepted my son as part of the package without hesitation. He was a Godsend, no doubt, and I couldn't imagine my life without him, either. Tears filled my eyes as I sat there utterly exposed before Quinn. He was asking a lot of me, but in light of what he had given me, it was nothing.

I knew this.

But I was afraid. I'd seen women lose everything behind a man—jobs, relationships with family members, houses, cars, hair. I would *never* be that stupid.

I set my elbows on the table and pressed my fingers into my forehead. "How soon would we have to move?"

"I think I can hold them off until the wedding."

"You *think?*" My stomach churned. I just couldn't see myself doing all this for love. "You should have talked to me before you took the offer, Quinn. I hope this is not an indication of how you plan to operate once we get married."

He gave me that one. "You're right. I just didn't think it would be such a big deal for us to get married and move so I can take better care of you and Eric."

Those were fighting words to me. "Then you obviously don't know me. I don't need anyone to take care of Eric and me."

"Look, I said I was wrong. Thinking for two—or three— is new to me, too. I shouldn't have accepted without discussing it with you. I have one question, though: Do you really think it's best for me to stay at my position here in Dallas and pass up this opportunity because you're afraid to trust?" He called me out.

"This is not about trust!" I exclaimed.

"It *is* about trust. But I'm not going to argue with you." He pulled my hands from my head and held them. "I love you, Peaches. I want to marry you. I want to be a second father to Eric and a great father to our future kids." He stopped, licked his lips, then added, "And I can hardly wait to make love to you."

Oh, he almost broke a sistah down with that one. I had to catch the spit from falling off my bottom lip. *Help, Lord!*

He continued, "I want to grow old with you, serve God with you. Peaches, I want to spend the rest of my life with you. All I'm asking is that you let it begin in Philadelphia. We don't have to stay there forever. It's just a stepping stone right now."

I knew in my spirit that I should have kissed my man and said, "Whatever you want, Big Daddy." But I'm sorry. I could not go out like that. I needed Quinn to understand that I was not going to be the type of wife to ask. "How high?" when he said, "Jump." If I started doing it now, I'd be pole-vaulting for the next fifty years. I wanted him to sweat it out for a while, for the record. "Let me think about this some more," I finally said.

"Don't *think* about it, *pray* about it," Quinn suggested.

Chapter 3

I knew I would be late getting back to work, but I had to call my girl before I got out of the car. LaShondra was devastated at the news I might be moving to Philadelphia. "I understand, though," she succumbed. "You have to go where God is leading you."

"How do you know God is leading me to Philadelphia?"

"Well, let's take inventory: your job is trippin', Raphael finally has a steady schedule with Eric, and Quinn is finally in a position to support you. What's the problem?"

I couldn't believe the words that were coming out of her mouth. "I don't need his support, LaShondra!"

"Well, if you don't want somebody to have your back, what's the point of getting married? You could just stay single if you wanna fly solo," she reasoned.

"Oh, you've got it bad, girl," I cried out in my car. "Turn in your I-W-C."

"What's that?" LaShondra asked.

"Your Independent Woman Card," I said as yet another Northcomp employee walked by, waving at me like I was a long lost friend. I didn't even wave back.

LaShondra managed a laugh and explained herself. "Now, I'm not the authority on marriage since I haven't been married long. But let me say this. There's something about knowing there's someone else, a physical person, in your corner. And it's even better when you know God put the person in your corner. Stelson has been such a wonderful addition to my life . . ." blah blah blah.

She must have talked five minutes about her Superman-of-God before she took a breath and let me interrupt with, "Then why don't you just quit your job, kick off your shoes, and stay home with the chilluns?"

She went silent for a moment.

"You still there?" I asked.

"Yeah, I'm still here. Look, Peaches, I personally don't want you to move to Philadelphia." Her voice cracked a bit as she went on to say how much she would miss me. "But if you want my gut reaction, selfishness aside, I say pack your bags, pack your son, and go be with Quinn in the city of brotherly love."

Not exactly what I wanted to hear. I knew LaShondra meant well. I just needed to hear from someone else who could give me a more down-to-earth perspective on things. Deniessa to the rescue.

"Don't do it, girl!" she advised. "If I had known then what I know now about marriage and about Jamal, I would have doused my wedding gown with gasoline and set it on fire!"

Now that's what I'm talkin' 'bout. Keep it real. It was humanly impossible for anyone to be as perfect as LaShondra made Stelson out to be.

I returned to my office and found someone from Yancey waiting to meet with me. Theresa smiled as she introduced us. "Patricia, this is Michael Yancey from The Yancey Group. Michael, this is Patricia Miller. She's the head of our human resources department."

We shook hands politely, sizing each other up all the while. He was a tall, thin man in his midforties with a pair of glasses that would have been the bomb in the '80s. Well, maybe they were coming back in style—but not that comb-over. Aw, who was I kidding? He could have come up in there looking like Denzel and I wouldn't have liked him because he was in my way. I had a pretty good idea of who was just sitting on the payroll and who was indispensable. Why I gotta have this son-of-a-golfer breathing down my neck?

Michael seemed content with me taking the reins on this project, which was exactly what I figured he'd do since he didn't know diddly-squat about how to calculate severance pay or navigate the particulars of termination for unemployment insurance purposes. He kept reiterating the phrase "structural realignment" so I would think he was somehow soaring above my knowledge, looking down at the big picture. It's a shame when people just won't admit they have no clue. I felt like telling him to get out of my kitchen.

By 4:30, I was ready to call it a day. I went to the restroom at 4:31 and stood in a stall until 4:45, when I returned to my office just in time to power down my computer and straighten up my desk.

"It looks like you've got a pretty good handle on things, Patricia," Michael said as he stood to shake my hand. "If you'll just get back to me by Thursday with your recommendations for early retirement and release, I'll review them and let you know my thoughts Friday so you can move forward."

I shook his hand. I figured the less we spoke the better off I would be.

"Have a good week, Miss Miller."

"Mmm-hmm," I barely mumbled.

I was not in a cooking mood when I left the office that day. Eric's day care was the first stop, McDonald's was the second, and my jetted Jacuzzi tub was nearly the last. If only I could come up with some kind of way to make a Jacuzzi-bed, I could start my own Jacuzzi-bed company and partner with Quinn to run it. Then he wouldn't have to leave me to follow this big marketing opportunity.

Something about the water swirling around me pulled

my feelings to the surface. Suddenly, I was crying. I didn't want to lose Quinn. I didn't want my son to lose touch with Raphael. And for as much as I despised the fakeness at Northcomp, I still didn't want anyone to lose their job.

Why was so much riding on me? Who got the big idea that Peaches Miller was capable of deciding everything? I was the same little fat girl who was picked last for every team in P.E. and the first one "out" in dodgeball. Shoot, I never even caught up with the duck in duck-duck-goose. How on earth did I end up being the shot-caller for so many important things in the real game of life?

Quinn called to say good night to Eric and pray with me. I was too broke-down to put up a fuss about Philly. The more he tried to talk me into it, the more I cried. "Baby, what's wrong? I really thought this was a good move for us."

I wish I could have told him it wasn't just about Philadelphia. It was about . . . I don't know . . . life. Me, him, Eric, us, everybody and everything. There was no way I could articulate my feelings. They were was too confusing, too convoluted.

"Peaches, talk to me," Quinn pleaded.

"I can't right now," I said truthfully.

He sighed. "When can you talk?"

"I guess . . . when I know what to say." I wasn't trying to be difficult. It just "be's" that way sometimes. Plus, I was tired. And hungry. Again.

Quinn led a prayer on our behalf. We said our amens and our I-love-yous, then hung up the phone with no real resolution in sight. I lay there for another thirty minutes looking around my bedroom, counting the six blades on the ceiling fan spinning around on the lowest speed. Were there really six or were there only five? Did I count one more than once?

My soul ached for some Heavenly Father–Daughter time. I wanted to pray. I needed to pray. But I was afraid I wouldn't like the answers.

Chapter 4

Working with Michael for the rest of the week at North-comp was, to say the least, nerve-racking. There were so many employees who had been there and worked together for so long, it was hard to determine who was vital and who wasn't. Well, it wasn't hard to do if I just looked at the numbers—but I couldn't help but see the faces that went along with those numbers. Don't get me wrong: I didn't have anyone I would consider a "friend" at Northcomp (not since Deniessa left), but there were still lots of good people here.

When I got to Northcomp in the late '90s, we were riding the technological gravy train, blowing up big time as a premier software company. The CEO retired in 2002, and the company was sold. People were a little worried, but the transition actually went smoothly.

But now, things were different. Companies were folding left and right, and Northcomp was on the way to the chopping block. According to Michael, it would be my job to first offer retirement to those who had been there longest and were making, to quote him, "ungodly amounts of money with so little education."

Okay, I, too, had been surprised to learn that some of those people out on the production floor had nothing more than GEDs but were making six figures, with overtime and all. But these were the same people who had stuck with Northcomp back when the CEO was struggling to keep it alive. They laugh now, but they still remember when the former CEO's car got repossessed right out there in the employee parking lot. Those people had stuck with the company's founder, helped him build the company. And he rewarded them for their loyalty.

I had to ask Michael the obvious follow-up question, for the record. "And if they don't accept?"

"Well, I suppose we'll offer them a voluntary layoff. If they don't accept the layoff, our last resort will be to release them. We hope, of course, many will take the money and run." Michael laughed. I didn't find his joke amusing, so I looked him dead in his eyes like this-ain't-funny.

I watched his face turn bright red as he cleared his throat nervously and turned his eyes downward again, focusing on the charts and graphs strewn across my desk.

He continued, "As for the hourly employees, the ones who are still under the six-month probationary contract must be terminated, preferably before the next pay cycle, to circumvent unemployment claims." Michael began to gather the papers we'd been analyzing. He filed them into his briefcase.

"Is that it?" I asked.

"Well, it *is* Friday, and you've got some firing to do."

He was right. It was Friday, and the pay period would end at midnight. I knew this was coming, but I wasn't ready. I was familiar with corporate downsizing and such; took classes on it, went to conferences about it. In my day, I had fired plenty of people for tardiness, lack of production, absenteeism, failure to do this or that. I had even fired a few people who just weren't getting along well at Northcomp. In the case of the latter, I always felt like it was best for those people to move on and find a place that better fit their personality styles.

But when it came time for me to fire my first person under *these* circumstances, I was sick to my stomach. With the economy in a slump, it might take them months or even years to find other comparable jobs.

I couldn't eat lunch before my 1:30 meeting with Alfred Putnam, the last man I hired. When I sent word to Alfred's floor manager that I needed to see Alfred in my office, all I could think of was James Evans on *Good Times* and how many times he got fired for no reason at all. Always keeping his head above water, making a way when he could. I wondered if Alfred had a good pool hustle.

It didn't help to see Alfred was wearing one of James's old plaid shirts when he walked into my office. And he was so friendly and respectful. Alfred always called me Miss Miller, even though he was old enough to be my father.

"Mr. Putnam, please have a seat," I offered.

He scrunched his eyebrows in concern. "What's wrong, Miss Miller? Did I forget to fill out a paper?"

"Oh, no, Mr. Putnam. You've done nothing wrong," I assured him as I took my seat across from him. He breathed a sigh of relief and gave me a grandpa-like smile.

Now it was my turn to be nervous. I gave myself an internal pep talk: *Peaches, you are a human resources executive. This is what human resources executives do—we fire people. Get it together, girl! Do your job!*

Mr. Putnam waited patiently for me to finish my self-lecture. His light brown, weathered hands were folded in his lap. His hooded eyes fixed solidly on me as I fidgeted in my leather chair.

I guess Mr. Putnam got tired of waiting on me. "You're firing me," he said, bearing his same sweet smile.

My shoulders dropped and I spilled out an unexecutive-like apology, "I'm so sorry, Mr. Putnam. The company is downsizing—"

"I understand, Miss Miller," he consoled me with a soothing tone. "I worked thirty years for the electric company before I retired. I know how these things go. I just thank God I've still got my retirement income, you know?"

"Yes, thank God," I agreed. My stomach settled a bit and I found the resolve to go through the rest of the termination spiel with him. As a final step, we confirmed his contact information to make sure his last check would be mailed to the correct address. "Do you have any other questions, Mr. Putnam?"

"No questions here. Hallelulah anyhow," he nearly sang as he let himself out of my office.

I was almost embarrassed to see Vernon, the head security officer whom I'd told Theresa to summon, standing just outside my doorway. It was standard procedure to have Mr. Putnam escorted off the premises immediately following his termination, but that didn't make me feel any better. I wanted to just slither under my desk, I felt so badly for him and everyone else I had to fire that day.

Once I was sure Mr. Putnam was out of the vicinity of my office, I stepped out to use the restroom. Collect myself. Not everyone was going to sit there and comfort me like Alfred Putnam did, because not everyone had retirement money coming in every month. And, certainly, not everyone knew to give God the glory no matter what. I had to get my game face on and *keep* it on until five o'clock.

My mother called me in the interim and left a message about the wedding plans. I had almost forgotten about my big day in all this Northcomp chaos. Her message, however, was a poignant reminder. "I got word from the caterer. Pretty reasonable estimate. I'll talk to you about it tomorrow when you bring Eric over."

I loved my mother, but she was worrying me to death with this wedding. Some people dream about their wedding for years—pick out the colors, the dress, and everything. My cousin, Walesha, always wanted to play "wedding" when we were little. She would put a white sheet on her head and act like it was a train—had us standing up under the swing set like we were at a chapel. Just crazy!

Left up to me, I wouldn't have even been thinking about a wedding. I had seen too many people go all out for elaborate ceremonies and then end up divorced before the debt had a chance to revolve one good time.

Alas, there was my mother. She would have disowned me if I popped up on her doorstep married without giving her the benefit of bragging about my upcoming nuptials to all the church folk. Since my siblings were so much older than me, several years had passed since she'd played a major role in a wedding. If everyone stayed hitched, I'd be the last child to tie the knot. She wanted to go down the aisle one more time in style, I suppose.

Returning her call was not the drama I dreaded. Her voice mail picked up after the fourth ring, and I left a quick message, "Whatever you think is best is fine with me. I'll call you when I get off work."

With my cell phone set on silent and my office phone forwarded to Theresa, I was able to concentrate on the task at hand. I fired four more people, and it was ugly. One lady cursed me out, and another one told me I was just "doin' the white man's dirty work." If I hadn't been depressed about the whole thing, I might have gone off on them. I didn't have it in me to kick them while they were down, though. Who knows? I might have said the same thing if I had been sitting on the other side of the desk.

Quinn sent me a text message at exactly quittin' time: U MADE IT! I replied: BARELY! Seconds later, as I was leaving the building, my phone rang and I explained to him how completely awful it feels to fire people in the middle of a recession, knowing they were just beginning to believe things were looking up because they'd recently been hired at Northcomp.

"It's not your fault, Peaches," Quinn reminded me. "Don't take their insults personally. They're just frustrated and scared."

"I know, I know." I sighed, angry with myself for letting this situation get under my skin.

Quinn must have heard the tension in my tone. "Baby, you can't let this get you down."

"I just need to unwind, that's all," I said as I shut the door to my car and started the engine.

Quinn laughed a bit and said, "That's what I love about you."

I needed some love at the moment, so I purred, "What do you love about me?"

"Underneath it all, you really do care."

Not quite the compliment I was looking for. "Underneath all *what?*"

"The fussing and the sarcasm and the attitude."

"I beg your pardon. I do not have an attitude. Just because I'm a strong, independent black woman who speaks my mind does not mean I have an attitude. If I was a white man, you'd call it confidence. Society is crazy with these double standards."

He gave a condescending cease-fire. "Okay, Peaches."

I didn't have it in me to take on another confrontation at the moment. Quinn wasn't the first person to accuse me of having a bad attitude, and he probably wouldn't be the last. No matter, he knew everything about me—the good, the bad, and the ugly—going into this marriage. There would be no surprise psycho waiting to ambush him after our wedding.

"You want me come by and pick up Eric so you can have some time to yourself?" he offered.

"That would be great," I accepted. This brother sure came in handy. "He wants to go see that new Disney movie."

"Cool. I'll find out what time it's showing and I'll call you, all right?"

"Okay. Love you."

"Love you, too" he echoed.

The next call was to my mother, who was all bent out of shape about the flowers. "Momma, I told you to get something simple. A single rose will be just fine."

She huffed, "When Early Mae's girl got married, every one of the bridesmaids had a full bouquet! Full, you hear me?"

"Momma, I don't have any bridesmaids. Quinn and I will be the only ones at the altar."

"Well," she said, and I already knew what was coming next, "I've been talking to LaShondra and she said she's more than willing to be the matron of honor. And I know you got other single friends from college who could be the bridesmaids. We could ask Walesha to be in the wedding. You know she loves weddings—"

"Mother." I had to stop her. "Quinn and I have a budget, and we intend to stick to it. Adding all these other people will take us way over our limit."

"You know"—she paused for effect—"if your father were here, he'd be so happy to see you walk down the aisle with you surrounded by your friends on one side and Quinn's on the other—along with your brothers. Don't you think your daddy would have loved that?"

My father's passing was still a sensitive topic for me, but I couldn't let it get me off track. "What Daddy probably would have loved more than anything would be for Quinn and me to be able to send Eric off to college one day."

She sighed. "Well, if that's the way you want it."

"That's the way it is." I held my ground.

"Fine. I'll call LaShondra back and tell her you said 'no.'"

I smiled to myself and offered to make amends. "Don't worry. I'll call her."

Before I called LaShondra, I called all of my siblings and told them my side of the story before my mother had a chance to get them all riled up over Daddy's memory. I'm sure things would have been different if Daddy were alive. He wouldn't have insisted on anything elaborate, but he would have helped, financially. What little thought I had given to a wedding centered around him walking me down the aisle; with that possibility gone, there wasn't much left to think about. I wasn't a real daddy's girl. I did, however, want to look like one for a day.

LaShondra knew I had a bone to pick with her, so she answered the phone with a loud apology. "I'm sorry, okay! Your momma got me all excited!"

"Don't blame it on her," I fussed, but before we ended our conversation, we both laughed about it. She confirmed our Saturday plans for a double date and told me she had to let me go.

"My sexy husband is on his way home and I haven't seen him in four days," she said.

I announced, "T-M-I!"

"I'm just letting you know—all phones will be off tonight." She laughed.

"Hey, I'm right behind you this summer," I had to agree. "I'll see you tomorrow."

A Friday night all by myself was exactly what I needed. Since Eric was gone with Quinn, I was able to pick up a novel I'd put down before this Northcomp fiasco started. I freed my mind from the current-day stress and dove headfirst into another world. I barely stopped reading long enough to let my son back inside my condo and kiss my man good night. The longer Quinn and I dated, the less time we spent together in each other's apartments. Things could get heated real quickly if we didn't watch our boundaries, and tonight was no different.

After we tucked Eric in bed, we immediately walked to my front door to say our good-byes, followed by a kiss. Quinn's lips were so soft. His neck so . . . manly. Dang! Why did he have to smell so good? And it didn't help that I was at a part in the novel where the husband and wife who had been apart from each other for eighteen long, dry months due to a war were just about to "catch up" with each other.

I hugged Quinn one last time as I simultaneously opened the door for him to leave. "Good night, baby," I managed to whisper between my heart's thumps.

He looked at me with a pleading in his eyes. "We gotta hurry up and get married, Peaches."

My body was searching for marryusrightnow.com. Seriously, people do everything else online. Surely there had to be a way for us to circumvent all this hoopla.

I teased Quinn, "You're making me wonder if you're marrying me just so you can sleep with me."

He fired back, "Sometimes I wonder if you're marrying me for that same reason."

"No, you didn't!" I yelled as I playfully punched his arm.

He scurried out the door, laughing at me. "Good night, hot momma."

I stepped onto my balcony as he skipped down the steps. "Don't make me hurt you." My own giggling, however, overshadowed my threat.

Quinn always could make me laugh.

Chapter 5

Saturday night, Quinn and I made our first stop at my mother's house. She had a big pot of spaghetti and her infamous garlic bread waiting for Eric—we smelled it before we even got into the house. "You sure you don't want to eat here?" Quinn asked me.

"I know, huh?"

We were barely in the door when my mother pulled us both into a headlockish hug. "Oh, my baby! Getting married!"

Quinn gasped for air. "Hello, Mrs. Miller."

"No more Mrs. Miller, Quinn. Call me Momma now," she insisted as she finally released us.

Quinn beamed and practiced her new name. "Hello, Momma."

She hugged him again. Then she turned her attention to Eric, smothering him with kisses and hugs. Eric ate them up.

Momma tugged my ear for a moment about the wedding photographer. Apparently, my uncle Charles was trying to build his portfolio and had offered to take pictures free of charge. I was fine with it, but she wanted another photographer there for backup.

"Wonder, will Uncle Charles be upset?" she asked.

"Probably," I replied.

"Well, he's just going to have to get over it," she smacked off, leaving me to wonder why she'd asked me in the first place.

My mother then led us all to the kitchen and offered us food, though she knew Quinn and I were meeting LaShondra and Stelson at a north Dallas restaurant for dinner. "I don't want to ruin my appetite," I declined.

Eric sat down at the table, ready to devour the food, but I gave him a detour: Put your things in the room and wash your hands before eating.

"Well," my mother said to Quinn and me as she searched through the cabinets, "let me pack you up something to take with you." Before I knew it, she had two bowls full of spaghetti and two slabs of garlic bread wrapped in foil—one for me and one for Quinn. "I know you still a bachelor, Quinn. You need good food to keep you goin' till you marry Peaches and she start cookin' for you."

"Yes, ma'am. I'm lookin' forward to that good home cookin'," Quinn said as he nodded toward me.

I looked him up and down like he was crazy. He waited until my mother turned her back, and he pinched my side. I couldn't scream, so I coughed.

"You feelin' all right, Peaches?" my mother asked.

I mustered up a straight face. "Yes, ma'am."

She eyed Quinn and me suspiciously. If she didn't see it on my face, I know she saw mischief painted all over his. Both of us were about to bust out laughing, so I said, "We have to go now, Mother."

"All right," she said. "You want me to take Eric to church with me tomorrow or you want to pick him up early?"

"I'll pick him up," I answered.

"Okay. Y'all have a good time," she said as she narrowed her eyes, staring us down. "And don't be makin' no babies before the weddin' night."

My eyes got real big and my mouth dropped open. Quinn

answered for us both, "Yes, ma'am. I mean—no, ma'am. We won't."

"Well, bless the name of the Lord. Good night," she almost sang.

When we got into Quinn's car, he started in on me. "You got us in trouble!"

"You're the one who pinched me!" I yelled in laughter. "Don't be touchin' me all in my momma's house!"

He backed out of her driveway and we headed toward the highway, joking because neither of us was willing to take the blame for my mother's scolding.

Once we were in the flow of freeway traffic, Quinn turned on the radio. Marvin Sapp's "Never Would Have Made It" was playing. It took me back down memory lane— through the fat childhood, the reclusive teen years, the rebellious twenties, the single motherhood, and more recently the loss of my father. But I was stronger and wiser for it all. And now I was sitting beside the man I was to marry, looking ahead to much better days.

Quinn began singing along with the chorus, and I was suddenly reminded of his pleasant stage voice. He sang a few more notes and pulled me out of my trance with a question. "What are you thinking about?"

"Mmmm . . . just thinking about how good God is."

He grabbed my hand and kissed it. "All the time, baby."

I asked, "What do you think about when you hear this song?"

"You. Us. God. I think about a lot of things—all we've been through. When I lost my job and you helped me get a better one. How you encouraged me to keep directing stage plays when other people told me to give up my dreams. I think about Eric and what a blessing he is to my life. I never knew a relationship could add so much meaning and purpose to everything. I can't be anything but thankful."

My eyes were watering by this point. I wiped the tears

away with my stray hand but kept the other wrapped in Quinn's. We rode the rest of the way to the restaurant in a silence that spoke volumes about our relationship. We were beyond the stage where every moment spent together had to be filled with words. We could now speak the soundless language of love and just be together.

The upbeat gospel tune playing when we parked put us both in a cheerful mood. Stelson and LaShondra were waiting for us, and seeing them was a welcome sight.

Our men exchanged manly greetings while LaShondra and I met in an ecstatic embrace. Seriously, you would have thought it was the Celie and Nettie reunion from *The Color Purple*. I hadn't seen LaShondra in a minute because she and Stelson spent the holidays in Louisiana with his family. I believe her hair had probably grown a good inch since I saw her last, right before Thanksgiving. Her spiral curls swung freely as she did a little dance when she finally saw my diamond solitaire. She was still the same ole fun LaShondra, even if we didn't hang together as much as we used to.

When we came out our BFF world, she and Quinn hugged, but I complained to her husband, "Stelson, I don't know if I should hug you, seeing as you stole my best friend from me."

"Come on, Peaches. Give a brother a hug," Stelson joked as he held out his arms.

I couldn't help but laugh and return his gesture. "You are so wrong. You know you're the only white person who gets to call me Peaches, right?"

He put one hand over his heart and bowed slightly. "I count it an honor to call you Peaches, Peaches."

I shook my head and smiled. "I can't even be mad at you, Stelson." Aside from his sense of humor, it's hard to stay mad at someone who treats your best friend like a queen. If I had to lose LaShondra to anybody, I was glad that somebody was Stelson.

Since we had reservations, we were seated right away in a circular booth. The restaurant, a steakhouse, had been renovated to reflect a cowboy motif. Longhorn skulls and saddles were mounted on the walls, giving the restaurant a country impression.

The waiter brought our menu, and Quinn took the liberty to order a combination appetizer: shrimp, chicken wings, and stuffed baked potato wedges.

"So, what's up with you two?" LaShondra asked us. "Any more wedding plans I should know about?"

"Nope," I said. "Momma's still working my nerves."

"What's the date?" Stelson asked.

"July seventh," Quinn piped up. "Six more months."

"Awww," LaShondra cooed. "You are such a good fiancé, Quinn. You know the date and everything."

Then she gave Stelson a loaded glance. We all knew why. LaShondra and Stelson were deep into the wedding plans when Stelson suddenly recalled he had committed himself to a major business conference in New York on the same day as their wedding. They had to push the wedding back almost another month, which was thoroughly inconvenient, not to mention embarrassing. LaShondra almost called the whole thing off, but thankfully, I was able to talk some sense back into her. I don't think she'll ever let Stelson off the hook for his scheduling error.

"She's still got you on payment plan for that one, Doc," Quinn chided Stelson.

Stelson put his arm around LaShondra and apologized for the umpteenth time. "I'm sorry, sweetheart. I'll spend the rest of my life making it up to you."

Give me a break!

The appetizer arrived just as my stomach was turning flips. We all dove into the platter and could only hope our entrées would be as delicious. LaShondra and Stelson split the last potato wedge just as our waitress served our main dishes.

After all those calories from the appetizer, chopped salad was my best option. In the years since I lost eighty pounds, I had learned to eat in moderation. A little chicken wing never hurt anybody, but topping off chicken wings with a hefty steak would go straight to my hips.

Stelson blessed the food, and that's when the problem started. LaShondra said something about our honeymoon, Stelson said something about a seven-day cruise out of Miami, I said something about getting back to Dallas in time for Eric's annual youth camping trip with the church, and Quinn busted out with, "Well, there should be plenty of places for him to camp in Philadelphia."

"So you *are* moving!" LaShondra cried. "I knew you'd come to your senses, Peaches."

My mouth was full, so I couldn't respond before Stelson jumped in with, "Peaches, I've been meaning to tell you—if you need some help finding a job in Philadelphia, let me know. I've got lots of clients there. You won't have any trouble, that is if you want to work right away."

Quinn took advantage of my manners by adding, "See, baby, look how God's already worked this out."

I swallowed my food as quickly as I could without choking and put a screeching hault to this whole table trying to plan my life for me. "I have *not* made my decision yet."

"Oh," from LaShondra.

"I see," from Stelson.

The table endured an abrupt break in the flow of conversation. A few minutes later, I dismissed myself. "I'm going to the ladies' room."

"I'm coming with you," LaShondra insisted. She trailed me all the way to the restroom and patted her foot just outside my stall.

"I just haven't made up my mind, okay," I said to her and then flushed the toilet immediately so I couldn't hear what she had to say. Then I stepped out of the stall and washed my hands, taking note of how the cross pendant on my necklace had shifted out of place. I fixed the necklace, patted my do, and smoothed out my blouse. LaShondra watched me the whole time, arms crossed at her waist, leaning against the granite countertop.

"Are you finished?"

I clasped my hands. "What do you want from me? I mean, I just haven't made up my mind yet."

"What is there to think about?" She shrugged. "You have no options. You love Quinn, he loves you, his job is transferring him, you go with him. That's a simple as two plus two equals four, Peaches. What gives?"

"Okay, add one for a child, one for a baby daddy, one for a job—" I counted on my fingers.

"No," she interrupted, "subtract the job. Northcomp is going under. You need to jump ship while you can and you *know* it."

I ran my tongue along the top row of my teeth and then smacked my lips. "Thanks for the vote of confidence."

"It's not about you, Peaches. Stelson watches the stocks every day. The major stockholders in Northcomp are selling because they see the writing on the wall."

"Since when do you and Stelson sit around watching the company I work for?"

"Well, when I told him that you and Quinn were moving to Philadelphia, he said it was a good thing, because North-comp got a red flag in some report—something about volatility and moving averages," she explained. "He's always checking out stocks because of his corporate clients."

"Northcomp is simply downsizing, that's all. Don't you think I watch the stock, too?" I lied like a rug. I hadn't bit more looked at my company's stock in months, but I couldn't tell her so. The restroom's dim lighting helped cover my facial expressions.

LaShondra gave me the time-out signal. "Peaches, this is not about Northcomp and you know it."

"Well, why don't you tell me what it's about, then?" Now it was my turn to cross my arms, kick one leg over the other, and observe.

"It's about you being stubborn and independent," she mouthed off.

"Since when is independence a sin?"

"Since it gets in the way of you following God's will," she preached.

"Look," I took up for myself, "Quinn is a wonderful man, but I will not just up and leave everything on account of him. I had a life before I met Quinn—a very good life, mind you—and I'll have one after him, if something should happen to us."

"Something like what?"

I rattled off a list of worst-case scenarios. "Him cheating, losing his job, getting on drugs, acting like he done lost his mind. Anything could happen, and I don't want to be stuck out with my son, fifteen hundred miles away from home, looking stupid."

LaShondra laughed and grabbed my left hand. "Listen to yourself, Peaches. If you really thought Quinn was going to mistreat you, you would not be wearing this engagement ring right now."

"Being engaged and being married are two different things." I cleared that one up for her. "You know, if Stelson had said the two of you were going to have to move to California soon after the wedding, you would have thought twice about it."

The truth hit her, and she nodded. "You're right. I would have thought about it for a minute. And then I would have thought about the consequences of not going. Not having him in my life, always wondering what might have been. I can't imagine my life without Stelson in it, and I know you would be miserable without Quinn. Not to mention how Eric would feel."

She struck a low blow there. Everybody knew Eric was crazy about Quinn, and vice versa. Alas, there was another issue. "What about Raphael?"

"Y'all can work something out. You're not the first woman to get married and move out of state with a child. And you and I both know Raphael is *not* going to ask for custody."

We stood there for another moment, LaShondra staring at me, me staring at my feet.

I washed my hands again.

"Peaches, I'm going back to the table now. Wait—have you prayed about this, by the way? What did Daddy say?" she wanted to know.

I could skirt the truth about a lot of things, but not about God. "I need time to pray."

"Uh-huh." She'd read me. "Well, you pray long and you pray hard—but don't act like He hasn't given you an answer when He does." She walked toward the door. "And don't hate if I fix Quinn up with somebody else who knows how to appreciate a good man."

"No, you didn't."

A smug grin swept across her face. "Mmm-hmm. Now you wanna get mad 'cause you know I'm right."

"Don't play." I rolled my eyes at her and followed her back to our booth.

Quinn and Stelson were in the middle of a conversation that LaShondra and I obviously interrupted. We were all seated again and we tried to ignore the Philadelphia topic, but the elephant had plopped his behind smack-dab in the center of our table. We couldn't talk around it, so when the waitress asked if we wanted to see the dessert menu, I quickly spoke for our whole table. "No, thank you. We'll take our checks, please."

Chapter 6

You ever have a Sunday morning where you just didn't feel like going to church? My alarm clock went off and I must have hit the snooze button three times before I actually opened my eyes. The fourth time, I couldn't feel the clock so I opened my eyes and saw it: my bare ring finger. It hit me. I was no longer engaged to Quinn.

Honestly, when I look back on it all, I don't remember every mean word volleyed back and forth in his car on the way back from the restaurant. I guess I blocked them out. All I know is he asked me if I really wanted to marry him. I said, "Yes." He asked me if I wanted him to leave his current job and find something else in Dallas. I said, "No."

Don't ever let it be said that Patricia Miller told a black man to quit a job.

I suggested a commuter marriage. He told me I could not have my cake and eat it, too. Yada yada yada. Things got heated; I told him he was not going to run me, he assured me that he intended to wear the "biblical" pants in this marriage. Next thing I knew, the ring came off my finger.

Quinn refused to take it back, though, because he said he knew I didn't mean it. He was right. I didn't want to break up. I only wanted him to think about what his life would be like without me.

But when I looked at my sparkleless hand sitting on the clock again and felt the sting of tears, I couldn't tell which of us was suffering more.

My landline rang and I answered it, hoping to hear Quinn's voice. What I got instead was a good tongue-lashing from my mother, who picked up on my grogginess. "What you doin' still in the bed at this time on a Sunday morning? I thought you were coming to pick up Eric."

I checked the clock again. 9:24. "Oh, I'm not feeling so hot today, Momma." It wasn't a total lie. My heart was indeed sick.

"Well, if you're sick, you the main one need to be at church gettin' prayer. You want me to come get you?"

"No, ma'am. I'll be okay. Just take Eric on to church with you. I'll come get him this afternoon."

She tsked me. "Don't you start settin' a bad example for Eric by not going to church."

"I won't," I assured her. It was amazing how quickly my mother could make me question my own mothering abilities. "I'll be by later to pick him up."

I returned to the warm pocket beneath my sheets and tried to go back to sleep. No use. My mind could only play the argument with Quinn over and over again. The whole thing was so stupid. I loved him, he loved me. Why was it so complicated?

I got up, brushed my teeth, and tried to eat the sadness away. Whole grain waffles and turkey bacon quieted my mind momentarily. I needed a mental break.

Lifetime movies to the rescue. I watched two movies— one about a woman who fell in love with her high school sweetheart at their twenty-year reunion. The second movie was about a blind woman who regained her sight at the hands of a handsome surgeon. When he took off the bandages and they looked at each other for the first time, it was literally love at first sight.

Those two movies made me think: Could they make a movie about me and Quinn? I mean, we met at singles Bible study at my church. We started dating, he met my son, and it's been all good. There was unmistakable chemistry between us, and we enjoyed many of the same recreational activities: plays, movies, and reading. All my adult life, I had been waiting to fall in love and get married. Now that it was finally happening, though, it wasn't the *ooh-la-la* feeling I'd always thought it would be. It wasn't this huge earth-shattering experience, like the women in those movies. I wasn't naïve enough to think that things were supposed to be like the movies. It was just . . . I don't know. I couldn't put my finger on it.

Maybe it was cold feet. Cold feet don't mix well with a fifteen-hundred-mile move.

I had to put on my fat pants that afternoon—the ones with the elastic waistband. I was too young to own such garments, but every once-in-a-month I had need for flexibility. Maybe I was having PMS, which would explain my irritability and irrational thoughts.

Problem was, I couldn't remember when I'd had my last period. Call me crazy, but I didn't keep track of my cycles like I figured most women did. I wasn't having sex, I wasn't planning any beachfront vacations—no need to watch my period.

A thought struck me—what if I was on my cycle on my wedding day? Naw, I couldn't go out like that. I'd have to get with my doctor and work something out.

I made a mental note to set an appointment with Dr. Gonleeza in the next few weeks.

Wait a minute—am I even having a wedding? Again, the harshness of the argument hit me.

Okay, I decided once and for all: Yes, I was going to marry Quinn. The only thing we had to work out was the living arrangements. *That doesn't even make sense.*

The internal argument was on. What about the military women? They were gone for months and their marriages survived. Sometimes. People do it every day! Movie stars are off shooting for weeks at a time, marine biologists have to travel to the middle of the ocean in submarines for weeks on end. Truck drivers do it. *So what's the problem?*

It's because I'm a woman. If the shoe were on the other foot, no one would expect Quinn to drop everything and move to Philadelphia to chase *my* career aspirations!

But he would.

I had to agree with my conscience. He would indeed do anything to make me happy. He might even decide to renege on the job offer—but then he wouldn't be happy. In fact, neither of us would be happy, because then he probably wouldn't have a job.

I couldn't stand in the way of his progress, but I didn't want to put myself out there. A woman's got to be able to stand on her own two feet whether she's in Dallas or Philadelphia.

What about depending on God?

I didn't have a good answer except to say it's easier to depend on God when I knew exactly what He was doing, which would not be the case in Philadelphia. New job, new surroundings, new church, getting Eric acclimated. Throw in a new marriage with no family or friend as my support system? Not to mention the fact that Quinn's company was probably going to work him like a Hebrew slave for at least the first year.

"God, why did You give me the perfect man and then take him away?" I whined my pitiful prayer as I made my way back to the kitchen for something sweet. Or crunchy. I couldn't decide, so I had both in a bowl of rocky road ice cream.

Trying my best to look pitiful, I denied myself all soap and even allowed my lips to look a little crusty. My lounge clothes barely matched, and my hair was scarcely tucked be-

neath a baseball cap. The worse I looked when I got to my
mother's house, the more I could convince my mother I
really was sick. Maybe.

When Eric rushed toward me at the front door with my
mother only a few steps behind, I went into drama mode.
With one hand held out to stop him, I cautioned, "No, baby,
step back. You don't want to catch what Mommy has."

My mother looked me up and down, put one hand on
her hip. "Last I heard, hard heads weren't contagious." She
tied me up in a hug.

Eric kept his distance but offered hope. "Granny made some
soup for you."

I managed a weak, guilty smile. "Thanks, Momma."

"Mmm-hmm." She rolled her eyes and walked toward
the kitchen.

"Eric, go pack your bag. Make sure you have your toothbrush and *all* your socks."

He bounded off to fulfill my orders, and I traced my
mom's steps to the kitchen, where she instructed me to sit
down.

Her back to me as she washed her hands at the sink, she
asked, "So what happened between you and Quinn?"

"Wh . . . what are you talking about?" I blinked in rapid
denial.

She faced me now, slid her hand down my left arm,
stopped at my ring finger. "You're missing something."

My mother gives new meaning to the term "watch you
like a hawk." "Nothing, Momma."

"You listen at me, Peaches. So long as Quinn don't beat
you or quit workin', everything else can be worked out."

"What if he cheats on me?"

"Hmph. That can be worked out, too, if he don't make a
habit of it. Besides, you keep him busy in the bedroom, he
won't have energy for no other woman."

"Momma, that's gross."

"Well, it always worked for me, that's the truth."

"Change the subject."

Momma grabbed a bowl from the cabinet and com-menced to preparing me a generous helping of chicken noo-dle soup.

"The cheating I'm worried about is the cheating *you* do to *yourself.* Cheating yourself out of love and happiness. And you know what John ten and ten says. The enemy is the one who came to steal it from you. But in your case, he ain't got to steal it 'cause you servin' it to him, just like this here soup." She handed me the bowl.

I swirled my spoon in the stock, creating a little whirl-pool. "What makes you think this is all my fault?"

" 'Cause I know my child, and I have this funny feeling called the Holy Spirit that shows me little things here and there." She sat across from me now and flashed a furtive grin.

I focused on my bowl again, taking in the first spoonful of Momma's scrumptious soup. Already I was thinking of a way to send her out of the room so I could turn up the bowl and slurp the last drops when finished.

"You listening to me?"

"Yes, ma'am."

"So, what happened?"

Another sip. Another decision. Do I start this whole busi-ness of telling my mother what's going on in my marriage or do I keep it between me and my husband (assuming I'd actu-ally marry Quinn)? Seems that same "funny feeling" Momma had was telling me to keep my mouth shut.

"Nothing I can't handle." I stuffed my mouth with soup for the next minute as I watched her facial expression go from offended to understanding.

"Well, just do me a favor. Don't *you* handle it. Let the Lord handle it. Don't make no sense for you to come in here one week with an engagement ring on and then next time you come through the door, your hand is naked as a jaybird."

"Aren't *all* birds naked, Momma?"

"Don't start with me."

She reached into a pocket on her housecoat and produced an envelope.

"Peaches, I got this from the bank. I need you to look at it and tell me what they're talking about."

Reluctantly, I took the communication and deciphered it. More than anything, I hated how helpless she acted when it came to business matters. Last year, she would have missed the tax deadline if I hadn't said anything. Why didn't she insist on being informed about everything in their marriage? How could she—or any woman—just trust their husband so blindly? It was like they had never seen *Waiting to Exhale* or *The First Wives Club*.

"They're asking you to verify your social security number for tax purposes."

"How do I do that?"

"Probably with a certified letter, maybe a W-9. Why don't you just call them and see?"

She stretched the corners of her lips. "I suppose I could." She stuffed the envelope back into her pocket.

Eric entered the kitchen with bag in tow. I grabbed my purse and keys as he announced, "I got all my clothes and my toothbrush, but Granny washed my socks, I think, 'cause I can't find 'em."

"They're in the dryer with the clothes he had on yesterday. Sit back down. Give it about another thirty minutes."

I eyed Eric again. Obviously he hadn't taken accurate inventory of his apparel, because there had to be more missing from his backpack than socks.

His only defense was a crooked smile.

Now I'd have to wait awhile before we could leave. And knowing my mother, this was exactly the way she'd planned it.

Determined to escape another line of questioning, I made my way to the living room. Daddy's empty lounge chair stared up at me. The deep groove his weight carved in the bottom cushion made it look as though some invisible person was sitting there. I wanted to believe Daddy's spirit was still in that chair, but the more I thought about it I could only laugh. If Daddy's spirit was sitting in that chair, it wouldn't be doing anything except snoring.

It's not like he'd be telling me what to do about Quinn or giving me advice about the game of love. All Daddy ever told me about men was to make sure I didn't need one. "Go to college and get a degree, Peaches, so you can get a good job and you won't have to depend on anybody for anything. *Then* you can think about boys all that other stuff."

He never actually told me about the "other stuff."

Daddy was about as antiboyfriend as any other father. No one could ever really be good enough for me in his eyes, I suppose. But somehow I wished he was there now. I wanted to run some things by him, because he never told me what to do if the man I love asked me to make a sacrifice. *Should I move to Philadelphia, Daddy? Quinn's got a good job there and I can get one, too, I'm sure.*

No answer.

Maybe you're asking the wrong Father.

I exhaled sharply at the revelation, as though my breath could push this thought out and away from me. What if God tells me to go to Philadelphia? That's right up there with what if God tells me to run off to some lost tribe no one has ever heard of and plant vegetable gardens for the natives. I'll support a missionary financially from now till every non-believer gets dunked in Jordan, but I couldn't see myself touching dirt—on purpose—any more than I could imagine myself jobless in Philadelphia asking for Quinn's permission to use *his* money to splurge on a pair of red pumps.

That's just not the Peaches Joe Miller raised, and it certainly wasn't the way I pictured myself.

Chapter 7

Security was visibly heightened at Northcomp for the next month. I, for one, was happy to see extra guards monitoring the parking lots and buildings. The office gossip wire questioned how the company could afford to pay for extra security but not salvage jobs. The guards were temps, of course, with no potential for full-time employment. Still, people were angry, and hostility slithered through the hallways.

I whisked past Theresa's empty desk, checking my watch to make sure I wasn't too early. Theresa should have been in place by 8:00. If she didn't arrive by 8:15, I'd call to make sure she was okay.

Mr. Hampton's bad cologne hit me before I actually saw him sitting in the guest chair of my office.

"Mr. Hampton?"

"Good morning, Patricia." He swirled the chair toward me and stood, rearranging his jacket.

"Is everything okay?"

"Yes. Well, no. I had a chance to speak to Yancey. You're not dismissing employees quickly enough. We need to lower the head count, Patricia. The sooner the better."

I let out a breath I'd apparently been holding. *Not quickly enough?* "We released thirty-two hourly employees who were still within their ninety-day probationary period last month. I was planning to run reports this morning so we can analyze the next round—"

"We don't have time for you to run every stinkin' stat. Yancey says it's pretty cut and dry." He crossed his arms and looked down at me.

Yancey doesn't know squat! It took everything in me to keep my neck from rolling and my hands from my hips. "Mr. Hampton, there are well-researched practices we need to follow in order to be able to prove why we're letting certain people go and others stay. If we rush this process, we put ourselves at risk of being sued for bias or discrimination."

"Neither the board nor the stockholders care about policies at this point in the game. We need to tighten up. Freeze raises and fire everyone we can. Quickly."

He brushed past me without formally dismissing himself.

Was he crazy? Yes. He *had* to be crazy if he thought I was going to ignore industry standards and fire people without set criteria so Northcomp could hang me out to dry when the lawsuits and unemployment hearings came flying in! Granted, I could have moved the process a little faster if I didn't have to check in with Yancey—but firing people in a highly litigious society like the entire United States of America is not a quick and easy task. Though it might come suddenly from the employee's perspective, it's rarely a sudden decision for the employer.

I knew this. Yancey had to know this. On second thought, maybe I was giving him too much credit. Well, even if Yancey didn't know it, Hampton knew it. This whole thing smelled of a setup, but I wasn't falling for it. If they wanted to fire me, they would have to fire me for following the rules, not for breaking them, because when all was said and done, Mr. Hampton could conveniently forget about the pressure he'd just put on me to free up the payroll. He'd never put such words in writing—precisely why he chose to come to my office rather than send an e-mail.

Where are those hidden cameras when you need them?

My cell phone rang, highlighting the fact that I hadn't even put my purse down since entering the room. I fished through my oversized bag, retrieved the phone, and read the name on the screen.

Quinn. Again, my heart started its shenanigans. *Is there no limit to life's drama?* "Hello."

"Hi, baby. How are you?"

"Not so good right now." I closed the door to my office and caught a glimpse of Theresa's still-vacant desk. "But let me call you back. I've got to find out what's going on with my secretary."

"Okay. We need to have another serious talk. My boss is really gearing up for my transfer." I'd done a pretty good job of dancing around the topic for a while. Alas, everything seemed to be coming to a head.

I sighed. "I'll call you back."

I searched through my digital phone book, pressed Send on Theresa's name, and waited for her to answer.

"Hi, Theresa, it's Patricia. Are you coming in today?"

"Mr. Hampton said . . . um . . . I'm part-time now. Twenty hours a week tops."

I must have stood there with my mouth open for a good ten seconds before I figured out what to say next. "Okay, so, when *are* you coming in?"

"I was thinking from ten to two. I'm sorry, Patricia, I thought you already knew. I'll come in now if you need me," she offered.

"Yes, I need you."

"Okay. Let me finish feeding my daughter and I'll be there in about an hour."

I heard Theresa rustle, heard her daughter's gurgle, and

caught myself. Just because Mr. Hampton was unreasonable didn't mean I had to be unreasonable, too.

"That's okay, Theresa. Just come in at ten like you'd planned."

"You sure?"

"Yeah."

"Okay. Thanks."

"Uh-huh."

Elbows plopped on desk, face buried in hands, I took a moment to process. This was ridiculous. How was I supposed to do twice the work in half the time with a part-time secretary? Not to mention, it was totally wrong for Hampton to make HR moves without consulting me. Making Theresa part time meant we'd actually *lost* money, since we'd gotten her through a temp service and paid quite a hefty sum to retain her. Financially, it would have made better sense to lay off a less essential secretary and let a few other administrative assistants pick up the slack. That's what *I* would have done, but did anybody ask me? Nope.

I couldn't waste time lamenting, though. I logged on to my computer, accessed information, and configured the reports I needed to help made personnel decisions. What would have taken Theresa five minutes took me nearly half an hour, which was long enough for Quinn to get impatient and call me back.

"I'm sorry I didn't call you back. It's crazy around here."

"Oh." He seemed satisfied with my blurted apology. "Is your secretary all right?"

"Yeah, she's fine, except my boss cut her hours without telling me."

"Wo-ah. Is he supposed to do that?"

I sighed. "No, he's not. It's not right, it's not fair, but you know what? Nothing is fair these days. I've got to fire a bunch of people who didn't do anything wrong. No fairness there."

"That's the way the ax falls sometimes," Quinn tried to

reason with me. "People have to find their security in God—not a job or a crazy boss."

Maybe I was in a nasty mood. Maybe I was just lashing out at the one I loved. Either way, I responded, "Funny—*you* sure seem to think there's a lot of security in Philadelphia."

"Well, since you brought it up, we do need to talk about it. I am moving to Philadelphia." His voice was calm and even. Settled.

"With or without me?"

"I want to go with you *and* Eric. Look, I'm truly utterly, eternally sorry I didn't talk with you before I accepted the position. I was wrong. I was inconsiderate. Can we just let this be my big goof before the wedding, like Stelson's conference incident? I mean, what else can I say, baby?"

"But you're still moving to Philadelphia, right?"

"Okay—let's do this. Let's reverse the hands of time and have the conversation we should have had when I got the offer."

I sighed. "Impossible."

"Humor me, all right?"

"Whatever."

"Peaches, I need to talk to you. I got a great job offer today, but we'll have to move to Philadelphia soon after the wedding. Since this decision affects me as much as you, I'd like your opinion."

If Quinn could have seen the look of stank on my face, he wouldn't have kept talking.

"So, what do you think?"

"I don't have time for games this morning, Quinn. I've got people to fire right now."

"You firing me, too?"

My stern expression melted as I considered his question. How could I fire the man who made me believe in love again? "Quinn, I am not firing you. I just have to . . . think things through."

"What's the big deal? I don't get it."

"You wouldn't get it 'cause you're a man. I will not end up like my mother, okay? Always depending on my father—he always made the money, he paid the bills, he ran everything. And now that he's gone, she's . . . pitiful." I threw my head back to stop the tears from racing down my face. "Always asking me to help with bills and taxes. It's really sad."

"I'm not asking you to go be June Cleaver—or your mother. If I wanted a passive woman, I wouldn't be marrying you. I love your strength, intelligence. I need you in my corner." Quinn's voice escalated now, reminded me of either a preacher or an actor in one of Shakespeare's plays.

"So what if I say yes. What if I put in my notice at Northcomp, walk down the aisle, pack up, and move to Philadelphia. Then what?"

"It's whatever you want. Go back to school, get a job, whatever. I got your back while we're making the transition. What's so hard about this?"

I have to admit, if I were my friend listening to this conversation, I would bop myself on the head and say, "Girl, are you—no, *is* you—crazy! You've got a good man who wants to support you spiritually, emotionally, professionally, *and* financially. You betta follow his happy behind to Timbuktu if you have to!" After all, that's what any woman with any kind of sense would reason.

But you know how we do. We could have the opportunity of a lifetime sitting right there in our faces and talk ourselves right out of the best thing. It happens every day. We get a choice—an apple or a cinnamon roll. The apple is good for you, has nutrients and everything. And the doctor already told us we need to lose twenty pounds. But what do we do? We will inhale a cinnamon roll like the doctor ain't said a mumbling word.

Or it's a dress. We know we need to be saving money for retirement, for the college fund—shoot, for next month's electricity bill! But we'll sit up and buy a red dress in a minute. Even if the red dress is a little too small because we've been eating all those stupid cinnamon rolls.

Then we choose not to go to the gym and exercise the next day—it never ends!

So, before anybody gets sick of me, let me just say: At that point, I was sick of myself, but I didn't know how to stop sabotaging my own life. I didn't know how to step out, choose the good thing, and run with it. Or maybe I was just too scared to do so.

"Quinn, I really can't deal with this today."

"I need to know what your plans are, Peaches. My whole life is on hold right now. If we're going to officially call off the wedding . . . then . . . I'll let my boss know so we can proceed with the transfer as soon as possible."

My mouth quivered. Stomach tightened. "Are you serious?"

"Yes. Why belabor the issue? If you don't want to marry me, there's no need in me staying here."

I squeaked, "I don't want you to go."

He laughed slightly. "You can't have your cake and eat it, too, baby."

"Well, can we talk tonight? Like, over dinner?"

"No. I'm finished talking. I've prayed, I've apologized, I've let you know where I stand. Either you're going to trust God enough to trust me or you're not."

Is he serious? Are we breaking up? "You're not willing to . . . see me anymore?"

"No. I can't do this. You have to make a choice. And if you don't make a choice, that, too, is a choice. Good-bye."

Click.

Okay, you know what I should have done? I should have called him right back and said, "Please, Big Daddy, don't leave me!" But you know what happened instead? The first thought that entered my mind was, "How can he just dismiss Eric so quickly? Hmph. He must not have loved Eric all that much in the first place."

It was, of course, a lie from the pits of hell. But right then, I needed that lie to take the spotlight off myself.

Better yet, I shoved this whole matter to the side and switched modes altogether.

I was at work. I had a job to do. Time to take my ax to the chopping block.

Chapter 8

Another Saturday, another event. If it's not a child's birthday party, it's a baby shower. If it's not a baby shower, it's a Mary Kay extravaganza—the list goes on and on. People must think single folks have nothing better to do on Saturday between ten in the morning and six in the evening.

One of the things I looked forward to doing on Saturdays as a married woman was just slicking my hair down with conditioner and cuddling up with my man all day watching *Good Times* reruns and eating lasagna. Hopefully, people would leave us alone in our newlywed world for at least a few years before they started imposing on our precious Saturdays.

Oh, well. My Saturdays might be open for a very long time. Several weeks had gone by, and despite LaShondra's, Stelson's, and my mother's attempts at intervention, Quinn and I were both too stubborn to give in. Yet I couldn't convince myself that it was actually "over" with him. Our only link was Eric, and I secretly thanked God for my son's church and recreational activities with Quinn, because I don't know if I could have quit Quinn cold turkey.

This particular no-life-on-Saturdays event was a wedding.

Considering my circumstances, I was not in a wedding mood. There is something about wedding cake, however, that rouses even the least romantic spectator. Eric wasn't much of a sweets eater, so between the two of us, I could probably secure a piece of the bride's and the groom's cake without anyone noticing. You gotta have a plan for stuff like this, you know?

There was also the issue of my mother. While she was perfectly capable of driving herself to the wedding, she insisted on riding together. Eric was thrilled, of course. No weekend was ever complete without seeing his grandmother.

Okay, Peaches, stop being silly. I had a little self-talk in the hallway mirror while adjusting the belt in my khaki coatdress to allow more slack. *No more acting ugly toward your mother.*

I exhaled, slumped my shoulders down, and let my abdominal muscles go. Who was I kidding? This dress was too tight. I didn't want to hear it from my mother.

I released the strained buttons one by one and dragged myself back to the closet. None of my dresses fit right. I resorted to a skirt and jacket combo. There was no room to grow in the skirt, but a shell top camouflaged the muffin top enough for me to breathe comfortably.

One fire extinguished, one to go.

My mother sashayed to my car in classic church-lady style—floral print dress, stockings a shade too light, with coordinating clip-on shoe decals. She was stuck in the '80s. Or was it the '60s? I couldn't be sure.

Once she finished fussing over Eric, she said hello to me.

"Hi, Mom," I languished.

"What's wrong with you?" She pressed her back against the seat, and I felt her eyes scrape me up and down.

I fixed my gaze on the road ahead. "Nothing."

She glanced at Eric in the backseat and then back at me. She leaned in toward me and whispered, "I don't know what's wrong with you, but I'm gonna ask the Holy Spirit to reveal it to me and then I'm gonna pray it out of you, you hear?" Then she sat back in her seat and began humming a generic gospel melody.

Truth was, I wanted to know what was wrong with me as much as she did. I just knew if I went to God about it, He'd tell me to lay myself out like a doormat for Quinn to walk all over. Not gonna happen. I had to have some kind of leverage.

"You got a gift?"

I motioned to the backseat. "Yes."

"Eric, baby, hand me the present."

My son followed his grandmother's orders and passed the white and silver gift bag forward.

"I like this bag, Peaches. What's inside?" Before I could answer, my mother proceeded to ruffle the tissue paper I had expertly, painstakingly arranged to cover the contents. "Oh, picture frames! This is nice."

"Thanks."

She smashed the tissue paper back down.

"You get them anything?"

"No siree. I ain't got money for no gift." She reached inside her purse and pulled out a pen. "I'm just gonna put my name on the card with you and Eric."

Kinetra, my twenty-one-year-old cousin who was still matriculating in college, mind you, decided to marry some boy no one had ever seen. I say "boy" because he couldn't have been any more than twenty-two himself.

Reliable family gossips said he had a good job, though, and Kinetra was on track to graduate with her teaching degree in just a few months.

The cause for the rush was the usual impetus. Pregnancy. Actually, Kinetra lost the baby early on, but the couple decided they wanted to marry anyway, hence this Saturday wedding on what had to be the rainiest day of the year.

There was certainly a lot of whispering and head-nodding

in the sanctuary as the bride walked down the aisle in a simple A-line off-white gown. Her groom fidgeted nervously at the altar—almost breathless at the sight of his bride. And despite the feelings of a few holier-than-thou family members, Kinetra exuded a beautiful, beaming smile quelling any doubts about their young love.

"Who gives this woman to be united in holy matrimony?"

This was the moment I had been dreading. My heart fell down to my lap, and my eyes followed. I couldn't bear to watch my uncle Hemmie raise Kinetra's veil and plant one last, gentle kiss on his daughter's forehead before giving her away. To me, this is always the sweetest moment in a wedding.

This moment would never happen for me.

The tears came swiftly. I managed to muffle the cries in my throat and keep my shoulders from twitching as the emotional tidal wave washed over my body.

Eric caught sight of my distress and shook my left arm. "What's wrong, Momma?"

"Shhhh." By this point, the preacher was well into the vows.

I grabbed a tissue from my purse and dabbed while my mother, now alarmed, looked on.

She touched my arm. "You all right, Peaches?"

I blinked rapidly, composing myself. "Yes, Momma, I'm okay."

"That'll be you up there in a few months if you get off your high horse." She peered at me through eye slits. So much for empathy.

I wanted to say, *That'll never be me because Daddy is never coming back.* But if I spoke anymore, I'd have to dash out of the building and steal attention from the bride. No, this wasn't my day. This was Kinetra's and what's-his-name's day. I'd have to suck up my sorrow and keep it moving.

Whether or not I'd ever have a day was anybody's guess.

★　★　★

The reception was held in the church's adjacent fellowship hall. Kinetra's husband had a big, country family, so this was not your ordinary reception. There were pork chops, chicken wings, ribs, mashed potatoes, three different kinds of cornbread. It felt more like a family reunion than a wedding reception. Actually, the atmosphere was kind of nice. This way both families could get to know one another and spend time in genuine fellowship rather than the uptight atmosphere generated by hors d'oeuvres and flowing drink fountains. It's kind of hard to be pretentious when you're picking chicken out from between your teeth.

The cakes didn't let me down. I ate my piece, Eric's piece, and a little of my mother's piece until she slapped my hand away. "You eatin' for two?"

No, she didn't! "Mother, why would you ask something so insulting?"

"I'm just saying—"

"Please don't *say*, okay?"

She threw her fork onto her plate—though the room was so loud I'm sure no one heard it—and announced to her audience of Eric and me that she was ready to leave.

She wasn't the only one.

The silence on our drive back was perforated only by her mumblings. She was holding back, for Eric's sake, but it was only a matter of time before she let it all go.

Maybe it was time for her to let it go—and me, too. I was tired of her obsession with me getting married. This was my life, not hers. Besides, I wouldn't want her life in a million years.

I dropped my mother off and followed the short path back home with almost no thought. Eric looked out the window, mouthing a noiseless conversation with himself about the cars we passed. An only child, Eric's imagination was his closest companion.

When we got home, we changed clothes and went to the

park to work off some of the food we'd eaten. The nippy spring air promised a natural fan to keep me from sweating out the curls I had so painstakingly crafted with a flat iron before the wedding. Eric fussed because I made him put on a jacket, but he forgot all about the inconvenience when he spotted a little red-haired boy playing alone on the playground equipment.

Eric quickly made friends with the boy, and they set off to conquer the task of climbing up the winding slide without slipping back down. Since there were no other children present to be annoyed or endangered by their activity, Eric heard no objections from me.

I took the opportunity to walk a few laps around the trail, keeping Eric and his easy-to-spot, red-haired companion in sight. A woman—obviously the genetic source of the boy's distinctive hair color—was now fully visible between the sparse trees along the route, huffing heavily as she paced the trail. The course narrowed at one point, and she briefly addressed me as we passed each other.

I wondered if people would be as friendly in Philadelphia. Would they speak? How many days of the year could I expect to be able to go outside in such a cold region of the country? I laughed, though, at the question. I didn't go outside much in Texas, with the heat and all. I'd probably just be exchanging one set of extremes for another.

With my increased rate of breathing, I could almost feel my mind clearing. Like my heart was pumping out the stress of recent days. *Why don't I exercise more often?*

Fifteen minutes later, I'd worked up a decent sweat—not decent enough to strike the hairdo, mind you, but enough circulation to clear the cobwebs. I thought about how Eric had walked onto the rocky play area and so easily gained a playmate. He was flexible. Adaptable. He could survive the move to Philadelphia.

Northcomp crossed my mind, too. What if the company folded?

And what if Quinn decided not to wait on me? Maybe I deserved to be left. God knows I deserved a lot of judgment He'd spared me from. Somebody was standing in the gap for me. Probably my mother, as nosy as she was.

For the first time in days, I talked to Him. *Thank You, Lord, for your grace.*

My cell phone vibrated and I checked the screen. *Raphael?* He never called out of the blue unless there was some kind of problem. Usually a child support remittance problem.

I slowed my pace and braced myself for a sob story. "Hello?"

"Hi, Peaches."

Sterile help-desk tone. "How can I help you?"

We held the phone for a moment before he continued. "Um, what are you up to?"

"I'm at the park with Eric. Why?"

"Nothin'. What's my son doing?"

"You feeling all right, Raphael?" I couldn't resist.

He laughed slightly. "Yeah, I'm cool. I'm just . . . calling."

"Oh. Alrighty then. I'll tell Eric you called."

"Can we talk?" he blurted out before I could snap my phone shut.

"Eric is on the swings right now. He's too far away from me to call him over. I'll have him get back with you—"

"No, I mean *me* and *you*. Can *we* talk?"

"About what?"

"Just talk. Like friends."

My legs came to a halt. "Nega-tyv. We're not friends."

"We were, in the past. And there's no reason—"

"To bring the past back now," I completed the sentence for him. "Look, Raphael, I don't *befriend* engaged men. I'm not going to be chitchatting with you, and I don't expect you to call me for any conversation outside of Eric once I get married to Quinn."

Never mind my wedding might not actually happen.

Besides all that, I didn't even *like* Raphael. How could I be friends with the man who stomped my heart to pieces and then tried to send me a bill for it while I was pregnant with his child? Raphael should thank God every day that I even tolerated him because if Jesus hadn't commanded us to forgive our enemies, I would have been content to hate Raphael forever.

He clucked a few more times, obviously trying to find a convincing comeback.

I didn't give him a chance. "Bye."

One glance toward the playground confirmed Eric was still busily playing. Satisfied that he was enjoying himself, I resumed my walking pace and called LaShondra to get her take on Raphael's sudden desire to be friends.

"Girl, he's acting silly because you're getting married."

"I don't think he has to worry about that anymore."

"Whatever," she snapped. "I'm praying the stubbornness out of your heart."

I stopped her before she could start on another rampage. "We're talking about Raphael, here. Crazy Raphael."

"Maybe he's not so crazy. He knows he lost a good thing."

"He didn't lose me—he threw me away. Stuffed me in the bottom of a trash can."

We laughed at my silly illustration, then she cut the conversation short. "I gotta go, girl. My hubby is pulling into the garage."

"Oh, barf. Here we go again." Though LaShondra couldn't see me, I rolled my eyes in disgust. "The king has returned."

"Peaches," LaShondra started, but then she stopped. We'd had this conversation several times since she married.

"Let me just go on the record and say that when I get

married, I will not get off the phone with you when my husband walks through the door." Women all over the world cheered, I'm sure.

"I just want to greet him when he walks in." She rushed her words.

"I used to have a dog who did that."

"All right, Miss Smarty Pants, you keep this up and all you'll *ever* have is a dog to meet you at the door."

She disconnected the call and, once again, I stopped in my tracks. *Did she just say that and then hang up in my face?*

I wanted to call her back. Let her know that this was one giant step back for womankind. What about our rights? The fight for equality? This girl done put us back fifty years, neglecting our lifelong bond of sisterhood for a man. If statistics held true, both of our husbands would be dead six years before we died, then where would that leave us? Back together again. And then she'll want to talk to me—but I'll not listen. In fact, I'll turn my hearing aid off and roll out on my Hoveround.

Chapter 9

Since my mother was hardly speaking to me—she didn't call to say "good morning"—she didn't get the chance to scold me about missing yet another Sunday service. I needed the rest. Going in extra early to cover Theresa's job and mine was wearing me out. Something had to give.

Plus, rain and thunder kept me up most of the night. Well, tell the whole truth and shame the devil, the rain and my own thoughts had me counting sheep.

I wondered what my father would want me to do. I wondered if I would look back and kick myself in the behind for not following Quinn to Philly. I was also bugged by Raphael's words. And since when do twenty-one-year-olds have more happiness and love than their thirty-four-year-old cousins?

I probably owed my mother an apology for my bad attitude. Sometimes she just made me so angry.

Maybe if there weren't the thirteen years hanging between the first round of kids and me, I could have been closer to my siblings and vented with them. I was the "surprise" child, having snuck up on my parents when my mother was in her forties. Certainly, I was thankful for life, but I lay in bed that night wondering why God let me be born so late in the game. I didn't get to have my father for as long as my sisters and brothers had him. Never really got to know my grandparents before they passed.

It wasn't fair. Sometimes I looked at Eric and thought, "I was just like him, all alone most of the time." When my siblings came back to my parents' home for Thanksgiving, they always told these wonderful stories about playing hide-and-seek, riding some huge dog our family apparently used to own, and fighting with the Townsend kids down the street. I had my own share of neighborhood fun, but not with them. Not with my own peeps.

The only constant companion I ever really had was food.

It just wasn't fair.

So when my alarm buzzed, I reached over and smacked it one good time. I wasn't finished resting, thinking, or both. Eric, however, wasn't quite so easy to pacify.

"Sweetheart, we'll just have house church today, okay?" I rolled over to face my son, who had already taken the liberty of putting on a shirt and slacks. Though he had missed a button, he was still a healthy sight.

"What's *house* church?"

"It's when we serve God at home. Sing songs, read the Bible, and pray. God is everywhere, Eric. You know that, right?" I bugged my eyes and nodded, hoping to see him reciprocate.

"But Momma, I want to go to *real* church. You didn't go to church last Sunday, either." Eric assumed his grandmother's place. Those little brown eyes weren't quite as accusatory, but they still held the power to convict.

I shook my head. "Well, we went to church yesterday, at the wedding. Remember?"

"Now I'm going to have two weeks in a row with no star for attendance in Sunday school." A scowl crossed his face.

"You better put your little lip back in," I commanded him.

"Can I call Mr. Quinn and ask him to take me to church?"

I pulled the covers over my head, feeling like a snake in a hole. Here was my eight-year-old son practically begging me to go to church, and I didn't want to take him. *Lord, what am I doing? My life isn't unwonderful. It's actually pretty good, and I thank You for it.*

I pushed the covers back, prepared to tell Eric that I had changed my mind about church, but he was no longer standing there. I figured he must have gone back to his room to sulk in silence. He'd be so happy when I gave him the good news—we were indeed going to church.

Since it took me twice as long to get dressed as Eric, I decided to go ahead and take my shower. The water seemed to rinse off all the regrets I'd wallowed in most of the night.

We were going to church.

I stepped out of the shower and threw on a robe, then found Eric sitting at the kitchen table eating a bowl of cereal, still dressed in his church clothes.

"You know, Eric, you were right."

He held up his index finger and hurriedly chewed the food in his mouth so that he could tell me something, but before he could speak, the doorbell rang.

Eric swallowed. "It's Mr. Quinn."

My eyebrows shot up.

"I asked you, but you didn't answer."

"That doesn't mean—"

The doorbell rang again. I shook my head as I stomped toward the entrance.

Sunlight spilled onto my face when I opened the door, and there stood Quinn looking like a handsomely radiant ebony hero. He sported a fresh shave, a maroon button-down shirt, and black slacks.

God was not playing fair.

Quinn removed his shades, and his eyes took me in. "You're beautiful with nothing on."

I pulled my robe even tighter.

"All natural, I mean." He laughed at his blunder. "No makeup."

"Thank you."

He looked past me toward the dining area. "Is Eric ready?"

"I'm perfectly capable of taking my son to church, you know."

Quinn looked at his watch, sucked in air between his teeth. "He wants to be on time for Sunday school. Sister Evans won't give him a sticker if he's late."

"Mmmm."

My son skipped up to us, Bible in hand. "I'm ready, Mr. Quinn."

"Hold up. We gotta fix you up, man." Quinn instructed Eric to get his button situation together and cinch his belt up a notch, making Eric presentable. Watching them was always funny to me. If it had been me, I would have unbuttoned Eric's shirt and repositioned it for him. Quinn taught Eric how to do things for himself.

"You got money for offering?"

Eric reached into his pocket and pulled out a dollar. "Yes, sir."

"All right." They gave each other dap.

"You're coming later, right?" Quinn asked.

"I guess—"

"Momma's going to house church today," Eric interrupted.

Now it was Quinn's turn to question me. "*House* church?"

Eric started to explain, "Yeah, it's when—"

"I'm going to my mother's church today," I lied smartly.

Quinn gave a slow nod, as though he didn't quite believe me. "Okay. Well, if you don't mind, I'd like to take Eric with me to Brother Riley's house after church. We'll eat there and watch the game with his boys. Cool?"

"Yeah."

"We gotta go, Mr. Quinn."

Quinn grabbed his car's fob and unlocked the door so Eric could get in the passenger's seat. With my son safely out of hearing distance, Quinn turned his attention to me.

"I've missed you."

I had lied enough for one day already. "Missed you, too."

He took my hand in his, quickening the pulse throughout my body. He leaned over the threshold and kissed my cheek. "Peaches, what happened to us? What's wrong?"

I removed my hand from his grip, crossed my arms. "I don't know how to answer your question. I'm just . . . in a funk, that's all."

"I'll be glad when you come out of it."

I looked up at him. In the next moment, his image was blurred by my tears. Quinn stepped into my home and pulled me into an embrace. I broke down in his arms, inhaling the heavenly scent of his cologne between sobs.

"Woman, I love you. You understand that? I love you, Peaches."

I nodded.

"Now, let's do this thing, you hear? We're getting married, we're moving to Philadelphia, and we're going to be a family with the help of the Lord." He pushed me back and bent down slightly so that we were eye to eye. "Are you with me on this or not, baby?"

The four inches of distance between us was killing me. I couldn't imagine what fifteen hundred miles would feel like. "Yes."

He closed the space again and kissed my forehead profusely. Then my cheeks again, and finally my lips, where we both sealed the passionate deal.

Eric's whining interrupted our reunion. "It's hot in here!"

"We have to go." Quinn stepped back.

I reached out for his hand, and he reciprocated. "I'll see you at *our* church."

I nodded. "I love you."

"I love you, too."

"Then put the ring back on."

Sunday with my men and my Heavenly Father was sublime. I was back on track. You know that feeling—when you've been running from God for a while and then you come to the end of yourself and just stop and say *Uncle?* Well, that's where I was. I just said, "Forget it, Lord, I'm not going to throw away this gift You have given me." Forget myself, my pride, and my fears.

Matter of fact, forget Northcomp. I walked in the office Monday with a new attitude. I wasn't going to be there much longer, so there was no undue pressure. I wasn't sweating the job or Hampton. Integrity and common sense dictated I carry on as though nothing had changed. And yet, without the stress of trying to make myself seem invaluable to the company, I felt pleasantly at ease.

That is until around eleven o'clock, when Eric's school called.

"Miss Miller, this is Mrs. Clocker. I'm the counselor at Wayman Elementary. I'd like to speak with you briefly about Eric's academic progress," she began in a most clinical tone. She went on to tell me Eric had failed the state reading assessment and was in danger of repeating third grade if he did not pass it on his second try next month.

"How can he fail third grade when his report card grades are passing?"

"It's not that simple. A grade given in the classroom isn't quite the same as a cumulative state test." She went on and on trying to explain things to me.

"Mrs. Clocker, the school year is more than halfway complete. Why am I just now being informed of my son's problem?"

"We've been practicing, benchmarking, throughout the year. Third grade is the first year for standardized testing in

Texas. Eric's scores have been in the seventies, so we've been keeping an eye on him."

"But *I* didn't know to keep an eye on him. All I ever see is the report cards, and they look pretty good to me. Do you think he's just not trying?" I knew my son was smart, but he could also be lazy.

"Well, we do teach students strategies throughout the year, but we can't actually make them use the strategies on the day of testing. You might want to ask what Miss Norman observes of him in the classroom."

My head was pounding—my baby fail the third grade? I had never known anyone to fail a grade in elementary school except this one boy named Kenneth Cooper, and he ended up going to the pen before we were even in high school. Besides, what kind of school flunks a third grader based on his first big test?

"I'd like to schedule a conference."

We set up a meeting. Tuesday at 11:30.

I could not wait to tear into Eric when I picked him up from the after-school program. He hopped into the car and gave me his usual, "Hi, Mom."

"Eric, did you use the strategies they've been teaching you when you took the reading test?"

He twitched his nose. "Yes . . . sometimes."

That was a lie if I ever heard one. "You think they're teaching you those strategies for their good health?"

"But those strategies are dumb. You gotta underline all this stuff—"

"You failed the test, Eric!" I shot down his excused via my rearview mirror.

His eyes fell to the floorboard, sadness etched into his face.

I focused on the road again, regained my composure. "You're a smart young man, but no one will ever know it unless you do your best on these tests."

"I *did* do my best."

"Not if you didn't use the strategies."

"But—"

"But my *foot*. If you plan on passing the third grade, you need to play the game the way they're teaching you to play it." The sooner he learned life's rules, the better. I was not going to raise one more little black boy who thought the world revolved around him—that everybody else's way is wrong and he's right. We had enough Raphaels in the world already.

And speaking of the devil, he happened to call my cell phone as Eric and I walked through the garage entry door.

"Speak."

"Hello to you, too."

"Raphael, what do you want?"

"If you don't want to talk to me, maybe Eric does."

I could have used a little tag team at that moment. Raphael might have been a nuisance to me, but he was coming around for our son. "Uh, you might want to ask him about his state test."

"Put him on the phone."

I called Eric to the kitchen and told him his father was on the phone. Eric nearly flattened me taking the phone from my hand. Why children can't see what's wrong with their fathers is beyond me. Must be some special kind of father forgiveness God gives them.

"Hey, Dad!"

I left Eric in the kitchen to carry on the discussion while I went to my bedroom to get out of my suit. I think I fired three people while on autopilot that day.

Maybe Quinn was right. Perhaps I should take some time off when we got to Philadelphia to help Eric with his reading. Better yet, I needed to help Eric now. No way was I going to walk into Eric's new school in Philadelphia and enroll him as a third-grade flunky. He'd be fighting an uphill battle from the start.

My shoes landed in the closet with no particular accuracy. I plopped down on my bed and took a deep breath. I looked at the clock. 6:27. This time yesterday everything was just fine and dandy. Now this mess. *Does it ever end, Lord?*

I took a moment to pray, asking God for His guidance in this academic situation. I asked forgiveness for appearing callous during the day's terminations at Northcomp. I asked a little forgiveness for my being a bit short with Mrs. Clocker. *They just caught me at the wrong time, Lord.* For some reason, I was also compelled to repent for the way I spoke to Raphael. *Forgive me, Lord. I know I need to be nicer. He just irks me, though. Amen.*

First real prayer I'd prayed in weeks.

Eric knocked on my bedroom door and entered once I granted permission. "My daddy wants to talk to you." He handed me the phone and then left the room.

I tried to remember what I'd just prayed about. I must be kind. "Yes?"

"So, what are they saying at the school?" At least he was asking.

"We've got a conference scheduled tomorrow at eleven-thirty. I'll let you know what happens."

"I can get off early and come to the meeting."

I sat straight up in bed. "For what?"

"I'm . . . his . . . father," he strung out, "and I'd like to know what's happening in my son's life."

Since when? I almost said the words running through my mind, but since the prayer for Eric was hooked onto the prayer for a gentler tongue, I had to refrain. "Fine. You remember how to get to the school?"

"Yeah. I'll see you tomorrow. Bye."

"Adios."

My ears detected a television blasting from Eric's room.

"Turn that off!" I jumped from the bed and marched into my son's room. "You will not be watching television on school nights until you pass that test."

"Momma, I finished my homework while I was in after-care," he whined.

I motioned toward his closet. "Get one of those books down and start reading. And write me a one-page report on what you learned."

"But I hate reading!"

"You gon' hate bein' in the third grade again if you don't quit being so lazy and pass that test!"

Chapter 10

It pays to have a school principal for a best friend. LaShondra told me what to ask and, in essence, how to act during the conference. "Don't be defensive, Peaches. Everyone's looking out for Eric's best interests."

I set the phone on my bathroom counter and turned on the speaker so I could use both hands to wrap my hair. "Do you think I should request a different teacher for Eric?"

"Did you not hear what I just told you about being defensive?"

"That's not being defensive. He's never had a problem before. Maybe he's just not getting it with Miss Norman."

LaShondra sighed. "Go to the meeting and have a discussion. You don't want to get a reputation as one of those moms who blames everything on her child's teacher."

She must have forgotten who she was talking to. "I don't mind sacrificing my reputation so long as my son gets a good education. He's going to be a black man someday. He can't afford to be uneducated."

I brushed the last of my hair in place and set it with a silk scarf.

"This is not us versus them. Don't go in there with a bad attitude."

★ ★ ★

Raphael didn't get to Wayman until almost a quarter till noon. Our meeting was well under way. I was mentally prepared to ignore him, but at that moment I welcomed his presence. The physical layout of the room had me on one side of the table with everyone else—Miss Norman, Mrs. Clocker, and the vice principal, Mr. Savelle—facing me. Granted, there are only four sides to a table. I just didn't appreciate the feel of it all—like they were teaming up to tell me my child wasn't up to par.

"Hello, Mr. . . . um . . ." Mrs. Clocker's voice trailed off as she apparently tried to avoid an awkward situation.

"Lewis." Raphael relieved her confusion with an outstretched hand. He wore a pair of freshly starched jeans with a striped, button-down shirt and a T-shirt underneath. Almost too casual for a conference at school, but his tight edge-up and sharp glasses gave an aura of confidence overriding strict protocol. He always did clean up nicely.

Mrs. Clocker reintroduced everyone in the room, and the meeting resumed as Raphael pulled a chair from the corner and sat next to me.

"I was just telling Miss Lew-, I mean, Miller, that I have been working with Eric very closely so far this year," Miss Norman reiterated proudly for Raphael as she passed around samples of my son's work. "He's very conscientious and he doesn't like making anything less than a B. It takes him a little longer to get finished, so sometimes I give him extra time or assign him a shorter passage, but he does eventually catch on."

She looked around the room, receiving understated nods from her colleagues. I, on the other hand, was not pleased. I might have been pleased if I hadn't talked to LaShondra the night before, but I knew better. "So what you're saying is, you've been modifying Eric's work?"

Oh, the shock that fell on their faces. "Modify" was, evidently, a four-letter word to these people.

"Oh, no, no." Miss Norman tried to backtrack.

"If you've been giving him extra time and shortening his assignments, then you *have* been modifying for him." I faced Mrs. Clocker now. "Correct?"

She bobbed her head side to side for a moment. "Well, technically . . ."

"Yes," Raphael tagged in as though we'd rehearsed this.

I continued, "And if you've been modifying his work all along, then number one, his report card grades aren't a true reflection of his mastery of third-grade skills. And number two, you cannot expect him to be able to pass a test that other kids who *haven't* had their work modified are expected to pass." I was back on Miss Norman now, who was turning bright red with every word I said. I almost felt sorry for her. She couldn't have been more than twenty-two or so, probably fresh out of college.

The vice principal jumped in. "We should probably revisit some of the things we've been doing to help Eric succeed." He shot a worried glance at Miss Norman. "But I can assure you, we'll do everything within our power to make sure Eric passes the next exam so he won't be in danger of failing third grade.

"We will need your help, however. Miss Norman has tutorials after schools on Tuesday and Thursdays."

Raphael shook his head. "We'll have to see."

I read the expression on Raphael's face and immediately knew we were on the same page. The last thing Eric needed was more time with Miss Norman.

"We'll probably look into Sylvan."

Mr. Savelle nodded. "That's a good idea."

Miss Norman was on the verge of tears. Now I felt sorry for her for real. Only a few days ago Mr. Hampton hung me out to dry, just as Mr. Savelle had all but done to her. "Yeah, Tuesdays and Thursdays aren't good for me." I had to throw her a rope, woman to woman, subordinate to subordinate.

A bell rang and Miss Norman stood. She averted all eyes in the room as she gathered Eric's papers, her notebook, and a pen. "I'm sorry. I've got to get back to class." She left without looking back.

Mrs. Clocker tried to cover for her. "The children do get restless when they're out in the hallway waiting for their teachers."

Mr. Savelle scooted to the edge of his chair and laced his fingers. "Let me assure you again, we'll be doing everything we can to help Eric."

"So will we." Raphael ended the meeting by rising and giving a manly handshake to the principal.

What was this—*man* day? I'm the one who's always handling things between the school and Eric. Now the principal wants to get all goody-goody with Raphael? I wanted to say something smart, but then I remembered what LaShondra told me about keeping a good reputation. So long as Mr. Savelle feared that Raphael might put a foot on his neck, there was no need in both of us coming across as threats. Raphael's foot was much bigger than mine, anyway.

We signed out at the front desk. Raphael held the door open for me as we exited the reception area. We took two steps into the main office and heard "Dad!" from behind us.

Eric was in line with his classmates, calling all the way down the art-lined hallway to get his father's attention. Raphael turned and waved at Eric as Miss Norman stood ushering the students into the room. Eric was busily pointing out his father to his little friends. When he finally reached Miss Norman's doorway, he must have asked her if he could say hello to us. She looked down the hallway, nodded at Eric, and watched as he quickly approached us.

Raphael lowered himself to receive Eric's hug. "Hey."

"Hey, Dad. What are you doing here?" I couldn't help but notice the way my son's face brightened when he spoke to his father. Like he was talking to Santa.

Raphael eyed me as he responded, "Your momma didn't tell you I was coming to meet your teacher today?"

Now why would I tell my son something I thought was a lie up until about fifteen minutes ago?

"Nuh-uh." Eric shook his head.

"Well, I did. We'll talk about it later. Get back to class now."

"Okay. Bye, Dad."

Eric jogged toward Miss Norman's room. Halfway back, he whispered, "Bye, Mom."

It's so nice to be an afterthought. I don't know what kind of spell Raphael had over our son, but the man was definitely sprinkled with magic Daddy dust.

Raphael walked me to my car, asking me to let him know how much tutoring would cost. His generosity surprised me, seeing as I thought my next call would be to the attorney general's office to see if I could have this additional financial support mandated.

"I'll let you know." I stepped into my car and shut the door.

Raphael stood next to my car for a moment while I turned the ignition. I didn't want to roll over the brother's foot, so I lowered my window. "You gonna step back or what?"

He shifted his jaw to one side, just like Eric does when he's thinking. "Can we do lunch?"

I rolled my eyes in their sockets for a moment. *Twilight Zone* music played in my head. "Why?"

He bit his lower lip and looked away. Another one of Eric's gestures, making me question the whole nature versus nurture theory.

"I need to talk to you."

Clearly, whatever he had on his mind had been there for some time—at least since he found out I was no longer on the market. Or maybe he needed an organ from Eric, which he wouldn't be getting. Either way, it was time for us to have this big come-to-Jesus meeting. Set everything straight, for the record.

I checked my watch. I had been gone almost an hour, but Theresa could hold down the fort. "We'll have to do fast food because I need to get back to work."

"Okay."

Quinn called as I followed Raphael's car through a busy retail area. "How'd the meeting go?"

"It was special, but I'll have to tell you about it later. Right now I'm on my way to eat lunch with Raphael."

"Why?"

Though I didn't appreciate the tone of his inquiry, I had to concur. "My question exactly."

"So what was his answer?"

"I'm not sure yet. He's got something up his sleeve. I'll let you know."

Quinn persisted. "I'm not hanging up this phone until I know where he's leading you."

I wondered if Quinn was in control mode or protective mode, not that I had enough sense to welcome either one. "I'm following him right now—wait. Okay, looks like we're going to McDonald's. The one down the street from the church. I'll call you later."

"Yeah."

My phone signaled the disconnection before I had a chance to say good-bye.

Mickey D's would have to suffice for what I figured was my last meal with Raphael before the one we might eat together at Eric's wedding. I ordered a kids' nugget meal and Raphael got a Big Mac combo. He offered to pay for both meals, but I really didn't want to endear myself to him. This conversation could get ugly.

We sat across from each other discussing as much as we could about the tutoring without having the numbers in front of us. I assured him I would know something by the end of the week. As far as I was concerned, we could have worked this out via e-mail. Alas, I had to be civil.

I was on my fourth nugget when Raphael finally decided to get down to the nitty-gritty. He grabbed a napkin and swiped the sesame seeds from his lips. "Peaches, have you ever regretted something?"

Picking you for a baby daddy. "Yes, I have."

"I mean really, *really* regretted something so bad you could kick yourself for doing what you did."

"I repeat, yes, I have."

"I messed up when I left you."

I nodded. "Yes, you did."

"And I'm sorry." All the muscles in his face surrendered, unveiling the sincere apology I could have used eight years ago when I looked around and found myself the single black mother of a young black male.

Enough with these true confessions. There was no priest stamp on my forehead. "Raphael, build a bridge and get over it. I forgave you a long time ago."

He laughed, looked down at his sandwich. "No, you didn't."

"Yes, I did. I went to the altar at church and everything. I was a snotty mess."

Arms crossed, eyes squared on mine, he probed, "If you've forgiven me, why do you hate me so much?"

On second thought, I could have used a priest's booth right about then. I wanted to hide behind a curtain, avoid Raphael's penetrating stare. I used to look into those eyes and see a great future. Now they only reminded me of a painful heartbreak. "I don't *hate* you, I just flat don't *like* you."

He threw his hands up, leaned back against the pleather booth. "I deserve whatever you feel for me."

"I'm glad you agree." I laughed and stuffed another nugget into my mouth. Only one left before I'd be out of distractions. I knew I should have ordered the ten-piece.

"Look, I know I can't erase the past, so I won't try. I would like to start over again. A truce?" Raphael presented a hand, but I left him hanging.

I cocked my head to the side. "What do you want from me?"

"I've been thinking." He hesitated.

"About what?"

"Me, you, and Eric. When we're together, it's like . . . this is the family I was supposed to have, but I threw it all away. I was young. Selfish. Didn't recognize a good woman when I had one."

All I could do was purse my lips, raise my eyebrows, and nod in agreement.

Raphael's eyes followed a little boy who struggled to walk back to his seat without spilling a Coke refill. "When you told me you were engaged to Quinn, my whole life flashed before my eyes."

"Raphael, you are engaged," I reminded him.

"That's only because of you. You held me to a standard. You made me do right by my Eric when I didn't even know how to be a father. I never had a father in my life. Look at me now, though. I'm getting married. I have a relationship with my son. None of this would have happened if you hadn't been the strong woman you are."

"You're welcome . . . I guess."

His eyes misty, Raphael pronounced, "Peaches, you made me a better man."

I can't lie—my heart was fluttering. Maybe even faltering. Before me sat the man I used to think lived inside Raphael's body. He was kind, genuine. Caring. He used to make me feel like I was the only woman in the world. And somehow he had managed to do it again in McDonald's, if only for a moment.

"All I can say is, I'm glad you've grown up. And if I had

any hand in that . . . well . . . let's just thank God and keep it moving, all right?"

A tentative smile crossed his lips. "I want to be friends again."

"No."

I'd meant for my answer to come out like Mufasa, but it sounded more like Simba. Raphael burst into laughter and I followed. My response seemed so juvenile. If we were going to have to communicate for at least another ten years, it might as well be amicable. Though I could probably never run out of sarcastic things to say to Raphael, there was always the repentance and frustration with myself afterward.

I had forgiven Raphael by faith, knowing one day God would make my feelings match my confession. Maybe I figured that day was as good as any.

Or maybe some of Raphael's enchanted dust got on me.

Chapter 11

I didn't get a chance to call Quinn back when I returned to the office. For one thing, Mr. Hampton was fuming that I'd been gone for over an hour and a half. He probably wouldn't have noticed if Theresa had shown up. She called in sick sometime after eleven, leaving a message on my work phone instead of my cell. This wasn't like Theresa. She must have had an interview or something. I really couldn't be too angry with her, because I might have done the same thing in her pumps.

Since I had no receptionist, I had to personally receive everyone who walked in for the afternoon negotiations. Vernon had my back, though, so I carried on with business as usual.

Norma Jefferson was leaning toward early retirement. Walking her through all the options and forms took no less than an hour. She took it gracefully. I closed our meeting with a smile on my face.

Axel Rand, however, came within two inches of cursing me out before he finally accepted the reality of termination. If I'd wanted to be rude, I could have mentioned his poor attendance record and the report of sexual harassment against him still staining his employment record. To be honest, Axel was on my radar long before the cutbacks. But I didn't want to totally annihilate the man, so I kept my mouth shut and watched him turn every color of the rainbow. When he realized he was fired—as in past tense, not up for discussion—his skin returned to its normal peach hue and we talked through the cash payout for his unused vacation days.

Phillip Carley was supposed to be my last appointment for the day. He quickly decided to take the severance pay and run. It was a generous offer. He was a fairly young, smart man. He could do a lot with that money, and I got the feeling he had already been working on a business proposal. Probably the next big dot-com sensation.

Another successful firing. I sat back in my leather executive chair for a moment, proud of myself for separating my emotions from my professional responsibilities. Maybe I *was* cut out for this. The seminar certificates lining my walls backed me. It's an ugly job, but somebody's got to do it, right? And maybe people like Phillip needed a push off the ol' ledge to get them flying toward their dreams.

A buzz from the phone interrupted my peace. "Patricia, could you please come see me in my office?"

Hampton.

I looked at my watch. Four minutes till quittin' time. *Shoot!* "In a moment."

I packed up my stuff, shut down my computer, and put on my jacket. Hampton needed to understand, whatever ungodly problem he discovered at 4:56 p.m. would have to wait until eight the next morning.

Purse and satchel in hand, I approached Mr. Hampton's door and greeted his longtime secretary, Linda, as she was leaving.

"Go right on in, Patricia."

I entered his office and saw Axel sitting across from Hampton. How on earth he'd convinced Vernon to let him remain in the building was beyond me.

"Patricia, I was just talking to Axel about his termination. Are you sure there isn't anything we can do to keep him onboard?"

Both Hampton and Axel stared at me now. See! This is the kind of mess I didn't have time for. A puff of sarcasm escaped my lips. "I'm afraid not."

Axel turned his attention back to Hampton. He might as well have dropped down on the ground and begged for his job with all the whining he did for the next five minutes. He even showed Hampton a picture of his dogs, which he apparently carried around in his wallet. "Scooner has epilepsy. He's on medication."

I announced, "I'm leaving now."

"Wait just a moment, Patricia."

Hampton stood, apologizing to Axel for the abrupt end of the meeting. "I'm sorry there's nothing else we can do for you. If Patricia says the data have spoken, the data have spoken."

Axel stomped out of the room, but not before he shot me a killer's eye. I kept my eyeballs pointed straight at him because I needed him to think I was not afraid of him, even if I was a little.

The moment Axel was out of earshot, Hampton begged my forgiveness, in so many words. "Thanks for coming through."

"This is not a game, Mr. Hampton. I am not going to play good cop, bad cop with you. If I fire someone, I expect you to have my back." I hoped he understood the terminology. Too bad if he didn't. It was after five—no telling what unprofessional slang might come out of my mouth.

He nodded. "Fair enough. I respect your decisions."

"I can't tell."

"You have to understand. These people . . . want a shoulder to cry on."

I looked at him like he was crazy. Why would anyone in

their right mind choose Hampton's hard, cold shoulder for comfort in difficult times? He didn't even sign sympathy cards—he had Linda stamp them.

He cleared his throat. "I only wanted to reassure him I'd give him a strong recommendation for another job. Just as I would for you if you were leaving, which, of course, won't be for a long time. You're a valuable member of this team. I'm seeing a side of you I've never seen before, and I look forward to the day we can increase your salary significantly."

How significant is significantly? Suddenly my attitude wasn't so bad. Maybe this was the answer to my prayers. Okay, not really my *prayers*, but at least my wishes. If Quinn and I waited out this rough patch at Northcomp, maybe my salary could become the family's main salary. Then we wouldn't need to move to Philadelphia. Quinn's job on the East Coast was probably as shaky as any job in any industry, given the market. At least that's what I told myself, anyway.

"Well, thanks for the vote of confidence."

"You're welcome, Patricia. I meant every word."

Hampton might have been a lot of things, but he wasn't one for making promises he couldn't keep. He said he was hiring a consultant, he hired one. He told the board he'd make a reduction in force and he'd lit the fire under my behind to get it done. I had no reason to doubt him, and I was willing to bet my marriage that as soon as things got back on track at Northcomp, I'd be sitting on a fat paycheck. Perhaps even chunky enough to pay off the condo before Eric went to college.

Quinn did not receive my new and improved master plan well. He was already a little upset with me for taking so long to return his call. Maybe I shouldn't have sprung the stay-in-Texas idea on him so quickly. Alas, I put it out there Tuesday night as we were on our way to singles Bible study.

Quinn's car was always immaculate. Lord knows I needed

him on my team, because there was probably a serving of small fries stuffed between my car's seat cushions. "Baby, can you wash my car tomorrow?"

"Don't try to change the subject. We just settled the Philadelphia issue two days ago," he argued quietly so as not to alarm Eric, who was busy reading a mandated book while riding the backseat.

I rubbed Quinn's arm. "I'm asking you to consider my plan, that's all."

"There's nothing to consider."

"Is this how it's going to be when we get married? I toss up a suggestion and you shoot it down?" Now my arms crossed my chest.

He purposely slowed his breathing. I imagined he was probably counting to ten. Or a hundred. Quinn didn't say another word until we reached the church parking lot. He settled the gear, locking the car in place. Eric hopped out of the backseat, waved good-bye to us, and ran toward the entrance nearest his classroom.

As I retrieved my purse from the floorboard, Quinn ordered, "Stop. Don't get out yet. We need to talk."

Happy he was at least willing to talk through things, I dropped my bag and eased back into the seat.

"Peaches, every since we got engaged, you've been acting differently. I mean, I thought you wanted me in your life. I thought you wanted us to be a family, but I'm not so sure anymore."

"I *do* want you in my life."

"Look, this thing is bigger than Philadelphia. I don't know any other way to say this, so I'm just going to say it. Either you're going to Philly or you're not."

I threw my hands up in high-drama mode. "Okay, fine. Fine. Forget I ever brought *my* raise up. We're moving to Philadelphia for *your* raise and that's final."

"No, I don't want you going with *that* attitude."

I huffed a few more times and then settled myself down while Quinn waited patiently.

"Peaches, I'm not making you marry me—nor am I making you move to Philadelphia. But if you're not willing to follow me as I follow Christ, it would probably be best if we didn't get married. I'm not willing to be any less of a man than God called me to be, and I won't settle for anything less than a strong woman of God standing in my corner."

He exited the car, leaving me to pout for a few seconds before he opened the passenger's side for me.

Bible study was a bust. Since I hadn't been to Bible study in a minute, I felt like I owed it to Brother Johnson to be especially interactive that night. Quinn's refusal to look at me, however, carried far beyond the room.

Took me back to the early '90s, to be exact. I wouldn't exactly classify myself a rebellious teenager, but I gave my parents a run for their money. Especially my daddy, and he had a unique way of punishing me. He ignored me.

The record for his punishment was a month. When he found out I had taken the family car without his permission, he didn't beat me down or ground me. He just didn't look at me or talk to me for the entire month of May 1992. I'd walk into the kitchen; he'd act like I wasn't even there. Me, him, and Momma would be sitting at the table and he'd reach over me instead of asking me to pass the sugar.

I'm sure there's some sort of child abuse category for it by now. Emotional neglect? Psychological abandonment? Whatever it was, it darn near killed me to be shut out of his life. Like he just flicked a switch and—*poof!*—I was gone.

I don't remember him using this tactic on the older kids. They got whippings up until they left the house, it seemed. I would have preferred a whipping, actually.

I'd seen him do it to Momma, too. They never argued in front of me, so I have no clue why he did it. But I do know Daddy wasn't talking to her on my graduation day.

By that time, I'd learned that two could play the silent game. Maybe it was a rebellious thing, maybe it was a mode of self-preservation. Either way, I decided if he didn't want to talk to me, I didn't want to talk to him, either.

Momma hadn't arrived at my mindset, though. Every morning, she'd talk to him to see if he was going to answer. And when he didn't, her eyes sank a little. She'd have to wait for another day.

You can image what a great and glorious graduation day it was. Our family clumped together in front of the auditorium. "Come on, Momma, smile this time." I literally pushed up the corners of her lips with my thumb and index finger, determined to get at least one happy shot on this memorable occassion. She kept her fake smile in place long enough for LaShondra to snap. Immediately after, her muscles gave way to sadness.

I wanted to shake some sense into Momma, tell her not to let Daddy's sulking ruin the day. Wasn't she immune to it by now? Didn't she have enough sense to know that Daddy's silent treatment was stupid and childish? When was she going to get a backbone?

Fast-forward eighteen years. I, for one, was not going to let Quinn's silent treatment rain on my parade. Not that I had a parade—but if I *did* have a parade planned, it would be great with or without him. I wasn't willing to give him the power to mess my life up, not now or ever.

After class, Eric cried hungry so Quinn stopped and ordered him a kids' meal at Schlotzky's.

"You want anything?" His first words to me in two hours.

"Let me see," I chirped, studying the menu. "You know I don't usually eat this late, but I'll take a smoked turkey sandwich with everything on it." I wasn't really hungry. The food could be my lunch for the next day. My motive for ordering so happily was to let him know the silent treatment didn't work on me. I was immune to it, had been trained by the best.

We rode the rest of the trek to my place in silence. I hoped he would stop me again when he walked us to the door, but he didn't. He said good night to Eric, turned his back, and *walked* away. I stood on the porch for a second and watched him return to his car. Couldn't help but admire his backside.

The stone-cold look on his face when he got behind the wheel, however, was anything but pleasant. He froze for a moment. Stared back at me. Drove away.

What on earth was that? I swear, it was the expression Florida Evans had on her face when she finally realized she'd lost James forever, minus the infamous three words.

Thank God Eric's bedroom wasn't adjacent to mine or he might have heard me sobbing in my big, empty bed. I was always fine with myself until I got by myself and all the problems in my life ganged up on me. Firing people, finding a tutor for Eric, making the choice between losing Quinn or myself.

I wondered if I was normal. I mean, was I crazy or was this just the worst case of cold feet on record?

And why was everyone happy except me? LaShondra was always smiling. My mother was blissful despite having lost my father. My only miserable company was Deniessa, but at least she had someone to hold onto at night. Hampton was probably even better off than me. He had golf buddies and, actually, a quite handsome family. Even Theresa, who was living in total hot sin with her boyfriend, came in with a good attitude every morning.

I was 99.9 percent sure no one I knew was crying with me. *Where's the justice?*

My cell phone chimed, signaling a text message. I knew it

had to be from Quinn. The phone's light assaulted my irritated eyes as I read.

I love u, but u r not ready. This is my last time asking u 2 b my wife & move 2 Philly w/me. Y or N?

I powered down my phone, thankful text messaging is not synchronous. I needed time. My body curled into a fetal position beneath my linens, and the crying resumed.

When that didn't help, I tried to pray. I say tried because after three minutes, I didn't feel like I was getting anywhere. As though God Almighty was on Quinn's side. *Y or N?*

So I turned to the next best thing. The unconditional love of a loaded turkey sandwich.

Chapter 12

I'm not quite sure of the protocol for text message reply time, but assuming I had the same twenty-four-hour-window allotted for e-mail response, I could technically wait until late Wednesday evening to reply.

Wednesday came and went. Same for Thursday. Friday morning, I thought I was going to be sick from sleepless, worrisome, cry-some nights—not to mention the scratchy throat I'd picked up. I called in and left a message telling Hampton that I wouldn't be in. He called me back in a fussy mood. He didn't get over it until I assured him I'd finished all my loathsome firing for the week. The next round of recommended axing wouldn't come until Yancey ran another set of projections following month-end sales data. Forget Hampton, I needed a sick day.

I threw on a T-shirt with yoga pants, slid into a pair of threadbare house shoes, and carted Eric off to school. On the way, he asked if we could get donuts for breakfast. Since I wasn't in my usual rush, I agreed. An empty parking spot opened up near the shop's entrance and I beat out an Escalade. The driver clearly wasn't happy with me. I didn't care, though. He could just join the club.

The really awkward thing about getting into parking lot

skirmishes is that, unlike road rage incidents, you'll actually be getting out of your car in a few minutes, walking alongside the other driver heading toward the same entrance.

I chickened out. "Eric, here's the money. Get yourself a dozen donut holes."

"You want something, Momma?"

I wasn't really hungry, especially after the previous night's snack of chips and soda. Still, there's just something about donuts. "Yeah. Get me two glazed. No, three." One for later, you know.

Mr. Escalade walked past my driver's door and I pretended to change the radio station. My peripheral vision confirmed he was looking at me, probably had a few choice words for me. I ignored him until he entered the shop and got in line behind Eric, at which point I kept an eye on things. People *are* crazy these days.

Minutes later, Eric hopped back into the car. He handed me my change and my donuts and then scraped a donut hole past his lips. Sugar crumbs gathered on his chops. I brushed the pieces away. "Plop the whole thing into your mouth so you won't get sugar everywhere, okay?"

How little boys manage to turn everything into a mess is beyond me.

The school's circular drop-off route was packed with, presumably, stay-at-home moms at the wheel. I could see them from the chest up; their tight-fitting tees, hair pulled back into ponytails. They'd soon be off to the gym or to the grocery store, doing whatever it is that stay-at-home moms do after they drop their kids off at school.

Eric bounded out of my grasp before I had a chance to check his face one last time. He said good-bye over his shoulder and walked briskly toward the building's front entrance. Halfway to the door, another little boy yelled, "Beat ya!" and the race was on. The two of them sprinted the last fifteen feet. It was a tie.

I could only laugh at their impromptu competition. My boy was something else. He liked school, enjoyed his friends. I couldn't imagine what failing the third grade would do to my baby. How would it affect his self-esteem? His sense of worth? And what kind of mom lets her child flunk the third grade?

These questions plus a million more rolled through my head all the way home. Was this my fault? Was I so busy falling in love with Quinn that I forgot to be a mother? Would this be happening if I had attended more Parent Teacher Association meetings? I probably should have mated with a better father for Eric, too. Up until the stupid conference, I'd always thought of Eric as exceptionally bright. But maybe there was one delayed, recessive weird gene in Raphael's family . . . well, it wasn't too recessive—Raphael certainly had it. Or was *I* the one with the bad gene, seeing as I picked Raphael for a baby daddy, even if it was an inadvertent choice?

Perhaps this was postponed punishment for having a child out of wedlock, for bringing a child into this world without providing a stable home environment. There had to be a consequence for my sin, after all.

Somebody had to be in the wrong, because failing third grade is not normal in my world.

The donuts disappeared—simply gone by the time I reached my home. Specks of white trailed down my shirt and onto the driver's seat, and the drawstring in my pants needed loosening. *I can't believe I just sat up here and ate all those donuts.*

I scrunched the empty bag into a ball and threw it into the trash can as soon as I got inside my home. No sense in keeping the evidence. If I kept that up I'd soon have the thighs to convict me. I needed to go for a walk. No less than two miles.

I checked my phone for signs of missed calls or messages. Nothing. No Quinn, no Momma, no LaShondra, no Deniessa. *Nobody cares enough to call me?*

The only thing calling me was a shower. Stuffing myself always made me feel uncomfortable. Almost dirty. Reminded me of my fluffy days.

When I was a younger, I couldn't get enough of those catchy-sounding foods. Ho Hos, Ding Dongs, Twinkies. They *named* them for kids. Getting my hands on those was my life's goal.

Momma was trying to curb my weight problem by fifth grade, so she stopped putting deserts in my lunch kit. Wall Street ain't got nothin' on school cafeterias when it comes to trading. Chips for a cupcake. And don't let somebody have pure chocolate—I would straight up do somebody's homework for a Hershey's bar. No almonds.

The shower succeeded in erasing some of my guilt. I'd messed myself up, though. Now I couldn't work out, because I'd already taken a shower. Deniessa was the only person I knew who took a shower before a workout. Her logic escaped me.

After finishing my after-shower routine, I donned a pair of jeans and the *Covered Until the End* babydoll shirt I'd purchased last year at my church's women's conference. Both pieces fit rather snugly. Not she's-too-fat-for-that snug, but the kind of snug men do a second take to study. I wasn't planning to go anywhere, though, so it didn't matter.

The familiar phone beep lifted my spirits, which were promptly dropped when I saw Raphael's name on the caller ID. I took a deep breath, tried to remember the truce we'd agreed to earlier in the week.

"Hello."

"Oh, that's a different greeting." I'm pretty sure I heard him smile through the phone.

"I don't feel like fighting with you today, Raphael." I yawned and wondered why I'd even bothered to get dressed when it was clear I needed to get my behind right back in the bed.

"You okay?" Concern traced his question.

I sighed. What could it hurt to answer him? "I'm just tired."

"You sick?"

"Don't know yet." Why would he care anyway? "What's up?"

"I wanted to follow up on the tutoring. Did you call Sylvan?"

That was a twist. *Him* calling *me* about a potential bill? "Yeah, I did. They don't have any openings right away, so I called Frierson Learning Center. They're a little more expensive, but they have one-on-one tutoring. Eric's going in for assessment Monday at six."

I didn't want to tell Raphael right away how much this whole thing would cost. Doing so would mess up my strategy. The trick was to get him to commit to half and then spring it on him. Of course, I could only ask for him to reimburse me in small increments, because Raphael had a habit of crying broke and throwing himself on the mercy of the court. Or me.

"So how much is my half?"

As the kids say, O–M–G! *Did he just ask a sensible question?* "Um . . . I . . . I'm glad you asked." I fumbled through a response. Sarcasm begged to be released, but Common Sense knew better than to insult someone who's about to cough up dough. "Testing is $175. The sessions will cost $49 per hour, and he'll probably go twice a week."

"Mmm, that's not too bad."

I had to know. "You got a raise or something?" *A raise in integrity?*

A slight chuckle on both our ends. "Hey, if Eric needs tutoring, I think we can work together to make it happen."

"In addition to your *regular* payment?"

"Of course. I mean, it is an *additional* expense associated with our son."

Times like these I wished it wasn't illegal to record a conversation without the other party's permission. This was *not* Raphael on the phone. Shoot, this was not 99.9 percent of the entire child-support-paying population talking.

I blinked a few times. Pinched myself. "I have to admit, I am surprised by your"—*doing right without being court-ordered*—"offer." I almost said "thank you," then I remembered how silly it would be to thank a man for taking care of his own child. "I appreciate knowing I can count on you to support our son."

"You've got it."

That's what I'm talkin' 'bout! "How do you want to work this? I can text you the learning center's address and you can mail checks to them. Or I'll see if they can receive payments online. You want to take turns—I'll do one week, you do the next?"

"However you want to do it is fine with me. Just let me know."

"Will do."

"And, Peaches, get some rest," he advised. "You sound really worn out."

He was right, of course. "I'm one step ahead of you. I took today off and I'm about to hit the hay."

Raphael wasted no time. "You want me to . . . bring you lunch or something? I've gotta come out that way."

I fell silent.

He added, "I mean, since you might be sick."

"What makes you think I would ingest *anything* you offer me?"

"Dang, girl," he sulked, "why you gotta be so mean?"

I laughed at us. "I don't accept lunches from engaged men."

"I'm not bringing you lunch as an engaged man, I'm bringing you lunch as a friend."

I buzzed him. "*Anck!* Wrong answer."

He tried again. "How 'bout I'm bringing you lunch as the person who is partnered with you in raising our son."

"I'm not letting you inside my house, Raphael."

"I'll ring your doorbell and set it outside your door. It's really not that serious."

If LaShondra had been there, she would have told me to blow a whistle real loudly and then hang up the phone in his face. Deniessa would have told me to take the food as partial repayment for all the hurt and pain Raphael caused in my life.

I told me not to flatter myself. It was humanly possible for a man to bring a sick person lunch. The Meals on Wheels people do it all the time. The pizza man does it. If I didn't make a big deal out of this, maybe it wouldn't *be* a big deal. But if I refused, Raphael might think I had some kind of . . . feelings for him still, like I didn't trust myself with him. I couldn't let him think I wasn't in control.

"What time do you want me to drop it off?"

I don't remember agreeing to this whole thing. "Don't matter."

"Twelve-thirty?"

"Whatever."

Had a similar conversation with a used car salesman once. Worst deal I ever made in my life.

One cap full of NyQuil and four hours later, I was awakened by the door's chime. Still dazed, I'd forgotten about my arrangement with Raphael. I tiptoed through my living room, still not sure I was going to open the door for whoever it was. Panic struck me as I wondered if I'd slept past the time I was supposed to pick up Eric from school. I glanced at the wall clock to reassure myself. 12:30. No, I hadn't missed him. Then I remembered Raphael.

I looked through the peephole to make sure he wasn't standing on my porch. The coast was clear. Quickly, I opened the door and snatched the brown paper sack off my welcome mat. In the distance, a car's engine started.

There was no time to see if the car belonged to Raphael. The contents of that bag were screaming my name. A moment later, I literally felt something move in my heart as I realized Raphael had delivered the most coveted rib plate in all of Dallas. Rubbed, dry ribs from Queenie's Bar-B-Que, baked beans (the kind with meat in them), and potato salad so good it might as well have been dessert.

I hadn't been to Queenie's Bar-B-Que in years, partly because I darn near hurt myself when I ate there. But when I did eat there, I always ordered the same combo.

And Raphael remembered.

Chapter 13

I'd had no contact with Quinn in four days. The time had come for me to break the news to my mother. Not to mention Eric, who'd verbalized concerns about Quinn's sudden absence in our lives more than once. I calmed his fears with a little white half lie. I told him Mr. Quinn was out of town. I classified it a half lie because, in the next few months, the lie would actually become true.

"When will he be back?"

"I'm not sure."

Eric squiggled out of the dinette chair. "I'm gonna go call him and find out."

"Sit back down." I pointed toward the chair. "Finish your breakfast before we go to Granny's house.

"And don't you be calling Mr. Quinn. He's very busy right now. I'll let you know when he's back in town, you hear?" Eric had exactly six pre-programmed buttons on his cell phone. Pretty soon, I'd have to repossess Quinn's button.

Eric stuffed a piece of toast in his mouth and chewed, eyes downturned. My son came as close to crying as an eight-year-old boy can get before he covered his feelings with a "big boy" mask.

The drive to my mother's house seemed shorter than normal. Every light green, every four-way intersection bare. The dreaded moment was near.

My mother deserved to hear it from the horse's mouth. She'd put her heart and soul into this wedding. Aside from her heartbreak, she was going to hit the roof at the thought of all the money Quinn and I had put into it by way of deposits. The sooner we notified our vendors, the more money we could get back. Thankfully, I had managed to keep my mother's fantasies to a minimum.

Is there a way to write off a change of mind on your taxes?

I didn't call before I drove over. My mother never went anywhere, never did much on Saturdays except get clothes and food ready for Sunday. There was no one at home for whom she could cook anymore, so she had taken to donating dishes to the church kitchen. Her sweet potato pies and 7UP cakes garnered in a good chunk of the usher board's funding, one savory piece at a time.

No, there was no need to call first. Besides, I would have to hear my mother fuss enough when I broke the news. No need in hearing the lecture all the way there, too.

I used my key to enter her house. "Momma, it's me." I announced myself so I wouldn't scare my mother half to death.

"In the kitchen," she called back. Eric took off toward the smell of spicy fried chicken and I followed, albeit more slowly.

Eric grabbed a drumstick from a fresh plate of meat and kept truckin' to the back bedrooms.

Dressed in a housecoat with a multicolored scarf wrapped around her head, my mother kept her back to me as she stood at the counter. I studied her for a moment, wondering if someday I, too, would let my fashion sense crash and burn.

I thought of all my friends' mothers. LaShondra's mother was okay except for those glasses making her look like a straight-up librarian. All she needed was chain link flowing down either side of her face. LaShondra's mother was different, though. She had a little spunk to her. I'd seen Mrs. Smith stand up for herself when Mr. Smith started rambling—something he tended to do whenever there was a discussion about race. Shoot, if I had brought a white man home, my momma would have let my father throw me under the bus.

Deniessa's mother, also a fashion victim, was divorced. She played bingo every single moment she wasn't working at AT&T. I don't see how she does it. Bingo never appealed to me, because only one person gets to win at a time, and I like to win every time. Nonetheless, she did have some semblance of a life.

This is just wrong! I had to stop myself. I was downgrading my mother, here. The woman who raised me, loved me, taught me how to write my name before I ever went to kindergarten. This is the same woman my son adored, the one who comforted me when I became a pregnant single mother. She stayed up with my baby when I contracted a postpartum infection.

I was ashamed of myself. How could I be this angry with her? She hadn't done anything other than be herself. Perhaps her selflessness was what bugged me most since my father's death.

I heard a faint sniffle. Actually, I'd heard it a few times since entering the kitchen, but it finally occurred to me that my mother was crying.

"What's wrong, Momma?"

She shook her head almost violently, confirming my suspicion.

I repeated my question.

She wiped the same spot on the counter again. "Sometimes I just miss your daddy so much."

"What do you miss most about Daddy?" A psychologist might have asked the same question to get my mother to open up. I, on the other hand, asked because I truly wanted to know. Aside from the fact that my father took care of all the finances and received her cooking, I hadn't seen him do a whole lot more around the house. Their love for each other, from the outside looking in, appeared . . . what's the word I'm looking for . . . functional.

Still facing the window, her back to me, she answered, "Everything. The way he used to take charge of things. He always knew what to do. If he didn't know, he wasn't scared of trying. He would take responsibility if it went wrong, but he always had some kind of plan, you know?"

Momma faced me now, tears tracing a path down her face. She rushed into me, cried into my shirt—long, heaving sobs. "Your daddy is gone. He's gone, he's gone," she repeated.

The weight of my mother was too much to shoulder, physically and emotionally. "Sit down, Momma."

I pulled out a chair at the table and placed her in it. With both hands, she wiped her cheeks. Another stream let loose. She dried three times before she could get the flow to subside.

Time for a pep talk. Never mind I resented the fact I'd be doing the talking while my own mother did the listening. Totally backward. Someone had to do it, though.

"Momma, you need to get a life."

"I had a life. It's gone now 'cause everybody's gone—your daddy's gone on to be with the Lord, your sisters and brothers are spread out all over the country. You're about to move to Philadelphia with my closest grandbaby." She sighed, her face heavy with emotion.

"Maybe the life you had is over, but you can get a new one," I assured her. "There are lots of things for single women—"

"I'm not single. I'm widowed," she clarified.

"All I'm saying is—"

"Don't you miss your father?"

Her question pressed down hard on my chest. "Of course

I miss Daddy." If I was really honest with myself, I had to admit I missed him for the same reasons she did.

My father was not the touchy-feely type. He was a heavy thinker. He spent almost forty years of his life working two full-time jobs, but when he wasn't working, he either was in front of a television watching the news or had his nose buried in a book. I suppose that's how he knew so much about everything, because if I had a question about anything, he'd help me arrive at the answer.

I'd go into the living room and stand behind his chair for a moment, waiting for him to acknowledge me. When he did, I'd walk to the front of his chair, address him head-on. My father was a short man who looked even shorter in his big, cushy recliner. I couldn't remember a time when there was hair on the top of his head, though there were plenty of pictures to say otherwise. His cheeks were pitted, remnants of earlier years when he smoked heavily during his years in the military. His lips were wide, in stark contrast with an almost European nose. Momma always said Daddy's grandfather was white, which also accounted for my father's light brown skin.

"Whatcha need?"

"I need your help with something."

Most of the time, he'd tell me to come back in a certain amount of time. And when I did return, he'd click off the television or close the book, give me his undivided attention as though he had been waiting for this solemn moment all his life.

I remember the advice he gave me about choosing a college. "I've been thinking about UT Arlington or Texas Tech. Shondra wants us to go to Jarvis Christian College together so we can be roommates."

"If Shondra jumps off a bridge, you gon' jump, too?"

"No." I gave him the classic teenage balk to the classic question aimed at developing young adults.

"Listen, you don't pick a college because of your friends.

You pick a college because it has a good program in your major area of study. Have you checked that out?"

"No, not yet."

"Well, get on it. And another thing, don't ever build your life around what somebody else wants. You're a young black woman. Things aren't the same for you as they were for your mother's generation and before. This day and age, you have to learn how to make it for yourself, understand me?"

He waited for my nod. "Peaches, if you ain't got nobody else, you've got yourself."

I don't know why he never caught my mother up to this century, but her female liberation was long overdue. If she didn't have any strength of her own, I'd let her borrow some of mine for a while.

"Momma, you need to get out of this house and beyond the church. Find some things you like to do. Isn't there anything you always wanted to do but didn't?"

My mother looked straight through me. Past me. With the slightest upturn in her lips, she confessed, "I always wanted to be a teacher."

"Then be a teacher." My face shot up an inch. Already I was thinking about calling LaShondra and asking her what steps Momma should take.

"That was back in the sixties and the seventies. Kids are too bad these days."

She had a point. "How about working at a day care? Babies aren't bad yet."

She pursed her lips in thought.

"Or maybe you could run a small day care out of your home," I proposed. "You could make good money doing that, too." Visions of flyers advertising my mother's business danced through my head.

She wiped the last puddle of tears from beneath her eyelids, and drew in a deep breath. She composed herself and returned to the bowl of potato salad.

"Maybe I'll consider the day care idea later. I can't worry about it right now, though. I'm too busy planning your wedding."

"Oh, about the wedding." Sounded like the title of a bad movie. "It's . . . off."

My mother beat the wooden spoon on the edge of the bowl, clearing the food clinging to the gadget. She approached me, one hand on her hip, timber wand in the other. "What did you say?" She wagged the spoon left to right with each word.

"I said there will be no wedding." Admitting it to my mother was one thing. Hearing myself say it was another. I had to qualify my statement. "At least not anytime soon."

Her face morphed several times, displaying a range of sentiments. Shock. Pain. Anger. "What did you do, Peaches?"

"Me? What makes you think *I* did something?"

She leaned over me and pointed the spoon at me. " 'Cause I know you, Patricia Ann Miller. You ain't been yourself since your daddy died. Plus you can be downright ornery sometimes."

She paced around the table now, giving me the room to roll my eyes at her when she walked behind me. To this day, I don't know how she saw my sassy gesture, but the next thing I knew, my momma bopped me on the back of my head with that spoon.

"Ow!" I ducked down, crossing my arms over my head.

She faced me front and center. "I know you don't like the way I've lived my life. Don't like the way I let Daddy run things, do you?"

Should I speak? I still couldn't believe she'd actually hit me. "Do you?" she demanded.

"No, ma'am," a tiny, five-year-old voice within me replied.

"Sit up."

I followed her order. Cautiously.

"You don't have to like what I do or what I've done, but

you will not disrespect me in my own house." She slung the spoon into the sink.

"Yes, ma'am."

"Now, look. I don't have a college degree, but I do know a good man when I see one. That Quinn is a good man. He loves you, and he loves my grandson. You betta do whatever you can to keep him."

At the risk of another thrashing, I voiced my opinion. "I don't want a man who wants to control my life."

"And I guess you think you're doing a good job of controlling it right now?"

I shrugged. "Yes, I do."

"You gon' control yourself right into a miserable, lonely life. I know your daddy wasn't perfect. He didn't talk much— he was just like Grandpa Miller. And Grandpa Miller didn't much know how to be a father 'cause his own father was too ashamed to admit he had been carrying on with a black woman.

"See, it wasn't your daddy's fault."

I eyed the spoon's handle, mentally measured the distance to the front door. I was fast—I could make it out of there before she got to me. "You're just making excuses for him again. No matter what Great-Grandpa did or didn't do, Daddy could have learned not to distance himself from the people who loved him."

Momma crossed her arms. "Hmph. Now, ain't that the pot calling the kettle black?"

Chapter 14

Eric begged to spend the night at his granny's, so I granted his wish. He'd left more clothes over at my mother's house than he probably had at home, so there was no problem with his wardrobe. My mother had plenty of books for him to read, and she promised to make sure he kept his nose buried in one for the rest of the weekend, though I was sure he'd also have his favorite sweets to accompany him on the literary journey. Somehow, Eric always managed to secure great weekends with friends or family—more than I could say for myself.

There was no lump, no pain, but I could still feel the area where my mother spoon-whacked me. Like you can still feel a pair of glasses even though they aren't on your face anymore.

This incident bore repeating to somebody. My first instinct was to call Quinn and tell him my mother had flipped out on me. I was struck even harder by the realization that I didn't have Quinn to call anymore. We were finished.

I took the shortcut through my neighborhood streets, heading back to the highway. The alternate path, known only by those who understood the intricate workings of the dead ends and wraparound streets of my neighborhood, took me

by several of my childhood friends' homes, including LaShondra's.

I was pleasantly surprised to see her car in the driveway. I
rather hoped she'd be there alone, without Stelson, because I
desperately needed to talk to her.

I parked behind her Accord and threw my purse over my
shoulder as I rang her parents' doorbell. Mrs. Smith answered
the door and pulled me into a hug.

"Peaches, sweetie, how are you? Ain't seen you in a while!
Congratulations on your engagement—me and Mr. Smith
will be at your wedding with bells on!"

I didn't have the heart to look into her dancing eyes and
stop the music. "Thank you."

She stepped back, eyed me up and down. "Look like you
putting on a little weight there."

Was there some kind of Insulting People 101 class they
used to have in the '60s? I swear, LaShondra's mother and
mine must have earned an A in the course.

I denied her observation. "No, ma'am, I don't think so."

She waved her arm. "Don't worry about it. Everybody
puts on a little bit when they first get settled down. It's called
'happy fat.' " She nodded at me and led me into the house.

"I saw Shondra's car out front."

"Yes, she's here."

I followed Mrs. Smith to the family room, where
LaShondra was sprawled out on the couch watching television, remote control in hand.

She rose to a sitting position to allow room on the couch.
"Hey, girl. What you doin' here?"

"Nothin'." I hugged her, taking the spot next to her. "I
just went to my mom's house and gave her the news about
me and Quinn."

"Is this the news I think it is?"

"Yeah. The wedding is off. For now."

LaShondra rolled her eyes toward the ceiling and appeared

to send up a silent prayer on my behalf. "I don't get you, Peaches. I really don't."

"Don't judge me on this. I could use a friend right now." I stared at my empty hands.

She finally looked at me again. Or, rather, at the side of my face. Then she leaned back and asked, "What's this stuff in your hair?" She picked through my head and produced yellow mush.

"Oh. My momma hit me on the head with a potato salad spoon."

Shondra smacked her lips. "*Somebody* needs to knock some sense into ya."

"Look, I'm already under a lot of pressure at my job, with Eric's school, and with my mom. We have to try to get back all the deposits for wedding stuff. The last thing I need is drama from you, too."

LaShondra tugged a Kleenex from the box on the coffee table and carefully cleared my do of all food.

"If you take a step back, you'll notice you didn't have all these extra problems until you broke off the engagement with Quinn. It's not hard to put two and two together."

She balled up the tissue and set it down.

It's kind of hard to fuss at someone who just groomed you like I'd seen animals do for each other on those National Geographic shows. Only a true friend would fish potato salad out of your hair, or pick bugs from your fur.

"Let me live my life, all right?"

She lowered the television's volume.

"I don't have a problem with what you do with your life so long as it lines up with God. I wanna know—is your plan His plan?"

We sat in silence for a minute before I realized she wasn't asking rhetorically. She wanted an answer. I couldn't give her one. "I don't know. I mean, I really don't think it's a good idea to put a lot of extra pressure on a new marriage."

"Peaches, I feel you. This is a big decision. If you told me you'd prayed about it and your answer was His answer, I would back you, no questions asked. But you know better than to make a decision, especially a major one like this, without hearing from God."

I shrugged. "Well, maybe I'm just not in my right mind."

Shondra tucked her chin in. "Nuh-uh. The devil *is* a liar. I don't know what's gotten into you, but I'm interceding for you, girlfriend, whether you like it or not."

Gratefulness should have been on my lips, yet I wondered how she would intercede for me when she was so consumed with getting settled into her wife role. We were out of touch, thanks to her, and I really didn't appreciate her basically declaring me to be in a confused and darn-near backslidden condition.

Slinging my purse onto my shoulder, I stood and straightened my blouse flat onto my bulging muffin-top stomach. "I can pray for myself."

Her eyes started at my feet, traveled up my body, and landed squarely on mine. "You haven't been doing so lately."

My neck went into action, voice in defense mode. "You don't know what I do or don't do."

"I can look at your *life* and tell you ain't been prayin'," she countered. "I am your best friend, remember? We've been here and done this before, circa the year of our Lord two thousand?"

She referenced the crazy whirlwind relationship with Raphael. *No, she didn't.* "Oh, we can go back farther than that. James Perkins? Anthony Colbert? How about Phillip Valentine?"

"Junior high, Peaches? Come on!"

Shondra laughed, but I didn't see anything funny.

"Don't go bringing up my past if you don't want to relive yours, too."

She blew out a breath of air and made the time-out gesture with her hands. "Okay, I'm sorry. I shouldn't have gone there."

"Thank you."

She closed her eyes and pleaded, "Will you at least promise me you'll have a civil conversation with Quinn about this?"

Hearing his name was almost too much. I couldn't answer.

Shondra stood and put her hands on my shoulders. She watched as the tears pooled in my eyes, then pulled me into a numb hug. "He's miserable without you, too."

I talked into her shirt. "You talked to him?"

"Yeah. He called the other day. Asked if you and Eric were okay."

I pulled back and wiped my eyes so I could see her clearly. "What did you tell him?"

"I told him you both were fine as far as I knew."

"Did he say anything about, you know, us? The wedding?"

She shook her head in bewilderment. "He said he thought it was over. He doesn't understand what's going on with you, and I . . . didn't know what to tell him. He's wondering if this is a side of you he never knew existed."

A puff of air escaped my lips in frustration. "Of course it's a new side—even to me. I don't know the engaged-and-getting-ready-to-move side of me. I don't know the wife side of me, either. Every since my father died and I've been looking at my mom, it's like I really can't decide if I want the new me, whoever she might be. Especially if she turns out like my mother."

"God didn't give us fear—He gave us power, love, and a sound mind," Shondra paraphrased 2 Timothy 1:7. "Bottom line, I don't want to see you miss out on one of the best things that could ever happen to you because you're too afraid to be vulnerable."

Spoken like a true newlywed. If she and Stelson stood the

test of time, then I'd take advice from her. Right now, they were probably well below the average length of a Western marriage. As far as I was concerned, Shondra wouldn't be in a position to preach to me until she and Stelson had at least made it past the seven-year itch. I wished them all the best, of course. Still, they weren't there yet. How could she be so sure?

The keys jingling in my hand spoke on my behalf.

"Peaches, don't make this move without getting a firm answer from God. Okay?"

I wish I could have promised her I'd wait. Waiting, however, is much easier said than done.

Thoughts of all the times I'd asked God something but He didn't answer fast enough filled my head as I drove back to my place. I didn't know what to major in, so I prayed about it. The deadline to declare was approaching quickly, so I researched the top-paying careers of the future and followed the money to computer engineering. My grades dropped so low that I almost lost my scholarships because, money aside, I hated computers back in the day.

And then there was my first job at Crabtree Monitoring. I settled for a position in accounting after weeks and weeks of interviewing at several companies, only to find my immediate supervisor hired me because he had a fantasy about getting with a black woman.

Both times, I had lived and learned. Nobody's plans are perfect, right?

I had to give myself credit. I was smart, I had common sense, and I knew me well enough to know I could not, would not be happy depending on anybody, even if the sexily fine body belonged to the greatest man I'd ever known.

I needed love, but I didn't want to move. I wanted someone to have my back, but I didn't want to actually have to depend on that person to come through for me.

So I prayed to God—or somebody—that things would work out my way.

Chapter 15

Frierson Learning Center's lobby area could have been an art gallery for all the contemporary design. The only difference was a carpeted play area and a few inspirational posters. I hoped I'd be paying for quality tutoring rather than ambiance.

"Hi. We're here for testing. Eric Lewis."

The receptionist tapped a few keys, printed a document, and presented the paper on the flat counter between her space and the waiting room. "Since you completed his enrollment forms online, we only need to collect the assessment fee today."

She circled the amount due on the paper, $175, as though it were taboo to actually speak the number. A little, teeny tiny part of me was disappointed to see Raphael had not yet come through and paid his half ahead of time. I had to remind myself—depending on Raphael was like depending on a crackhead.

Eric and I were seated, waiting for him to be summoned. The layout reminded me of a doctor's office, only this time I wouldn't be going back with him. I had read the enrollment paperwork carefully—parental presence was a distraction to the students.

When the receptionist called Eric forward, he happily bounced down from his chair and followed. He looked back at me and gave me the thumbs-up. I returned the gesture and added a wink.

For all the pain and anxiety surrounding his birth, I wouldn't trade him for the world. He wasn't an accident—he was a surprise, something I didn't even know I wanted until I received it.

I'd packed the latest Kendra Norman-Bellamy novel to pass the time. With Eric beyond view in the glass door, I settled in for a rare hour of peace. Seven pages into the novel, I was feeling frazzled. The novel opened with a romantic scene, and my mind drifted to Quinn. I wondered what he was doing, where he was. Actually, he usually worked late Monday nights—except when the Lakers played. In the time we dated, I had grown from tolerating basketball to appreciating the sport in an effort to spend more time with Quinn. We even hosted the play-off parties at my place that year.

LaShondra and Stelson, Deniessa and Jamal, and a few other couples came over to watch the games. The men pretty much kicked us ladies to the curb, but we didn't mind. Watching them fuss and argue over a questionable foul was almost like overseeing children on a playground. They weren't our kids, of course, but there's a certain amity among moms mirroring the unspoken bond between wives. I wasn't a wife just then, but I was part of the clique that day. And it felt good.

I reached for my cell phone, flipped it open, and scrolled to Quinn's name. My thumb rested on the green Send button. *What do I say?* He probably wouldn't appreciate my calling just to say hello. *Maybe I should tell him about Eric.* No. Cheap trick.

With no game plan, I closed my phone and placed it back in my purse. The plush lounge chair suddenly felt like sinking sand. I wished I could pull a curtain around me and throw myself a big, huge pity party, but I was sure no one would come. No one was saving the date for me—not even my own mother.

The novel joined my phone—no need in making things worse. I grabbed a few pop-culture magazines from the adjacent stand and flipped through the celebrity news. Splitting couples, upcoming movies, half-naked singers, and the latest fad diet. Some woman was touting that she went from a size 8 to a size 2. I could wondered what woman in her right mind standing over five feet tall *wants* to wear a size 2?

Magazines were no help at all. I closed my eyes and set my head back on the wall. A semi-nap would suit me fine. I don't think I quite expected the drowsiness to take over me, but it most certainly did. With all the tension at Northcomp, my brain quickly took advantage of the chance to relax. The lobby was empty and the only children who entered the office went quietly to the receptionist who opened the door for them to proceed to the tutoring area.

I was approaching never-never land when the tug at my sleeve pushed reality back into place.

"Wake up, sleepyhead."

It took me a moment to put it all together. Raphael was present, sitting next to me in Frierson's waiting room. He wore a button-down denim shirt with khaki pants and a brown belt with matching leather shoes. Looked pretty good, actually, especially considering he rarely showed up for anything outside of Easter speeches and school plays.

"Hey." I was probably smiling wider than I should have been.

"I thought you were supposed to catch up on your sleep over the weekend," he recalled.

"I did get a little rest." It's hard to sleep with a broken heart sitting in your chest. "But then there's work, you know."

He threw one ankle over his opposite knee. "Tell me

about it. I never knew moving up in the company would be so difficult."

My interest piqued, I nodded for him to continue.

"I'm the supervisor in my department now. Most of my subordinates are my former coworkers, and it's not pretty."

"That was a bad move." I shook my head.

He looked down at me. I noticed again how tall he was. His skin a sheet of chocolate, dappled with well-formed features that, once upon a time, took center stage on some very steamy nights.

Snap out of it!

"What was so bad about my promotion?" he asked, presumably for the second time.

Shifting my eyes away from his, I answered, "Human Resources 101—never promote someone to be direct supervisor over their former peers. They should have moved you to another department. Makes for a very uncomfortable situation, decreases productivity, increases hostility."

His head bounced back for a moment. "Hmph. You always did know your stuff."

He glanced at his silver-linked, dia*mel*-studded watch. A step up for him. "How long has Eric been in there?"

"Not long."

"Well, if he's got a while, I'm gonna go next door to the bookstore. You want to come?"

I turned down the corners of my lips and his invitation. "Not really."

"You sure? They've got a lot of . . . books."

We both laughed at his lame attempt to entice me, but I wasn't persuaded.

Raphael left the lobby and I tried to return to my nap. It dawned on me that he hadn't said anything about the money. Probably didn't want to mention it. But if he could afford a nice watch and a new book, he could afford to go half.

What was he doing here, anyway? Sure, Eric would be overjoyed to see his father, but beyond that, what was his point? Didn't he have a fiancé he needed to tend to?

Half an hour later, Raphael returned, sack in hand. He promptly produced a copy of *Essence* magazine from the bag and handed it to me. "I see Frierson doesn't particularly cater to its African-American clientele."

I gladly accepted the magazine. "Thank you." What I really wanted to say was, "I don't need no magazine—I need *half,* fool!"

Raphael set the plastic bag on the floor and began looking over my shoulder as I flipped through the magazine. I couldn't hold it in any longer. "Why are you here?"

"I want to know what's going on with my son."

"Did you bring your half of the money?"

He motioned toward the receptionist. "Already paid the lady."

"No, *I* paid the lady in full."

"She said she'd give us a credit toward future tuition. So, he won't have anything due for a while."

"Mmm." Eyes back on the magazine.

"Do you not want me here?"

I took a deep breath, considering his question. I wanted him there for Eric's sake—for the look in his eyes when he realized his father's presence. Other than that, no. I really didn't. "Raphael, I have to give you props. In the past several months, you have been doing better with our son. But what's all this other stuff—calling me just to say hi, bringing me Queenie's Bar-B-Q, buying me magazines? We've called the truce. What *else* are you going for?"

He leaned in toward me, close enough for our shoulders to touch. "Well, since you asked. I think I want you."

I nearly jumped, burrowing my back into the chair. "Are you crazy?"

"Maybe."

"I am engaged."

He shook his head. "Where's your ring?"

I tucked my hands under my thighs. "So maybe I'm not engaged. But I am . . . in love with someone. And so are you—you're the one who's *really* engaged." I turned the tables, unwilling to admit the situation with Quinn.

He squared off with me. "Peaches, I've been thinking some more. When you told me you were getting married, I swear, my whole life stopped."

"Is it me, or didn't we just have this conversation last week?"

Raphael surveyed the room, clicking his jaw in what I recognized as annoyance at the receptionist's watchful gaze. "Hear me out."

I searched his eyes for a hint of deceit. There was none, so far as I could tell—only pools of deep brown sincerity. He was either telling the truth or lying to both of us.

"I know I was a dog back then. I used you, I neglected my son, and I left you high and dry. I was wrong." He stopped, eyebrows raised, awaiting my response.

"No objections here."

He huffed. "I'm sorry and I want another chance to be more than friends."

"I think you're forgetting someone here—your future wife?" I reminded him.

Raphael shook his head. "I can't marry her knowing that I didn't turn over every possible stone with you."

I waved him off. "Let me just stop you right here." I began the count with my index finger. "Number one, you did not want me until you saw that someone else wanted me. Number two, I feel sorry for Cheryl. If you don't love her, you have no business marrying her. Number three, you are *living* with Cheryl, which tells me that you are in no way concerned about living a Christian lifestyle. I cannot be hooked up with someone who's not traveling down the same road

with me. And number four, I am still . . . connected to Quinn."
I held up my entire hand now. "And number five, I do not
fool with you—we're *barely* speaking now."

Really, I wanted to pop him on the head like in one of
those V8 commercials. He was living in la-la land if he
thought for one second I would give him a chance to break
my heart again.

He lowered his voice an octave. "You're saying you don't
love me anymore."

"I'm saying neither of us knew what love was when we
were dating, and apparently you still don't know what it is."

"And you do?"

"Yes."

"With Quinn?"

"Yes."

He gave me a smirk. "No, you don't. If you did, you'd still
be engaged."

"I'm not going to discuss this with you." I reopened the
Essence magazine, my toe tapping nervously on the floor. I
was approaching anger, though I wasn't sure why.

"Mmm-hmm. Look at your foot," he teased. "You only
tap your foot when you're upset."

I willed my shoe to a halt. "I don't appreciate you trying
to barge back into my life."

"So maybe I don't know what love is, but you're the closest thing I have to it. If it means I'll need to start going to
church, leave Cheryl, whatever—I'm willing to figure it out
for you. For Eric."

Mentioning our son was way below the belt. I cinched
my eyelids tight and allowed my head to make a soft thud on
the wall behind me. I wished Raphael would disappear, because I didn't exactly know what to say. These days, what
black woman *doesn't* want to be in a relationship with her
child's father? It was selfish of us to make Eric without sur-

rounding him with a loving family. Did I owe it to my son to try again?

I thought I was over the guilt, but every time I went to a school play or a soccer game and watched Eric perform with no man at my side, there it was again. And when I filled out paperwork for the dentist or program enrollments, there was always the additional section to complete if the other parent's home address was not the same.

Quinn was as good of a potential stepfather as could be, but only because he realized Eric was part of the package. In the beginning, the only glue holding those two together was me. They had their own bond now, of course, but it was in jeopardy. If Quinn moved on, I couldn't expect him to keep playing the father role for my son. Quinn didn't owe Eric anything. Raphael, on the other hand, did.

That made all the difference.

Against my wishes, Raphael was still sitting there when I opened my eyes. I had to face him. "I—"

"Shhhh." Raphael put his finger over my lips, and something happened. To this day, I can't really explain it, but when he touched me, I felt like Sleeping Beauty. All the anger, hostility, and resistance toward him suddenly made sense.

I couldn't stand him because I was afraid. I was afraid because I was still vulnerable. And I was still vulnerable because, underneath it all, I still cared.

Chapter 16

When Hampton cut Theresa's hours again, Theresa cut loose. And then there were two—me and Yancey—to finish lowering Northcomp's head count. Theresa had never been involved in the decision-making process, but I missed her terribly when it came to accessing reports and shielding me from countless phone calls and drop-ins. The extra workload had me coming in early, leaving late.

When Quinn walked straight up to my desk unannounced, I was completely unprepared. I suppose security must have remembered him from previous visits, otherwise Quinn couldn't have waltzed in without a buzz here or there.

"Michael, could you excuse us for a moment?"

Michael looked from me to Quinn, then back to me. Obviously concerned, he asked me, "Is . . . everything okay?"

With my assurance, Michael left the room.

Now for the second time in two days, I was completely lost. Seeing Quinn conjured up a thousand good memories intertwined with a longing for intimacy with God. I couldn't think about Quinn without thinking about my spiritual growth.

Quinn stepped into my office, closed the door behind

him, and then put both hands in his pockets. Him, me, and the four walls. He hadn't said anything yet, so why was I feeling like one big cell under a microscope?

I broke the silence with, "Hello."

"Hi. I just wanted you to know I'm leaving next week."

My insides turned to slipped an inch. *So soon?* "Mmmm." I swallowed, thankful I was sitting already. "I thought you said it could wait until after July."

"I don't have a reason to wait anymore, do I?" His flat tone said he wasn't really expecting an answer.

"I . . . guess not."

"We need to talk about Eric."

I rolled my lips between my teeth and lowered my chin. Now was as good a time as any to let Quinn off the hook. "You don't have to play the father role for him, Quinn. Children are resilient. He'll adjust."

Quinn shook his head. "I wasn't *playing*. I love Eric like my own son. I want the best for him. I'd like to spend time with him when I come back for holidays and such. My nieces and nephews are always asking about him."

A pang of shame coursed through me, followed closely by anger. "Are you trying to make me feel guilty?"

He chuckled lightly. "Don't flatter yourself. This is about Eric, not you."

After I picked my face up off the floor, I continued with, "Well, Eric has been spending a lot of time with Raphael, and I think it might be best to give their relationship some room to grow."

One hand came out of a pocket and he rubbed it across his head several times, base to crown. I realized for the first time, ending our relationship posed two breakups at once for Quinn.

He cleared his throat. "I have to respect your judgment since I don't have any legal rights. If nothing else, I'd like to say good-bye to him. I was hoping I'd see you both at church this past Sunday, but I guess you . . . went to your mom's church or something."

My lips flatlined, neither confirming or denying his hypothesis.

"Does he even know I'm leaving?"

"Not totally."

The floodgate holding back Quinn's frustration gave way. He held out his arms, palms up. "When were you planning to tell him?"

"I don't know—I haven't even told myself, really, let alone my son."

He clicked his cheeks. "I didn't want to have to tell him over the phone, but you leave me no choice. I'll call him." Quinn walked to the door.

"Quinn."

His back to me, he stopped. "What?"

I pulled my purse from the side drawer. I found the ring in the secret zippered compartment where I'd left it, secure in its black velvet box. Slowly, I approached him, presenting this treasure I once would have killed to possess. Quinn really hadn't done anything wrong; he deserved to have it back. He deserved to give it to someone who wanted to be the woman Quinn probably needed in his life all along. I used to think that woman was me, but I couldn't tell anymore because my definition of "me" was changing.

When I placed the ring in his hand, Quinn grasped mine. He lowered his arm, pulling me closer to him in the process. Suddenly, we were face-to-face. I sucked in the air around me, held onto it for dear life while my very spirit seemed to melt.

"I loved you, Peaches. Remember that."

The ring box slipped from my hand to his. He tucked it into his pocket and opened the door. And with that, Quinn Robertson walked out of my life.

★ ★ ★

Rocky road ice cream was my only comfort that week. My mother was furious I'd officially cancelled the wedding. Said people from the church were calling, asking nosy questions. LaShondra had no sympathy for me, and I had to fire three more people by Thursday—one of whom had been my foot-in-the-door at Northcomp. T.G.I.F. took on a whole new meaning for me.

Raphael sent me a few text messages asking if we could get together, but I told him I wasn't ready. I was all shook up, for lack of a better term. I promised I'd call him back when things settled down at work.

I just wanted to crawl into a cave and hibernate until everything blew over. Were it not for Eric, I might have done so. I can only marvel at how many full-blown depressive episodes have been averted by the sheer fact that mothers have to keep on ticking no matter what's happening around them.

One of Eric's classmates had a birthday party Saturday, so I went through the motions of buying the gift, showing up at the bash, and singing the birthday song. Even after the event was over, Eric and I stayed at the miniature golf center for another hour. I didn't want to go home.

"Ma'am, we need this table for another party," the hostess barely whispered. She was fifteen, maybe, and wore her blond hair in a floppy ponytail on top of her head.

I'm guessing my face must have been a mirror of my soul—tormented, unfriendly—because relief spread over her face when I gave up the booth and went to find another seat. Both my mother and LaShondra called me while we were there. I sent them to voice mail.

I ordered myself another hot dog and purchased more tokens to keep Eric busy while I sat and people-watched. There were a few married couples present—most with more than one child, which made me wonder about having more children. Quinn had said he wanted one pretty soon. Then we'd have the whole two-different-last-names-in-the-house issue. My mother used to call that "mixing up the family." How would it make Eric feel to be the only Lewis in a house full of Robertsons? And how would my other hypothetical child feel when his or her big brother went away for a weekend every month?

No matter. This whole thing was nothing but conjecture. Quinn was gone now.

My phone buzzed in my purse. The screen showed Raphael's name and "1 Text Message." It read: You free?

I flicked my phone open and called him.

"Hi. I'm glad you called," he said.

'Bout time *somebody* was glad to hear from me. "What's up?"

"I've missed you this week."

I moaned, "Things have been pretty crazy for me."

"Anything I can do to help?"

"No, I don't think so. I just need to sit down somewhere and get my thoughts together."

"What's on your mind?"

I hesitated, not really sure if I should tell Raphael everything. I generally followed the relationship rules—no talking to a man about another man. I realized then I had thrown myself back into the market to play these silly games again. "Nothing you can help me with."

"Try me."

What did I have to lose? Besides, Raphael had a fiancée anyway. Until he got rid of Cheryl, there were no rules. "Quinn is leaving town without me, and I'm . . . a little down about it."

Raphael huffed a few times. "You're upset over another man?"

"I don't exactly have you. Nor am I even totally sure that I *want* to be with you." There. The truth was out.

"How can you say that?"

"Because I don't know. And because you're still engaged, remember?"

I heard his breath catch in his throat.

"Hello?" Sarcastic Peaches spoke up for me.

"I'm still here."

"So, that's what's on my mind."

The phone went warm against my face as I waited for his response.

"Can we get together tomorrow?"

"Yeah," I replied.

"I mean just me and you?"

"No. I don't have a sitter for Eric."

"Oh." He seemed surprised. "How about I pick you two up for the movie grill?"

"Works for me.

"When are you going to tell Cheryl?"

"As soon as I can. I've got to get my ducks in a row first— get my name off the car she's driving, see about breaking our cell phone contract, you know. Technical matters."

No, I didn't know. "Whatever."

"Peaches, I know you gave up a lot to give me another chance. I promise, you won't be sorry."

"I have not agreed to give you a second chance."

He backed up. "Okay. Then, I'm glad you agreed to give me a chance to *try* for a second chance. See, I got you there."

It felt good to laugh out loud again. "Whatever."

Chapter 17

I smothered myself in work to avoid thinking about Quinn. Hampton took notice of my sudden rededication to North-comp. "Don't work yourself too hard," he'd warned one evening as he breezed past my office on his way out the door. It was already close to six o'clock, and I probably could have worked until eight, but there was still the steady job of mothering Eric that had to be done.

With Quinn out of the picture and my mother not even talking to me, I was a single mom for *real* now. Raphael hadn't requested any more regular days with Eric, aside from time with me included.

And where was this whole thing with Raphael going anyway?

The day care closed at six-thirty, so finished or not I had to leave my place of work and head toward the center. Those folk don't play about their extra ten dollars for every five minutes you're late picking up your child.

Eric's sullen face didn't even tilt upward at me when I called him toward the sign-out area. He slung his backpack over his shoulder, held it in place with one arm, and trudged over to me.

Actually, he looked like I felt, but I didn't want to say so.

"Well, you sure look happy today," I chirped as we walked out the door, headed back to my car.

"I talked to Mr. Quinn today."

"Oh." My pace quickened. When we were both buckled into our seat belts—bracing myself for the impact. "What did he say?"

A coarse wail escaped my son's throat. I peeked at him through the rearview mirror to verify the horror. Yes, my baby was crying. Crying like a big boy who was ashamed to be crying but couldn't hold it in any longer. Between sobs, Eric managed, "He's . . . hmt . . . he's moving away."

I slanted the rearview mirror up, denying Eric an angle to view my reflection. He wasn't the only one crying now. It took everything in both of us to avoid an all-out breakdown. I started the car, cleared my throat, and tried to offer some comfort. "Eric, you can still talk to Mr. Quinn. And you've still got me, and your daddy—"

"But Mr. Quinn is like my bestest . . . hmt . . . friend in the whole wide world, except for God."

I didn't have an answer. No comfort. No solace. A gaping hole filled my chest area. This business of breaking up ain't no joke. I hadn't suffered this kind of pain since . . . well, since Raphael dumped me, if I wanted to be honest with myself.

But I couldn't be honest, because if I heaped the memory of Raphael leaving me on top of the pain of me leaving Quinn, I wouldn't be able to breathe. I had to forget one or the other, and then Raphael's was the easiest to subdue.

What happened between Raphael and me took place a long time ago. I wasn't the same woman, he wasn't the same man. Starting over with him would, hopefully, be like starting with a new person altogether. Only this new person happened to be my child's father. I didn't have to worry about whether the man would try to molest my son or if he would treat Eric any differently than he would treat the child we might have together. This was a win-win. Right?

It had *better* be right. The very idea that this heartache over Quinn might all be in vain was too much to even consider. If my potential relationship with Raphael didn't work out, I would be totally devastated, not to mention embarrassed and guilty for taking away my son's bestest friend next to God.

No. I had taken the driver's seat like a good, independent black woman was supposed to do, and I wasn't going to let anything or anybody try to make me look a fool while gripping my life's steering wheel.

"Hush up crying now, Eric. Everything's gonna be all right. You want some ice cream?"

He sniffled, wiped his face with the back of his sleeve. "No."

"Well, I sure do. I'm going to stop at Braum's. You sure you don't want anything?"

Eric remained silent.

I ordered the sundae as well as dinner at the drive-thru. No sense in cooking when I could just get a quick fix. "Let me have a number three, a number seven junior size, both with Sprites, and a double-dip hot caramel sundae with nuts. No cherry."

The attendant's voice came back scratchy and loud. "You want to upgrade that adult meal for seventy-nine cents more?"

I poked my lips out. *What's seventy-nine cents?* "Yes, please."

Eric asked for his fries and I passed them back to him. I normally don't allow eating in my car, but French fries are the exception. They're at their best when that hot, fresh grease is still glistening on every side. Eric and I both enjoyed the treat as I drove home.

"Momma, can we go visit Mr. Quinn one day?" my son asked with a full mouth.

"Swallow your food before you speak."

I heard him gulp down what must have been a gob of fry mush. "I want to see Mr. Quinn. Is Philadelphia far?"

"Yes."

"Like *far* far?"

"So far you have to get on a plane to get there."

Eric squealed. "Ooh! I can't wait!"

"I never said we were going there. Stop putting words in my mouth." *No sense in belaboring the issue.* "Eric, Quinn and I have broken up. Do you know what that means?"

"Is that the same thing as a divorce?"

I sucked in my neck. "What you know about divorce?"

"Like you and my daddy got."

"Your daddy and I were never married."

Eric begged to differ. "That's what my daddy said. He said you and him were married, and then you got a divorce, and now he wants to marry you again, but he told me not to say anything around Miss Cheryl."

It's a good thing I was at a stop sign because I might have had an accident otherwise. My head swerved around almost more than humanly possible, allowing me the opportunity to look into Eric's eyes. "Your daddy said what?"

"Oops." Eric put a hand over his mouth. "He told me not to tell you, either. Momma, please don't tell Daddy I told you."

The driver behind me blew his horn and I was forced to turn back around, but my mouth was still wide open. How dare he tell our son that we were getting remarried. That's got to be the most confusing thing to tell an eight-year-old who knows his mother is engaged to another man. I wondered exactly when Raphael had told our son this presumptuous tale.

I wondered even more how Eric thought I was going to pull this off. "So, baby, what did you think I was going to do? Marry Raphael and be with Mr. Quinn, too?"

"No. But some people at my school have, like, two moms or two dads or like . . . and I kind of have two dads, so . . . I thought it would be the same."

Good Lord! What is the world coming to when kids

don't even understand the basic institution of marriage? "Well, let me clear something up for you. The Bible says let every man have his own wife and let every woman have her own husband."

"So how come you had two men?"

I jumped to my own defense. "I don't have two men. I only have one. Maybe."

"Who?"

"Your daddy—*maybe*. But he's not nor was he ever my husband."

Eric was really trying to figure this out. "But what about Miss Cheryl? I thought *she* was Daddy's wife."

"They're not married, either." I sighed and shook my head. "Eric, we've talked about this enough, okay?" I had to close off this conversation because if I wasn't careful, this would work its way around to how I managed to get pregnant if his father and I were never married. Not a conversation I wanted to have with Eric just yet. I'd always told myself I wouldn't lie about what happened. I would tell him when he was ready—whenever we started having talks about God's desire for His people to remain pure until marriage.

Eric pressed once more. "But if they're not married, how come they live together?"

"Eric, this is grown folks' business, you hear me?"

I got a glimpse of him through the mirror again. His eyes squinted, one finger resting on his temple. My baby was thoroughly confused.

And he wasn't the only one.

Chapter 18

Going out to a movie on a school night was a huge no-no when I was growing up. We couldn't do anything on school nights except maybe go to a revival, and even then we'd leave early sometimes if the preacher was too long-winded.

When Eric was younger, I tried to establish that rule for him, but Raphael was so sheisty back then, I had to take him up on his offer to spend time with our son whenever he put it out there.

Eric was somewhat distracted from his Quinn funk by spending time with his father for the evening. Eric was, however, a bit discombobulated by me hanging around with them at the combination movie theater/restaurant.

"May I take your order?" a teenage boy with a huge hole stretched into his earlobe asked.

Raphael ordered for us all. "We'll take the family-size large pizza." He directed his attention to Eric. "Pepperoni, right, son?"

"Right."

Family. The word sounded almost as good as wedding bells. I don't think I'd ever ordered a family size of anything in recent years, at least not since I'd lost eighty pounds in my twenties. It seemed only right to order one now that I'd suddenly found fifteen of them again. If my scale, which I finally found the nerve to step on that same morning, didn't tell the truth, my jeans did.

I was getting to the point where I only wore loose-fitting shirts. Nothing tailored, certainly not anything with a belt. The less definition, the better. Raphael had never known me as a big girl, and I had no intention of painting the picture in his mind. But for the life of me, I had no recollection of how I'd gained those fifteen pounds. I had to get myself together soon or I wouldn't be able to wear anything in my closet.

When the server brought our pizza to the table, I knew *that* night wouldn't be the night I'd return to healthy eating habits. For a second-rate eating joint, this place had its pizza recipe down—the thick, flaky crust, nice blend of cheeses, and fresh pepperoni slices pushed my diet off another day.

I hadn't said much to Raphael since we got there, and I was thankful when the lights dimmed. With Eric sitting between us, there wasn't much chance of awkward conversation. Every once in a while, I snuck a peek at Raphael. Then I pinched myself to make sure this was really happening. I was really sitting somewhere with Raphael again. With our son. Our family. And, I have to tell you, it was one of those situations where you know it's probably not right, but it is what it is and you want to make the best of it. In fact, one time I heard Dr. Phil say, "Sometimes you don't make the right decision, but you can make the decision right." I hoped his wisdom lined up with God's Word . . . some kind of way.

Through stolen glances, I was reminded of what attracted me to Raphael in the first place. Momma would say he had "good hair," well, what was left of it. Wouldn't be long before he'd have to shave it off because it would be hard for him to pull off a toupee. Raphael's eyelashes were longer than mine, and his face sported hearty cheekbones, a thick chin—both features passed on to our son. I'd noticed more than one woman doing a double-take as we stood in line for tickets earlier. Their eyes scrolled down and noticed his bare finger, too. Goodness! The investigative skills we single women possess should be bottled and sold!

Halfway through the show, which—for the record—was a lame flick about a kid who wished upon a star for magic bike, Eric's eyelids got heavy. Slowly, his head tilted forward, then jerked back when his reflexes kicked in. The whole routine was pretty funny. I reached over Eric and tapped Raphael's shoulder so he could check out his son's unconscious antics. Raphael cracked up, startling Eric out of his sleep.

He whispered, "Is it boring, Eric?"

Eric shook his head "no" while rubbing his eyes with his fists.

"You sleepy? Ready to go home?" I was all for leaving if Eric had had enough.

He denied the obvious. "No. I want to stay here with you guys." Eric took my hand in his right and Raphael's in his left. He sat up in the seat and refocused himself on the movie, apparently determined to make this evening last as long as possible.

This has got to be the corniest human moment on file, and don't even asked me why I decided to look Raphael's way. The darkened theater only afforded a glowing profile, just enough to see him watching me, too.

A spark of hope gushed through me, filling my mind with dreams of the future. I'd never wanted Eric to be an only child. Truth be told, no little girl says to herself, "When I grow up, I want to have *two* baby daddies!" Raphael wasn't the worst man on earth. Okay, maybe he used to be, but nobody's perfect, you know?

Maybe one day I'd sit down with our grandchildren and tell them how they almost didn't come to be because Grandpa Raphael and I broke up for several years before God brought us back together. Maybe one day we'd all sit around on the back porch laughing, eating warm peach cobbler, and

I'd look over at Raphael—just like I did tonight. Hey—stranger things have happened. People remarry their exes every day.

On top of it all, I guess I figured I at least owed it to Eric (who did not ask to be born) to be open to the idea of giving him the family I'd failed to secure for him before I got pregnant. Yes, we were in the new millennium, but some of the old-school terms like "broken home" and "stepfamilies" still stung.

They say God works in mysterious ways. Maybe this was just one of those ways.

Raphael walked us back to my car when the movie was over. The lack of light outside said it was way past Eric's bathtime, nearing his bedtime. I wondered how my own body managed to make it through the movie without snoozing.

Raphael buckled Eric into the backseat, closed his door, and then stood beside me as I opened the driver's door.

"Wait."

I stopped with my door half-opened, one foot on the floorboard. "What?"

"Don't you want to talk?"

Really, what man wants to *talk?* "Talk about what?"

He scanned the passing traffic over the hood of my car. Shrugged, and returned his eyes to mine. "About what just happened back there. I know you felt it, too."

I leaned into my car, started the ignition so I could get air going in the car for Eric. I instructed my son to pick up one of the books we now kept handy in the car, then closed the door and returned to a standing position so I could have a private conversation with Raphael. I pressed my ample behind against Eric's window so he wouldn't be all up in our business.

Shame I had enough butt to almost cover a whole window.

Raphael inched into my personal space, his hand resting on my car. "I had a good time with you and Eric tonight. This is how it should have been all along."

Lips pursed, I was silent.

"You look nice tonight." He started with small talk.

I rolled my eyes. "Try again."

"No, I'm serious. Any man would be proud to be seen with you."

Whether or not Raphael really meant the compliment, my slightly impaired sense of self-esteem slurped it up like a pool of water in a dry desert.

"Peaches, are you going to try to be in this relationship or not?"

"I'm here, aren't I?"

He motioned toward my frame. "Your body is here, and I know your heart is here, but your mind . . . it's somewhere else. Maybe it's with old boy."

Maybe it was. Honestly, did I have the nerve to pick up where I left off with this man? Was that spark really there, or was I imagining it? Willing it? I had to know. "Kiss me."

"Huh?"

"Kiss me. Now."

Raphael's eyes were cue balls, wondering what on earth I had just requested. He didn't wonder for long, though. He took one step toward me, closing the gap between us even more. For a moment, I hoped Eric wasn't looking. But when Raphael steadied my chin with his hand, I didn't care. His soft lips met mine. The kiss was tender. Tentative. Flashbacks of our intimate moments together played in my mind. He always was a gentle, attentive kisser. An even better lover. Raphael might have been selfish in many arenas, but never in bed. After our first rendezvous, I understood what all those lovers' songs meant. The O'Jays' "Stairway to Heaven," "Whip Appeal," and "Let's Do It Again" all made perfect sense to me from that day forward.

He must have sensed my surrender to his lips, because Raphael's kiss became stronger, deeper. I matched his pressure with my own as a delicious heat coursed through my body. I could almost feel myself turning to Jell-o from my lips on down.

Okay, maybe the kiss wasn't *that* long, but it was long enough for me realize there was definitely something to the adage: you never actually get over your first love.

Raphael put both hands on my hips and pried himself from me.

The smile on my face must have been a mile wide. I shoved my hands into my pockets and took a deep breath. "That was . . . nice."

"That was *more* than nice and you know it."

No use in me lying—that felt *good. Real* good. "Yeah, you're right."

He pulled me into a cozy embrace, conjuring up even more memories of the good times we had together. Sinful times, mind you, but the facts were still the facts. People can say what they want to say about wonderful personalities and warm attitudes, but there's no substitute for good old-fashioned chemistry.

Not that I didn't have it with Quinn, just I wasn't sure how it would all work out . . . you know . . . when it came down to it. I'd imagined how it would be, but I couldn't be 100 percent sure. I'd heard about couples going to sex counseling and sex therapy. Who's to say Quinn and I wouldn't end up there?

Anyway, Raphael and I had more in common than sex. We had a son. We had a history. We had a bunch of other stuff once upon a time, I was sure, but I couldn't name them right off following our intoxicating kiss—made me doubt whether it was safe for me to drive afterward.

"I'll call you tonight." He pecked me softly on the forehead.

"Okay."

After I was safely strapped into my seat belt, Raphael walked back to his car. I peeked at Eric through the mirror and noticed him dozing off, and I was glad. Only a few days ago, he'd seen me hugged up with Quinn at my doorstep. Now I was with Raphael. What would he think of me? No wonder he was so confused.

Well, I, for one, was no longer perplexed. I wanted my family—me, Raphael, and our son. Though my heart was still leaking at the point where Quinn exited, I'd have to sew it up.

And then, again, there were thoughts of Quinn. How much I loved him. How much he loved me and my son. I wondered if he would find someone else, or if he would become one of those bitter brothers who held women at arms' length because of one sister who burned him.

For the record, did I actually burn Quinn—or did he burn me? *He's the one who left you—not the other way around.* He could have stayed. I don't know exactly what would have happened with his job if he'd reneged on the offer, but he could have taken the risk just like he was asking me to take the risk. Yes, he could have stayed. He chose not to. He left me. *So actually, he dumped you!*

Rather than marvel or feel guilt at my heart's ability to switch gears so quickly, I sighed and declared to myself, "It is what it is." Shoot, I know a lady who got divorced and then married somebody else before the season changed.

Eric slumped through his nightly routine and quickly jumped into bed. His eyelids must have been ten-pound weights. The sight of him struggling through his nightly prayers was nearly funny. When we said our "amens," he shuffled beneath the sheets and whispered a weak, "Good night, Momma."

"Night, baby." I walked toward his door and turned off the light.

His voice creaked through the dark. "Momma?"

"Yes?"

"Did you kiss my daddy?"

Thank God for darkness, curse the nosiness! "Did you *see* me kiss your daddy?"

"I don't know. I couldn't see 'cause your b . . . body was in the way."

"Go to sleep, Eric."

"Yes, ma'am."

I stepped into the hallway, out of his view, thanked my lucky stars for my behind. That boy did not miss *anything!*

My showerhead was in dire need of replacement, but I suffered its scanty stream so that I could get in and out of the bathroom quickly. I didn't want to miss Raphael's call.

Perhaps fixing showerheads was one of the tasks I could delegate to my future husband. Wait a minute. Was I in marriage mode again? And to Raphael of all people? He'd said he wanted a relationship with me. A family. What else could he have meant?

Bathed, lotioned, and powdered, I sat in bed awaiting a late-night chat laced with flirty laughter. When Raphael and I were dating, we used to turn our radios on the same old-school station and listen to every song together as we talked on the phone. We played a game we called "That's My Jam" where we shared the first memory conjured up by the first few lines of each song.

Aside from all the drama with Eric and the raggedy way Raphael ended our relationship, we were actually friends once upon a time. For a few weeks at least.

I turned on my radio, switched the dial from AM gospel to an FM smooth R&B, and slid beneath the covers with a smile on my face. My stomach fluttered with giddy anticipation.

The phone's vibration nearly scared me out of my skin. I laughed at myself for jumping when I'd been expecting a call the whole time. But instead of a ring, I got a bleep. A text message?

Can't talk 2nite. Cheryl is here.

Chapter 19

My attitude was so jacked the next day at work, firing people was almost therapeutic. Everyone in the building knew what was happening—no need in waiting until the end of the day. I felt like the army commercial—I did more by nine o'clock that morning than most people did all day.

And it didn't help that there was something wrong with my computer. My login wouldn't work, so I had to call IT and see about getting it fixed. Michael Yancey was there that morning, so we used his laptop to access information.

By lunchtime, Raphael had called and left so many messages I had to scroll down on my alert screen to view them all. Was he crazy? Did he really think he could play me like this? Cheryl had to go. And I mean G-O with the quickness, because I was not going to be woman number two in line. Matter of fact, there better not *be* a line!

That Michael man sat in Theresa's empty space all morning looking crazy and coming into my office after each person left to say silly things like, "You really handled that well" and "It had to be done." If only I could terminate *him,* I would have been satisfied.

The sooner he left Northcomp the better, so I asked Michael if he would mind a working lunch. He readily agreed. I pulled out the Snickers bar I had in my purse and cracked it open right over a stack of papers. I swiped away the slivers of chocolate that landed on top of the pile.

Michael laughed quietly. "Do you . . . keep those handy?"

I mumbled, "What?"

"Candy bars."

After forcing the gob of carbohydrates down my throat, I quickly responded, "You ain't ever seen a black woman pull a candy bar out of her purse?"

An apology gushed from his lips. "Oh, I'm sorry! I didn't know. Is this cultural? Like . . . hair grease?"

"No. It's a Snickers bar. I like them and I eat them. It's not about being black."

"*You're* the one who said black."

I let my arm drop to the desk now. "You got a problem with black people?"

"No!" Michael held up both hands defensively. "That's not what I'm saying." He grabbed the top chunk of paperwork. "Let's get started on the first batch of data."

Y'all, I know I was wrong to play the black card, but there was something about him I never liked, and he was getting on my last nerve! Plus, it's just wrong to question a woman about what she eats unless you are a certified health expert.

Michael and I got busy crunching numbers and analyzing data. Really, I should say I got busy, because all he did was agree with everything I said. Two secretaries would now take on the work of three. A part-time employee's hours would be cut even more to, hopefully, force a voluntary resignation. And with a little luck, I might be able to retire my chopping ax if the next quarter's reports were favorable. Then maybe people would stop looking so frightened when they saw me in the common areas around Northcomp.

Michael was right about one thing—I knew my stuff, and I did handle myself well in the midst of the downsizing. I liked to think the "midst" was over and we were headed toward the light at the end of the tunnel. The end of firing people was definitely near.

We finished up at around two, and I fully expected Michael to start packing up his little duffle bag and head on out to wherever consultants congregate while they're still billing companies for a full day's work.

But instead of his usual speech about having to go do something immensely important, he asked, "Why don't we go see Mr. Hampton for a moment."

And he really wasn't asking, now that I think about it. He was directing me, holding my door open, standing back like "ladies first."

"I don't need to see Mr. Hampton."

"Well . . ." Michael's eyes dropped to the floor. "I think it would be best if we did."

Whatever. Michael must have had a reason to see Hampton. Probably wanted to prove himself useful. Maybe even invaluable.

I strolled down the short hallway to Hampton's office with Michael following closely behind. A little too close, now that I'm remembering it.

Linda didn't bother to ask why we were there. "You can go on in, Patricia. He's expecting you."

Michael stopped, gave me a sad nod, and gestured toward Mr. Hampton open door. "I'll see you . . . next time."

Michael knew good and well there wasn't going to be a next time, because the moment I walked into Mr. Hampton's office, he promptly fired me. "I'm sorry it came to this, Patricia, but we're going to have to outsource your position."

The objects lining Hampton's walls—his family, his parents, his degrees—suddenly became blurry. *No! You will not cry in front of this man! Rule #1! Rule #1!*

Before I knew it, my hand was resting firmly on my hip

in classic sister-girl stance. "What about all that talk of promoting me when the smoke cleared? Moving me up and giving me a pay raise?"

He stuttered a few times and finally came up with, "The numbers said otherwise."

The good ole blame-it-on-the-numbers excuse. *What about loyalty? What about honesty?*

Okay, I had to consider my next job. I quickly let my hand slip so it dangled at my side. The game was still on. "Is it safe to assume I can expect a glowing recommendation from you?"

Hampton's smile returned as he realized I was not going to do the fool on him. "Absolutely—I'll have Linda get started on it right away. She can e-mail it to you by tomorrow if you'll give her an alternate e-mail address." I'd never been anything except professional with him, but I think Hampton always suspected that a sho nuff clown could pop out of me if he turned my handle long enough.

Maybe that's why he refused my suggestion to be the outsourced contractor for the position. I told him it would only take a few weeks for me to establish an LLC and get myself certified as a woman-owned business, which could only help Northcomp in terms of compliance. Come to think of it, contracting was my ultimate professional goal. Maybe this was God's way of opening a door for me sooner than I'd imagined.

Hampton slammed the opportunity door shut without hesitation. "We've already got a contractor in mind. But if it doesn't work out, I'll certainly consider your offer."

Yeah, right. Like I've got a chance against one of his golfing buddies.

I tell you, this world does not play fair! Maybe while I was spending so much time trying to learn how to be an exceptional human resources executive, I should have been taking up golf so I could get out there and wheel and deal on the *real* playing field with those good ole boys.

Inside, I was a ball of emotions. Outwardly, I kept my stone countenance and my dignity in place. I've had to reschedule a meltdown many a day. "Well, I suppose I'll get my things and be on my way."

Turning my back to Hampton, I found myself facing security. *Et tu, Vernon?* He couldn't even look me in the eyes. Just told me he'd follow me back to my desk so I could gather my belongings and then he'd escort me out of the building through the back door.

I'm sure if I were white, my face would have been beet red, because every square inch was burning. *How could he use me like this? They waited until I finished all the dirty work and then fired me!*

Back in my office, I grabbed a plastic grocery bag from the stash I always kept in my drawer and began stuffing my personal items inside. This was nothing less than humiliating. I'd been at Northcomp for seven years. *No kind of notice or anything! I mean, they're treating me like I'm some kind of hourly employee with no vested interest in the company!*

Vernon stood guard at the door but refused to watch me directly. Over the years, he and I had a nice little working relationship. He helped me when I needed folks off the premises, and I did my best to make sure he always had work to do.

He must have felt bad about the whole situation. *He ought to feel bad! This whole company ought to feel bad!*

Everything made sense now. They'd brought in the Yancey Group so I could teach them my job. Then they got rid of Theresa. *And no wonder my login didn't work this morning! That was just dirty!*

I grabbed a brand-new box of high-quality ballpoint pens from the lower drawer and threw it into my sack. Yes, I was stealing. I figured they owed me *at least* a pack of pens after all I'd done for them. I grabbed a stack of sticky notes and some binder clips for old times' sake, too. I wanted to take the electric stapler, but just then my plastic bag gave way and all of its contents spilled onto the floor.

"Dang it!"

Vernon offered to help but I refused him. "I've got it."

Frustration took its toll and the tears began to flow freely as I quickly pulled two more bags out, stuffed one inside the other, and transferred my rightful property and the loot into this fortified knapsack.

Michael rapped on my door, putting a halt to my last-minute pilferage. "Patricia, I just wanted to say it was very nice working with you."

There was no time to dry the tears from my face. What did it matter, anyway? Reckon I'd never see him again. I stood tall and decided on a simple "Thank you."

Michael's eyes, loaded with compassion, dropped. "If it helps, I structured a very generous severance package for you."

Sarcasm bubbled in my stomach, but it's kind of hard to act tough when you're crying in front of someone, so I quelled the urge to bite him. "Yes, it does help." That was the truth—the money would certainly come in handy. As a single mother busy doing the job of two parents, I didn't have too many zeroes in my savings account. My Benz was my only big splurge. I had a few long-term investments for Eric's college, but touching those accounts came with huge penalties.

Vernon asked, "You all packed up?" My cue to get to steppin'.

I took a deep breath and looked around one last time to make sure I wasn't leaving any of my things. This whole office used to be my thing. Now it would belong to someone else.

Michael offered his business card. "If you think of anything you forgot, just call me. I'll be sure to put it aside for you."

I took his card and placed it in my jacket pocket. I swiped another tear away.

"And if you need some work, I'm sure I could use your help on some of our projects. Your level of expertise is a very hot commodity these days."

Not hot enough for Northcomp. I pressed my lips together in a semi-grin. A straight face was all I could give Michael without busting out in great sobs. I hoped he understood. People on the verge of a major breakdown are in no position to smile.

Vernon and I bumped into Hampton on my last walk down a Northcomp hallway. I probably should have kept my mouth shut, but I had to stick it to him just this once. I knew why he didn't tell me he was firing me before today. Ever since newly terminated ex-employees started going postal, it was a commonly held belief that people (particularly executives) should not be notified of impending termination. Folks have been known to do all kinds of crazy things before their final dates of employment—erase hard drives, sabotage projects, download and spread viruses, sell company information. I understood the concept.

What I didn't understand was why he had to butter me up like Northcomp would have my back if I had theirs. I had to know. "Why did you have to lie about the promotion? That was really unnecessary."

He shrugged and plastered a fake frown on his face. "All's fair in love, war, and a bad economy."

Chapter 20

It was 2:47 PM when I walked out of Northcomp for the last time. By 3:30, I was sitting at home in front of the television watching *The People's Court* while downing a bacon cheeseburger, large fries, and a diet soda. The reality of being fired hadn't hit me yet, I don't think. Maybe Hampton would call me tomorrow and say it was all a big mistake. Michael Yancey had reconsidered, they were terribly sorry and wanted me back, with the raise he'd promised. Perhaps they'd call and say we'd gotten a major contract with the government and everything was back on track. Or, better yet, maybe they would call next week and say that business was so slow since I left, they'd obviously been cursed for firing me.

I think I liked the last reason best. Picture it: Hampton and Michael running around my office trying to make heads and tails of the data, trying to figure out why productivity was down, why contracts with vendors were falling through. Just like Joseph—his brothers set him up to die, but they ended up needing *him* when it was all over with! *That's what I'm talkin' 'bout!*

Thoughts of the Bible brought an unexpected sadness to my heart. I hadn't been to church in weeks, couldn't remember the last time I prayed *for real.* The words I'd been whispering to God lately were rote and empty. The usual "Thank You, God, for another day" and "Now I lay me down to sleep." I suppose they were better than nothing—probably bought me some grace for acknowledging Him.

Still, I missed His presence. Alone in my bed, surrounded by leftover trash from foods I hadn't eaten since I was well over two hundred pounds, I cried out, "God, what am I going to do?"

Then I waited. And I waited. And I waited for that small Voice to speak but He didn't said nary a word.

His silence was heartbreaking. I mean, I'd just lost my fiancé and my job, and I was on the verge of rekindling a relationship with Raphael. Why was He speechless in all of this? Why wasn't He there when I needed Him?

Reminded me of my natural father's quiet spells. I understood Daddy had his own emotional issues, but what was God's excuse? Why wasn't He "showing up and showing out," as the old saints say? I wanted Him to, number one, get me a job. Number two, get Cheryl out of the picture so, number three, Raphael and I could have the family I always wanted. And the quicker He moved on these things, the better.

I slid down my sofa until my knees hit the floor, then positioned myself in classic prayer form—hands folded, waist bent at a ninety-degree angle. I prefaced my prayer by asking God to forgive me for anything I *might* have done wrong. Then I got down to business. "Father, You know the desires of my heart—and You said in Your Word You would give them to me. So, here they go." And I fervently rattled off my list of wants like a child talking to Santa Claus the week before Christmas.

I added a little prayer for Eric, too, in anticipation of the results from Frierson. I was thinking about praying for Quinn, but I didn't know what to pray. Maybe I should have prayed that God would send the right person into his life. I couldn't bring myself to do it. I simply prayed God's will for His life, whatever that was.

Judge Milian was about to render her verdict, so I wrapped up my prayer quickly and hopped back onto the couch to witness the outcome. Two cases later, I decided I'd go ahead and pick up Eric from day care early because, according to the news flash, a severe thunderstorm was headed our way.

While driving to day care, LaShondra's name appeared on my car's display, signaling her call. I pressed the Answer button on my steering wheel. "Speak, my sister."

"What you up to?"

"Going to pick up Eric before this storm sets in." I turned on my wipers as the first sprinkles announced its arrival.

"Oh, you left work early?"

Tell the truth and shame the devil. "Girl, I just got fired."

"What?!"

"Kicked to the curb."

LaShondra made a few noises. "Wh . . . when? Why?"

"Today. Because this is triflin' corporate America."

"Hmph." I recognized her smug tone. "I ain't gon' say it."

"You might as well, with that attitude."

"Nope."

"I'll say it for you." Then we both sang in unison, "I told you so," followed by harmless laughter.

"And since we're going here, I might as well speak my peace." LaShondra hopped on her high horse—the white stallion she got when she married Stelson, I think. "If this ain't a sign from God, I don't know what is."

"A sign about what? I'm going to move on. File for unemployment, live off the pot of tax money for a while. Lord knows I've been putting money in it long enough."

She smacked her lips. "The Lord also knows you need to beg Quinn to take you back."

I found a parking spot near the day care's entry and settled in for a good, long argument with LaShondra, the kind of spat you can only have with your best friend and know that things will still be all right at the end of it. Storm or not, we needed to have this discussion once and for all. "I'm through with Quinn, okay? I'm moving on. Keep up with me, please."

"You're saying you don't love him anymore?"

She'd hear it in my voice if I lied. "Don't put words in my mouth. All I'm saying is I'm going forward with my life. No looking back. Remember Lot's wife?"

LaShondra gasped. "Don't try to twist this. Lot's wife died because she looked back and longed for a hot mess—not because she took a second glance at her knight in shining armor."

"Whatever. I'm saying the *concept* of looking back is a problem."

She argued, "Not if you're looking back because God wants you to look back."

"When did God ever tell somebody to look back?"

"That's your problem, Peaches Ann Miller, you don't listen to nobody."

I stared at my car's display panel again. "Am I talking to my momma or my best friend?"

"Doesn't matter. We both know you."

"Well, if you already believe I'm a stubborn old mule, why can't you just let me live my life and do things the way I want to do 'em?"

I heard her take a deep breath. "You know what? You're right. This is your life. You have a God-given right to jack it up if you want to, but don't come cryin' to me when you look around and everything is to' up from the flo' up, okay?"

"Thank you, LaShondra Brown. I'll be sure to keep my problems to myself from now on."

"Fine. I'm not going to say another word about Quinn."

"Fine," I agreed. "Surely do 'preciate you dropping the subject."

"You need to call your momma, though. She's worried sick about you." Even in her contempt, my best friend was always looking out for me.

"I'll call her later."

"You do that. Bye."

"Bye."

Chapter 21

My double-chin was the last thing to go when I lost eighty pounds a decade earlier, and it was the first staple sign to appear when the weight returned. The extra fullness stared back at me on my first official day of unemployment.

Not only was I unemployed, I was officially fat again.

And the rain kept coming.

As ill-timing would have it, the next night was the evening Raphael and I were called in to meet with the Frierson folks and discuss the results of Eric's assessment. When the receptionist called to confirm that Raphael and I would be there, I spoke only for myself and told her she'd have to talk with Raphael personally. She seemed surprised, maybe even annoyed. Nonetheless, she must have called him because he beat Eric and me to Frierson.

Eric released my hand and flew to his father as soon as we entered the place. "Hey, Dad!"

"What's up?"

They hugged like long lost relatives who hadn't just seen each other in recent history. Raphael helped Eric out of his raincoat and hung it on the coatrack near the door. Then the two had a brief conversation before Eric tried to busy himself in the children's play area. I quickly redirected him to pick up a book instead of fooling with those toys.

"But Mom—"

No words needed. The *eye* stopped his whining.

I chose a different section of the waiting area to be seated. Raphael made his way over to me, invading my private space with his seductive cologne. That stuff ought to be illegal, smelling like strong, working, educated black man with swag.

"I'm sorry about the other night."

I kept my eyes downcast, pretending to browse the Web on my cell phone. "As you should be."

"Leaving Cheryl is not that simple. I have to get things in order. I can't just walk out," he tried to explain.

"Funny. You didn't have a problem walking out on me and Eric."

He grasped my chin and pulled my face toward his. "Peaches, I want you to leave the past in the past, all right? I'm not the man I used to be. I'm better now. I don't want to leave Cheryl high and dry. It's not her fault I couldn't get over you."

Hmmm . . . was this some kind of a reverse romance psychology? As a woman, I could appreciate his sensitivity. Getting dumped is brutal. But as *his* woman (if that's what I called myself), Raphael's consideration for Cheryl's feelings annoyed me.

A loud clap of thunder brought Eric back to my side. Eric was eight, but he was still very much afraid of storms and all their accompanying glory. He sat down at my feet, abruptly ending the tense conversation with Raphael.

When we were called to a meeting room to discuss the results, I assured Eric he would be fine waiting in the lobby area without us. He didn't buy my words of encouragement.

"You straight, man," Raphael pumped his son's confidence.

Eric inhaled his father's certainty.

I was again thankful to have Raphael at my side. Though I couldn't agree with LaShondra on the particulars of being hooked up with a man, I had to give it up on this one: When meeting with other people about your child, it feels absolutely marvelous to have someone else in your corner.

The briefing room looked more like a living room. Couches, coffee tables, a small aquarium. The lone beta fish swam gracefully, a calming gesture.

The person assigned to Eric's case, Evelyn Farley, should have taken a lesson from the fish. She was uneasy from the get-go. Red splotches started at the top of her silk shell blouse and climbed up her neck as she fumbled through the preliminaries. Eric is a well-mannered young man, he clearly has a supportive family, yada yada yada.

I couldn't wait any longer. "So, what's the problem, then?"

She cleared her throat and, with her fingertips, pulled her bangs behind both ears. "Miss Miller, the results of our assessment point to a possible learning disability."

Learning disability? "What?"

Evelyn nodded solemnly. "Yes. There are, of course, many different types of learning disabilities. However, we don't actually *diagnose* such disabilities here."

Raphael snapped at her, rubbing his hands on his knees. "So, how does this work?"

I rested my hand on top of his. No need in both of us going left.

The woman answered in a calm tone. "Well, once a learning disability has been either ruled out or diagnosed, we can formulate a plan to work with Eric and help him catch up to his peers."

Learning disability? Impossible. My son could read when he put his mind to it. "Evelyn, Eric can read. I've heard him myself. I mean, he stumbles on big words, but I think I would know if my own child had a learning disability."

She shrugged. "Not necessarily. Eric is an only child, correct?"

"Yes."

"Sometimes when you're only familiar with one child and how that one child reads or learns, you don't have the perspective to compare him with other eight-year-olds. Moreover, sometimes we can account for grade-level differences by maturity, months apart in age, and such. A child who starts kindergarten fairly early because he has a summer birthday may not enter with the same skills as a kindergartner who turns six in September. There are many variables, but by second or third grade, we can begin to see the gaps much more clearly.

"The good news is, we'll be able to catch this pretty early and work with Eric so that he doesn't suffer the rest of his school career with an undiagnosed learning disability. You'd be surprised how many children experience failure in school because their symptoms aren't recognized. Often they get labeled as behavior problems because their parents, for whatever reason, do not seek outside services to address the child's needs. Eric is lucky to have you two."

Evelyn took a break and we all took deep breaths.

Raphael's hand softened under my grip. Instinctively, my fingers laced with his and I asked, "What do we do now?"

"There are several resources in the Dallas area I can refer you to." She whipped out a list of hospital and clinics specializing in diagnoses for children. The weight of my heart in my chest doubled when I recognized some of the facilities' names from fund-raising appeals I'd seen on television. *My baby needs to see a doctor. A specialist.*

I tried to remind myself that I should be thankful Eric had a learning disability, not a life-threatening physical problem. Still, a learning disability would make him . . . different. People wouldn't treat him the same, his self-esteem would be shot. Kids who are like me when I was in third grade would tease him and call him names. Seriously, I can't even count the number of times I made fun of kids who rode the short bus when I was in elementary school.

Raphael must have sensed me sinking. He held my hand tightly. "Did you hear what she said, honey?"

God knows I needed to be somebody's honey right about then. "Huh?"

"She says she can help us get an appointment pretty quickly."

"By all means." My own sniffing caught me by surprise.

Evelyn pulled a tissue from a box I hadn't even noticed before. I wondered how many other parents had cried in this same room.

The scenario reminded me of the funeral parlor a few days before my father's funeral. It seemed like every room in the place was cry-ready. Everywhere I looked there was a box of Kleenex, like they were expecting me to break down any minute. I expected to break down, actually, but I didn't then. Didn't cry much at the funeral, either. In fact, I was still waiting for the moment people talked about—when the wave of grief finally overtook me and I could cry like a baby for my daddy.

There was no delay, however, in the case of my son's potential diagnosis. As soon as we stood outside the Frierson Center, the dam broke and I wept torrentially onto Raphael's shoulder while Eric tugged my arm pleading to know, "What's wrong, Momma? What's wrong?"

"Your momma's going to be all right, Eric," Raphael answered for me. Then he asked me for my keys so he could bring my car up to the port.

The rain had slackened a bit, so I turned down his offer. "That's okay. I won't melt."

Disappointment smeared his face. He was only trying to help, trying to be a man. Trying to model everything I hoped Eric would witness and practice someday.

"On second thought, I guess it's a good idea."

Moments later, Raphael parked my car, got out, and then tucked both Eric and me safely inside my vehicle. I rolled down my window and said good night.

"We need to talk."

I nodded, still too shaken to speak.

"The sooner the better."

Again, I silently agreed.

"Tonight?"

This time I shook my head, wiping my eyes and recomposing myself. "I'm pooped and the weather is pretty bad out here. I'm going home. Call me later—if you can."

He sidestepped my punch. "I can . . . follow you home. We can talk there, if that's okay with you."

"It's not okay with me."

Eric interjected, "It's okay with me!"

"We're not talking to you," I scolded, burrowing into him with a glare.

Raphael tried again. "We need to go over the papers, talk calendars, talk insurance. I promise I won't bite." He flashed both palms in a gesture of innocence.

His eyelashes were to die for.

I exhaled audibly. "I guess."

"I'll stop and get us something to eat first."

Eric hollered from the backseat, "Daddy, can I go with you?"

Raphael passed the buck with a shrug.

Once more, I relented. "Go ahead."

Eric threw off his seat belt and bounded out of the car.

True to his word, Raphael arrived at my home half an hour later with a salad for me as well as sub sandwiches and Cokes for us all. As we ate at my kitchen table, the feeling of parental doom was temporarily suspended. Eric and Raphael competed to see which of them could stuff his mouth the fullest—a dangerously disgusting game Eric used to play with Quinn. Gross.

I wondered if it mattered which man assumed the "father" role in my son's life. I wondered if Eric thought of them as interchangeable. I mean, are children really that flexible? Had he forgotten about Quinn so quickly? Had I?

Raphael supervised Eric's nightly routine while I straightened up the kitchen and relaxed with a little Maxwell flowing, checking my e-mail messages. I overheard Eric ask his father about a bedtime prayer. My ears perked up, and I turned down the volume on my computer.

For all the years I'd known Raphael, he'd never been a particularly religious person. He respected my "church girl" mentality, but he didn't trust preachers. Said they were nothing but crooked pulpit pimps.

"I'll lead the prayer this time," Eric suggested, "and you can do it next time. Or do you want to go first?"

Raphael chuckled slightly. "Naw. You got it, doc."

Eric then prayed the standard bedtime appeal, followed by a list of names—my mother, my friends, all the people who loved him. Including Quinn. He also prayed to receive a dog, which was something he'd have to keep on the list until he moved out from under my roof.

I guess with the stress and after all the junk I'd been downing lately, my stomach didn't know how to act with something green—namely, salad—in it. Throughout their semiprivate prayer time, I kept going to the restroom to pass gas. Perhaps it wasn't meant for me to eavesdrop.

With the prayer complete and Eric's night-light employed, Raphael rejoined me in the kitchen. He wore an uncomfortable smirk. I already knew he had something smart to say.

"What?"

He crossed his arms and leaned against the counter. "I don't know if I want my son believing all that church stuff. I don't have a problem with him believing in God and knowing right from wrong. But he has to realize if you want something to happen, you have to *make* it happen. He can't depend on God for everything, and he definitely can't put all his trust in people who claim to know God."

"I'm not going to argue with you about religion, Raphael. We've never agreed on it before and we probably never will."

"All I'm saying is, I don't want him brainwashed by a bunch of hypocrites."

I matched Raphael's stance, leaning on the opposing counter. "First of all, Christians are not *all* hypocrites. Second, if you understood anything about God's mercy and grace, you wouldn't be so judgmental."

A dent appeared just beneath his cheekbone. Resentment. "Is this about God or about Quinn?"

"Seems like they're one in the same in Eric's eyes."

I threw my dish towel in the sink and stored the plastic plates in the pantry. "Trust me, they're not."

"What happened between you and him anyway?"

A mighty fine question indeed. Problem was, the answer didn't make good sense. I couldn't very well say, "I got scared." So I did what everyone does when they want to be right. I gave him my version of the breakup. "He got a job offer in Philadelphia and he accepted it with very little consideration for me or Eric."

Now that I'd voiced my slightly truncated side of the story, it did sound like a pretty good reason to break off an engagement. Maybe if I said it to myself enough times, I'd believe it. Build up a whole story around it and replay it over and over in my head until it became my truth.

"Okay. So let's talk about the testing and tutoring." I left hot subject alone.

I pondered whether I should tell Raphael I'd lost my job, but I didn't want to scare away his newfound goodness by suggesting he might have to come off even more cash.

I didn't have to make the choice, because his cell phone rang.

"Shoot." He unhooked it from his holster and read the face. Meanwhile, I read his face. His lips flatlined, but his forehead crumpled enough to let me know it had to be Cheryl—or someone else he didn't want to hear from. He pushed a button that stopped the ringing, then put the phone back in its place.

I glanced at my watch. "It's late. Maybe we should talk about this tomorrow."

He readily agreed. "Yeah. I'll call you."

"Yeah." *Right.*

I walked him to the door, opened it. Wished I could have kicked his behind as he stepped across the threshold. Without a good night, I closed the door.

He knocked. "Peaches."

I yelled back through the door. "What?"

"Open the door."

"Who is it?"

"Imma," he played along.

"Imma who?"

"Imma need to use your restroom before I leave."

Lord knows I needed that laugh. I opened up and stepped aside. Raphael disappeared into the restroom.

A few minutes later, he burst out of there holding his nose. "Girl, you lit that bathroom up! Dang! You should have warned me!" He coughed, waving a hand in front of his face as though he had just stepped out of a burning building.

I was too tickled to be embarrassed, so I let it go. We fell into each other's arms laughing fully. Freely. I felt his solid abdomen, warm and strong, heaving against my chest. The deep timbre of his chuckle sent soft vibrations through me. I hadn't been this close a man in weeks, and it felt good.

The hilarity subsided, followed by reality. He pulled me

close to him and wrapped one hand behind my head, pressing me onto him. "I've missed you."

I appreciated hearing his confession. And I especially appreciated being so close to him. "Same here."

He stepped back, surveyed me. "And I like this new you."

Speechless, I pushed his forehead back with my thumb. How dare he.

Before I could provide him with a few choice words, Raphael explained himself. "No, I mean I like the curves. They're sexy."

"Fat as I am, I'm sexy to you?"

"Yeah." He drank in every ounce of me with his eyes. "It's sexy when a woman comes into her own body—lets the curves fill in her figure. You are definitely hot."

"Hmph. Tell that to the rest of the world."

"I don't want to ever say those words to anyone except you. You are beautiful, Peaches."

Seriously, some men are just smoooooooth, make a woman feel as though her life is straight from a sappy bestselling romance novel.

So you know what happened next. My eyes sank deeply into his. He kissed me tenderly. And all my good sense, scripture memorization—not to mention home training—flew right out of my mind, replaced by sensory images of passionate cries and recollection of uttermost satisfaction I *always* experienced when Raphael and I slept together. I'm talking dependable. Clockwork. Money in the bank, *capiche?*

That night, Raphael lived up to the memory. *Mmm, mmm, mmm.*

Chapter 22

Nine years of celibacy down the drain. Just like that. And after our two-hour tryst, Raphael kindly kissed me on the forehead, dressed, and headed home to Cheryl.

I'm tryin' to stay saved here, so . . . hmm . . . how can I describe my thoughts? Well, after my pulse returned to normal and my brain returned to its rightful place in my head, I could have just wrapped my hands around my neck and strangled myself! What was I thinking? How did I let this happen?

It was bad enough I'd given in to temptation. But the man I gave in to just left my bed to be with the woman he was living with! Shoot, if I had known I was going to blow it, I could have *at least* blown it with somebody who was at liberty to stay the night. Somebody like Quinn who was mine and mine alone. Or somebody like Morris Chestnut, whom I could easily justify as a once-in-a-lifetime guilty pleasure.

No, I had to go and do it with *Raphael* again. Traded nine years of walking in victory for two hours of flesh-fulfilling sex. In the heat of the moment, there was no questioning how good my body felt. Indescribable is the only way I can describe it. I suppose once you're on that path, there's no detouring. Well, maybe there is a detour, but I certainly wasn't trying to find it.

I couldn't sleep after he left. Certainly couldn't pray, not with all the guilt floating around the room. I hauled my sheets off my bed and threw them into the washing machine. Then I hightailed it to the shower and tried my best to get clean— lathering, scouring, rinsing, and repeating.

It wasn't long before the tears came. I was suddenly religious again, bombarded by scriptures and clichés nowhere to be found just a few hours earlier. I had given myself over to the enemy again. My body, God's temple, in ruins. *The Lord is far from the wicked. The wages of sin is death.*

Heaping on top of those realizations was the understanding that this incident was probably the final nail in the coffin for me and Quinn. I couldn't possibly hope to reconcile with him—ever—after sleeping with another man. This wasn't the kind of secret I could take into my marriage, and I couldn't expect Quinn to forgive me for something like this. Come to think of it, I wasn't too sure I could forgive me, either.

Unless this all worked out in the end. I mean, if Raphael and I ended up being together forever, this small glitch in timing wouldn't be so drastic in the grand scheme of life. It's not like we'd never done it before. If we got married, it would just be one of the many times we'd have sex, right? And the good? I was still the only woman I knew under the age of thirty-five who had slept with only one man. That had to count for *something*.

Okay, so plan B in action. *Regroup, Peaches, regroup and refocus.* I could still make this work.

Over a quick batch of Rice Krispies Treats, I devised a plan for my life that made the most sense. Maybe it wasn't right, maybe it wasn't God's best, but a sistah has to do what a sistah has to do.

Plan B, step 1: Get a job. Everything else would have to wait. I spent the rest of the week scouring the Internet for leads, registering with headhunters and temporary agencies.

Some of the people I called upon were former Northcomp vendors whom I knew well.

"We should be able to place you quickly," they said. "Your experience and people skills are definitely in demand," they promised. They lied. Three weeks after being terminated at Northcomp, I was just as unemployed as the next woman in line looking for work. Time to file for unemployment.

I thanked God for the severance pay, but I think He was mad at me, because a good little chunk of the money got eaten up by the central air unit I suddenly needed for my condo. I could have cried when I wrote out the fat check, but I certainly wasn't in the market for a heat stroke so I didn't have much of a choice. Don't let the spring season fool you in Texas.

Word made it around my camp that I was unemployed. In one of our rare conversations, LaShondra said Stelson was keeping an eye open for opportunities. My mother said she was thinking more and more about the day care business we discussed. She said I could work with her if I wanted to. The longer I went without employment, the more I wondered if it would come down to me accepting her offer. And with the extra expense of Eric's tutoring, there was no telling what I might end up doing before it was all said and done.

"Peoples been asking about you at church," my mother pried as she invited me into the house.

Eric ran ahead of us to the kitchen, presumably to find a bite to eat. I suppose if nothing else we could always come to my mother's house for food.

I dodged my mother's comment, refusing her invitation. "I've got to go." I handed her Eric's weekend backpack and stepped away from the door.

"You can't come inside and talk for a little while?"

I was already late for my date with Raphael—not that I wanted share this tidbit of information with my mother. "No, ma'am. I'll catch up with you when I pick Eric up after church Sunday." I had no intention of catching my mother up on my life. If she caught wind of me and Raphael, she might flip.

As I walked back to my car, I thought about my mother being the only one taking Eric to church these days. I remembered the girls who had babies while we were still in high school. I used to see them at the basketball games and at dances and wonder who was watching their babies. My mother told me straight up—if *I* got pregnant, *I* would be the one raising the baby. Back then, she couldn't understand why any mother would take on the responsibility of raising her "fast" daughter's child. And yet, she was doing it now, in a sense. Eric was a grandmother's dream, but I realized then she was taking on the charge of rearing him spiritually because if she didn't, no one else would.

Is that what I had become? Fast? Certainly felt like it. Since the back-down-memory-lane night with Raphael, seems like I'd put on a pair of banana peel shoes and made a habit of slipping. He knew I was a Christian and I knew I was a Christian. Our bodies, however, didn't get the telegram. And every time we slept together, it just got easier and easier to tuck my conscience away.

Plus I had all but lied to Eric about where his father slept when he spent the night once.

I simply wasn't the woman I used to be. I didn't even have a job, for crying out loud!

Even though Raphael was still living with Cheryl, he said they were no longer sleeping together. I wasn't stupid enough to believe that propaganda, but I allowed it for the moment. What else could I do? If I lost him, I'd just be stuck out looking like the big fool who let a catfish go for a minnow. The only good sense I can claim to have had was the sense to make sure we had "safe" sex, if there is such a thing.

Raphael and I met at one of those overpriced, swanky cafés—a place with far more decor than good food. Since I'd told Raphael I was trying to hold on to my little duckies for obvious reasons, he kicked in when it was time to pay the tab at the ordering counter.

We found a booth and settled in for a conversation that I knew would somehow lead back to my bedroom. These days, our talking always led to action. Couldn't blame it all on him, though. I did my fair share of flirting.

"So, what's on your mind?" I asked, then scooped a spoon full of broccoli cheddar soup into my mouth.

Raphael gave me a sexy smile and took a bite of his panini. He chewed but kept his gaze on me, prolonging our eye contact in the same way the brother knew how make what should only be a fleeting moment last much longer in bed. "Just you."

Already, my earlobes shivered, matched by a sensation on my thigh that fooled me for a moment until I realized my phone was vibrating. Using my index finger and thumb, I pulled the phone from my pocket and took a glance at the display.

After reading the name, I slid the phone back in place.

"Who was it?"

"Shondra."

"What—y'all don't talk anymore?" Raphael asked.

My salad fork couldn't hold enough food to stuff my mouth long enough for a good explanation to appear. How else could I say, "I'm avoiding my best friend?"

When I didn't answer, Raphael jumped in. "I take it you haven't told her about us yet."

Table-turning time. "Whom have you told?"

"Cheryl. My mother. Fabian."

Those people didn't really count, in my book. Cheryl had to know because it affected her directly. Both Raphael's mother and his brother were trifling. They lived in drama, so this would not come as a surprise in their worlds.

My world, on the other hand, was full of regular people.

"When do you plan on telling them?"

"When do you plan on moving out of the house you're sharing with Cheryl?"

"At the end of the month," he blurted out.

"Yeah. I'm moving out on the last day."

"Good, baby. Where you moving to?"

His eyes widened. "I *thought* I was moving in with you."

My neck slid over to one side. "I don't know where you got that idea. I didn't say you could move in with me."

"Peaches, I'm there almost every night." He swung his knife in the air.

"Irrelevant."

He let out a loud sigh. A sarcastic laugh. "I can't believe this."

I matched him with a laugh of my own. "What made you think you could move in with me?"

"We're dating. We're a family, planning a future together. Hello!"

"Okay, but we are not *married,* which is the prerequisite for living together in my book. I don't play house."

"So, what? You want me to propose now?"

"Don't get carried away."

"If we're not planning to move in together and try a serious relationship, then what are we doing?"

"I don't know. You're the one who started all this reconciliation, not me. You're supposed to spend the rest of your life repaying me for all the wrong you did, remember?"

He shook his head and tore into his sandwich looking like a teenager who'd just been told he couldn't have the keys to the car. His behavior reminded me of the childish Raphael I'd discovered when we dated the first time. He used to get angry when I beat him at Monopoly. I mean, he got seriously mad when he had to pay me for landing on *my* property! Guess old habits die hard.

Raphael shoved his straw into his mouth, slurped, and

then stared at me for a moment. He nearly choked on a condescending laugh. Or maybe it was a homeless laugh.

"What?" I had to know.

"You church folks are all alike, sinnin' and grinnin' just like the rest of us but acting like you've got some kind of standard."

A month earlier, his statement might have felt like a punch in the stomach. But, given my most recent fornication streak, I knew he had a point. For a moment, I wondered if it would ever be possible to talk to Raphael about God or church after I had given in to temptation so many times.

Still, he was *not* moving into my apartment. "This isn't just about religion. It's about . . . womanhood and . . . principle."

"I thought I'd be doing you a favor, since you don't have a job."

Okay, that one did hurt. And, again, he had a point. A sharp, stabbing point.

"But if you don't want me to move in and help out with the bills, I'll get my own place. Not a problem." He sat there pouting for another five minutes. If he was waiting on me to change my mind, he'd be waiting till the cows came home. I kept on eating as though nothing was wrong.

Then his phone chimed. I'd been around Raphael enough to know Cheryl's ringtone. Raphael practically glued the phone to his ear as he walked away from our table and toward the men's restroom area so he could have privacy.

Ain't this a blimp? How does one just presume he can move into someone's apartment? *Like he's entitled to sleep in my bed?* Besides, I didn't like the way he said "help out" with the bills. God forbid, but if I *ever* let my boyfriend move in with me—which wasn't about to happen, mind you—but if I did, he would *not* be "helping out" with a little water bill here and a cable bill there. Yeah, I caught Raphael's drift. His idea of helping out probably meant me paying the huge, static bills and him chipping in on the smaller, variable notes that could pile up for a while before disconnection.

And how would the whole setup look to our son? For all the times I'd had to sneak Raphael out before Eric woke up or hide Raphael in my room until I took Eric to school, Raphael should have known I wasn't the one for blatant cohabitation.

Then again . . . how could I have expected him to know? I was doing everything else like the world, why should this be any different?

He rushed back to our table. "I have to go."

"Why?"

"Personal business."

"Am I not part of your *personal* life?"

He didn't answer me. Just wrapped the fancy wax paper around what was left of his panini and secured it with a toothpick. He pecked me on the cheek, proceeded to his car, and peeled out of the parking lot.

I swear, that had to be some of the most bipolarest mess I had ever witnessed.

Chapter 23

The bad thing about a good friend is, she won't give up on you. LaShondra called me twice one particular Saturday and left nasty messages. "Your momma says she's gonna pray the spirit of rebellion right out of you." "I know you see my number on your screen, Peaches. Don't make me come over there."

At around six in the evening, she made good on her threat. The bamming on my door woke me from a good sleep. My first thought was fire. Seriously, she was beating that hard. But her voice on the other side calmed my panicky nerves.

"Peaches!"

This girl was going to wake up the neighbors—assuming other people slept as much as I had been sleeping lately.

"I'm coming," I yelled to her as I turned the locks.

I barely had the door open when she busted up in my place like a police officer in raid mode. She quickly scanned my living and dining areas and then looked me up and down. LaShondra dropped her purse on the floor and approached me, putting one hand on my shoulder and the other on my forehead. Still hadn't said a word to me.

"Hello to you, too."

She peered into my eyes, scrutinizing my very pupils until I could feel pools forming in my bottom lids.

I yanked my gaze from hers. "Stop it, LaShondra."

"Peaches, everyone is worried sick about you. What's going on?"

"Nothing." The corners of my mouth tightened.

She huffed, "You're not returning phone calls, not going to church. Eric is practically living at your mother's house."

No way was she getting away with that one. "Not true."

"Your mom says you've been taking him over there a couple of days during the week, in addition to weekends."

"Only on choir rehearsal nights, and when he doesn't have tutoring. And sometimes she even *asks* to keep Eric." Okay, so maybe there was some truth to her accusation. Still, I wouldn't have exactly called myself an absent mother. Maybe I was just having a . . . break. When married moms and dads go away for a while, they call it a "vacation." When a single mom does the same thing, oh, we're "negligent." The world is so full of double standards—or so I told myself to keep from feeling too badly about the situation.

LaShondra folded her arms across her chest. "I'm your best friend. I know there's something going on with you and I'm determined to help you through it."

Who died and made her Mary Poppins? "This is America. I have a right to be in a funk. Everybody can't be happy-go-lucky all the time like you."

She planted herself on my couch and crossed her legs defiantly. The tips of her open-toed tortoiseshell pumps pointed at me. *Cute shoes.* Those must have been new. Matter of fact, her whole outfit was new to me.

Before she got married, LaShondra and I used to shop together almost every weekend. We'd even taken a few road trips to suburban outlet centers and scooped up bargains galore. Sometimes Deniessa would tag along with us, but even if she didn't or couldn't come, LaShondra and I were wholesale warriors.

We used to attend the same singles Bible study, too, until one of us was no longer single. I really don't know how the Bible becomes different after one gets married. I guess if I had to put my finger on it, the different Bible studies were a point of separation for us. We weren't focusing on the same scriptures or readings anymore, so we didn't have our Word bond. Of course, I wasn't too concerned about it then, because I was busy falling in love with Quinn.

Quinn. Already, he seemed like a distant memory. Almost as distant as the good ole days with my best friend.

I paced the floor a few times and then offered LaShondra a bottled water because, clearly, she wasn't going anywhere any time soon.

"Yeah, I'd like water."

She caught the bottle, twisted the top off, took a swig. Small chat came first. We discussed Eric's upcoming birthday party to be held at Pizza Kingdom.

"Isn't he getting a little old for Pizza Kingdom?"

Never crossed my mind. Maybe she was right. I'd been wrong about his reading problem. I also remember the moment I realized Eric was too old to go into the women's restroom with me. Time flew so quickly with my son. "He still enjoys himself when we go there."

"If you say so. You haven't been saying much of anything lately, though."

"What?"

She slanted her head to the side, compressed her lips.

Shrug. I sat directly across from her, the coffee table marking where her territory ended and mine began. "What do you want me to say?"

"Say what's on your mind."

"I'm wondering why is my best friend is here conducting a one-woman intervention."

"You want me to bring the rest of the crew, 'cause I will if we can get you to talk."

A humorless laugh escaped my throat. "Are they all waiting on the other side of the door?"

"They'd be here in a minute if they thought it would help." She joined me on my sofa, breaching the imaginary wall between us. We were knee-to-knee now, and my eyes threatened to betray me. "Peaches, don't shut out everyone who loves you."

My body tilted and my head landed on her shoulder. Immediately, she wrapped me up in a hug that I'd been needing since I lost my job. Or maybe since the day I got the call from Eric's school.

Maybe even as far back as when I got the call about Daddy's heart attack. Sometimes the memory snuck up on me without notice. Momma's phone call. "Peaches, your daddy's been admitted to the hospital. He was having some trouble breathing." I honestly thought the reason she wanted me there was to handle business. Talk to the doctors, find out if he needed surgery, determine if we needed a second opinion. With my older brothers and sisters so far away and my father incapacitated, I figured I was the only person adept at handling this for my mother.

All the way to the hospital, I thought about insurance and co-pays, wondering where my father kept all of the financials because, surely, I would need to handle things while he healed.

I stopped off at Williams Chicken to get something for my mother and me to eat. No telling how long we might be sitting in the hospital, so I thought it best to be prepared. But when she called me back and said, "Get here as fast as you can, baby," the strain in her voice caused a wave of acid to well up in my stomach. My train of thought took a sharp detour, passing by the thought of my father's rare but treasured laugh and the way his feet could stink up a whole room. It's funny what you remember about a person when their soul is dangling.

There was so much I wanted to say to Daddy. I wanted him to know I loved him, and I understood he loved me in his own silent way. I vowed to whisper these thoughts into his ear when I got to his room. Then, hopefully, he would wake up and remember what I'd told him, and things would be different between us from that day forward because this near-death experience would soften him, make him appreciate me.

But when I got there, he was already dead. Nobody told me, I just knew it by the sullen eyes and furrowed brows. The cardiac surgeon was, evidently, finishing up the speech he had probably given dozens of times. "We did all we could do. I'm sorry, Mrs. Miller."

My mother collapsed into my arms, signaling the moment I added another weight to my great hold-up. Holding up for my mother and my son. Everybody, it seemed.

Quinn arrived at the hospital within the hour. I held onto him for a quick minute before my mother and I had to get busy with the documents and subsequent funeral arrangements. Things just got busy, and they never stopped long enough for me to process what happened. Or maybe I just didn't want to process it.

Somehow lying in my best friend's gentle embrace tore a huge scab off my heart. Handling the past pain with the present confusion was too much. LaShondra let me cry all over her new pink and black drawstring shirt. "My life is just crazy right now. Totally crazy."

She patted my back. "Life *is* crazy, girl. That's why we need God and each other. Here." She took a bracelet off her wrist.

I started at it for a moment and briefly glanced at the scriptures printed on three pink beads.

"It's called a WordWatch. Helps you keep the word of God close by," she explained.

LaShondra stayed at my house for another hour. We talked extensively about my job search and Eric's confirmed diagnosis of mild dyslexia. I boo-hooed again when I confessed my feelings of inadequacy as a mother. "When I think of all the times I punished him for not reading, and accused him of not trying as hard as he could, I could just kick myself. I actually punished him for something he couldn't help."

"Peaches, you didn't know. You can't blame yourself for now knowing." LaShondra comforted me with words and unyielding support. "Just be thankful you found out so early in his life. Some people get all the way into adulthood before they find out that they're dyslexic. And a lot of people will never know. They just figure school isn't for them, so they drop out or don't even give college a try.

"Same thing with depression and ADD. Grown people wondering why they can't focus long enough to follow their dreams, never stopping to think there might be a real reason for the problem. I see it every day and it's sad. Thank God, Eric won't be a statistic."

I know LaShondra too well. "So why are you talking to me about depression and attention deficit disorder?"

She guzzled more water. "Well, sometimes people do have problems. They need medical attention. I mean, if they could at least get a diagnosis, they would know what natural remedies to try and how to pray against the issues."

"People like who?"

Her eyes darted around the room. "People like . . . anybody."

"People like me?" Every ounce of energy I had was being used to keep my face set in stone.

She finally settled her stare on mine. "Yes, Peaches, even people like you."

"You think I need professional help, huh?"

"You might."

"Who *else* thinks I need professional help?"

She slid both hands under her thighs. "I don't know."

"You're a terrible liar."

LaShondra threw both hands into the air. "Okay, okay. Everybody knows something is up with you. Your mom is afraid of what's going on—that's why she's volunteering to keep Eric so often. And Quinn—"

"What does *Quinn* have to do with anything? He's halfway across the country!" I stomped circles around the couch, but she held her ground.

"Believe it or not, Quinn still loves you."

I thanked God my back was to her when she broadcast this news, because I know my face would have given me away. *Quinn still loves me? Why?* "He needs to move on."

"Well, he's trying, but you can't just flip a switch and turn off love. Not *real* love, anyway."

My pace halted with the refrigerator approximately five feet ahead of me. "You want some sweet potato pie?"

Whether LaShondra wanted a piece or not, I was certainly in the mood for a slice. She accepted my offer by taking a seat on a stool at the kitchen bar. I plunked two hunks of pie onto saucers and slid one over to her as I occupied the other stool. My behind was so big on that stool, I was hanging all over the edge, but I didn't care just then.

I toyed with her revelation. "So, Quinn still wants to get back with me?"

She frowned. "I didn't say all *that*. I just said he still loves you. He wants the best for you and Eric, whether he's in your life or not. Dang, this pie is so good," LaShondra commented, licking the tines of her fork. "Stelson's trying to lose a few pounds. He's got us both on this health kick—no sugar in the entire house. Cut me another piece."

I obeyed LaShondra's order, scoring her a generous second helping. "Sure you're not eating for two?" I teased.

Sadness suddenly claimed her face. A moment later, she tucked in her bottom lip to stop the quivering.

"Oh, my gosh, Shondra, what's wrong?"

She slid the pie aside and plopped her elbows on my countertop. All ten fingers slid beyond her hairline. "I can't get pregnant."

"*Can't?* What do you mean *can't?*"

"We've been trying. It's just not happening." Tears streamed down her face as I continued to watch her countenance morph from overbearing to overwhelmed.

I couldn't believe it! LaShondra—crying? Sure, I'd seen her cry before, but not since she'd met Stelson. I thought her life was picture-perfect now that she'd met and married the man of her dreams. Whose life *wouldn't* be perfect after such an event?

"Have you been to see a doctor yet?"

Worry puckered her brows. "No. We're going to give it a few more months before we make an appointment with a fertility specialist."

"Okay," I sang in a cheerful tone, "so you might have to go to a doctor to have a baby. Where's the grief in that?"

"Why me?" Now it was her turn to whine. "I mean, people who don't even *want* to have babies get knocked up every day. There's got to be, what, a thousand abortions a day. And here I am happily married and financially capable of rearing a child, and I can't even get pregnant. It's not fair."

"Welcome to the real world."

I cut my second slice of pie and probably would have eaten another one if LaShondra hadn't been there. As I listened to her explain what they had already done to try to conceive—ovulation monitors, thermometers, even a different set of drawers for Stelson. Probably too much information, I'm sure, but she needed to get it off her chest, so I listened.

"What bugs me most is when I think about all the times I tried all of those different birth control methods. You know, back when I wasn't really committed to the Lord? I wonder if those birth control pills and foams and patches caused my body to forget what to do."

My chin dipped, as did my voice, "Sounds to me like you're looking for a reason to blame yourself."

"And you know what else I wonder?" she asked, completely ignoring my last statement. "For real, Peaches, you can't ever tell anyone on earth I said this. But I wonder, in the back of my mind, whether this would be happening if I'd married a black man."

"You can't be serious. That's ridiculous and you know it."

"I'm just saying . . . the thought crossed my mind."

"Well, let the thought cross the street and go on over to somebody else's house, because this has nothing to do with race. I see tons of biracial kids at Eric's school. And I know you've gotta see them every day at your school, too. Right?"

She took a deep breath. "You're right. This *is* ridiculous. The Lord's mercy is new every morning. I've been forgiven for all my sins. And the black–white thing is irrelevant." In an instant, she wiped her tears and talked herself onto a higher emotional and spiritual plane. She whipped out her cell phone and pressed the screen frantically. "I've got to go online and find me some scriptures to stand on. You with me?"

It had been so long since I'd stood on any piece of the Word for anything, I wasn't sure I had the strength to stand. I couldn't say no, though. "Yeah. I'll stand with you."

"Let me use your computer so I can print." She hopped down off the stool and headed toward my bedroom.

Any other time, I wouldn't have thought twice about it—my bedroom used to be just as uneventful as every other room in my condo. Things were different now. Given the situation with Raphael, I couldn't afford to let her just bust up in my room of sin. "I'll bring the laptop in here and we can print later."

Her stride halted. "You got somebody in your room or something?"

I rolled my eyes. "No, I most certainly do not. I just have my, you know . . . my privacy. Besides, my room isn't clean."

LaShondra eyed me for a second, then relented. "You know what my momma says. If your house is a mess, your life is a mess." She returned to the couch while I retrieved the laptop alone.

It was a good thing I stopped her, too, because the first thing I noticed when I walked into my bedroom was one of Raphael's du rags hanging on my headboard. The evidence had to go. I stuffed it under my pillow. A quick visual inspection turned up a pair of Raphael's socks and one of his shirts draped on the back side of my desk chair. Both were quickly tossed into my closet in anticipation of returning to this room later with LaShondra to print.

The coast was clear, but my conscience wasn't. I had never hidden things from my best friend before. And yet, I didn't want her judging me about Raphael. *Would a real best friend judge me, anyway?* What about the unconditional love I was supposed to feel from her? And from my mother?

At that moment, it seemed like maybe the only person who loved me unconditionally (besides Eric) was the one person I'd kicked out of my life.

Chapter 24

Raphael's presence at Eric's birthday party was not a total giveaway. He'd been known to show up at this celebration with some small token of his love for our son. Every other year. Neither my mother nor LaShondra suspected anything when he arrived bearing a neatly wrapped gift. "How y'all doin'?"

"Fine, Raphael. How are you?" My mother had always been civil with Raphael. She didn't appreciate him getting me pregnant out of wedlock. That kind of thing takes two, though.

I think she'd been more angry with me than him, anyway. Her only words to me when he left me were, "You didn't have no business lying down with him before you got married, anyway. Did you really expect him to treat you like a lady *after* the fact?"

I had tried to tell her that men today don't think any less of a woman for having sex before getting married like they did back in her day. "It's just the way things are, Momma."

"Y'all can keep on believing lies from the enemy if you want to. Besides, any man who knows the Word of God but will still sleep with you before he marries you will sleep with somebody *else* after. If he ain't got control over his flesh with regards to you, what makes you think he'll suddenly be able to control that same flesh when the next woman swishes her behind in his face?"

My mother had a way with words. She was probably onto something there, I'll admit. Maybe her observation would have rung true if Raphael actually claimed to know the Word, which he did not, but I had kind of led my mother to believe Raphael was a churchgoing man. Actually, he was— when I dragged him along with me. I guess I just thought he'd change, with a little help from me, of course.

Almost a decade later, it seemed liked some of the seeds I'd planted in Raphael might actually be sprouting up through the heart I used to think was pure dirt. The little buds had bloomed into nice . . . flowerettes. Too young to pick, yet promising—if they stayed on the stalk awhile longer.

Raphael dropped Eric's gift at our booth and then went to search for our son. I was just thankful he hadn't tried to kiss me in LaShondra's presence. The other adults present, mothers of Eric's school friends, formed a nice little barrier between me and Raphael I hoped like crazy he wouldn't breach.

Idle "mommy" chitchat helped to calm my nerves a bit. Kierra's mother, Paige, talked about her daughter's cheerleading tryouts, and Jose's mom, Angelica, wanted to know where Eric would go during the summer months.

"Well, if I don't find a J-O-B"—I laughed nervously— "he'll be at home with me. Otherwise, I'll probably put him in the YMCA camp, unless my mother here finally decides to open her day care."

My mother sulked a bit but perked up when Angelica exclaimed, "Great plan! I'd rather leave Jose with someone who's mature and knows how to actually lend a hand in helping to raise kids. Here, let me give you my card. Any idea of when you'll open enrollment?"

"See, Momma. I told you."

My mother shot me an unspoken *shut up* while Angelica searched through her purse. "I'm not opening anything any time soon."

Angelica produced a business card nonetheless. "If you change your mind, let me know. Jose will be your first student."

"All right, Momma Miller! Got your first customer before you even opened your doors!" LaShondra cheered. "Look how God works!"

"Amen," Paige echoed.

"You guys are all believers, too?" Angelica clapped her hands on the table.

"Sure sounds like it," Paige confirmed.

"This is awesome! We just moved here and I've been asking God to introduce me to other women who love Him. Oh, I'm so glad we came to this party. What church do you all go to?"

We took turns naming our churches as Angelica questioned each of us about the different ministries and service provided therein. Angelica wanted to know which pastor preached series sermons and how often they took communion. I probably should have been taking notes with Angelica, because I hadn't been to church since I went with Quinn and Eric a month earlier. I was so far removed from the house of the Lord I was convinced I'd feel like a visitor whenever I built up the nerve to go back. My mother's church, which I frequently visited on Wednesday nights, would be the worst about speculation. Probably not verbalized, but certainly expressed through narrowed eyes and lowered tones. Or maybe they'd just hog-tie me and throw me on the altar.

Angelica said she wanted to visit each of our churches. She began probing through her purse again. "Where's my pen when I need it?"

"Sweetheart, looks like you need a smaller bag so you can find your things," my mother remarked.

A submissive smile swept across Angelica's face. "Yes, ma'am." A moment later, Angelica was busily jotting down addresses and service times. "My husband goes to work at two o'clock on Sunday afternoons, so we'll have to attend the earlier services. We're praying for God to open up a better shift for him at his new job."

Now it was LaShondra's turn to dig for pen and paper. She offered to add Angelica's family's needs to the prayer list she and Stelson had going for friends and family. Paige threw out her prayer requests, too, as LaShondra jotted notes in her ever-present prayer journal.

All this talk about the Word and God and church was getting to me. *Why does LaShondra have to turn everything into a big prayer meeting?* I wondered if she was turning into one of those holier-than-thou types. You know the kind—always bringing God into *everything*. Can't chew a stick of gum without saying grace.

Actually, those were the things Raphael used to say about me. Being on the other side of the accusation, I understood fully what he meant. LaShondra couldn't go anywhere without talking about Stelson or God. And I, for one, was good and tired of it.

"Would everyone who's attending Eric Lewis's ninth birthday party please return to your tables for pizza!" Our party hostess, a young girl named Jordan, announced the arrival of our food, but Eric and his friends were so busy playing they missed the news altogether. I took the mishap as an opportunity to escape the minirevival at our table.

One by one, Raphael and I pointed the children back to our party area. Paige's younger daughter, Alyssa, took my spot in the mommy booth. When I approached again, Paige told Alyssa to move so I could sit next to my mother.

"Oh, no, Paige. She can stay. I'll sit here," I said, scooting into an adjacent booth. With my back to LaShondra, I felt

much safer. Raphael inched in across from me and we com-
menced small talk, relieving my mind of the spiritual pressure
at hand.

Pizza and soda were served, followed by Pizza Kingdom's
goofy signature birthday song. While we were all standing
around Eric waiting for the mascot's cue for each birthday
child to blow out the candles, I took a glance around the
room. Eric was indeed the oldest child in the room celebrating a birthday. *Why does LaShondra have to be right about everything?*

Next, Jordan helped Eric open his presents. The gift my
mother brought was wrapped in blue metallic paper and
topped with a shiny silver bow. Far too extravagant for a
widow on a fixed income. "Momma, why'd you spend so
much on the paper?" I asked her as Eric ripped through the
covering with no regard for its beauty.

"I didn't. Quinn sent the gift to my house, already
wrapped. Told me he promised Eric he'd get him a Bible with
color pictures in it for his birthday." She reveled in this news.

Couldn't argue with her, though. Quinn always was a
man of his word.

Raphael glared at me like this was my fault or something.

I was more than ready to go by then, but we still had a ton
of tokens left. I distributed hands full of golden tokens to
each child and still had more to spare. "Let's go play some
games," Raphael suggested to me.

I leaned in and whispered across the table. "You know I
can't play with you."

"That's not what you said last night," he teased.

A quick kick to the shin should have done the trick, but
it didn't. He tried to kick me back, initiating a token-free
game of our own.

"Who is that kicking this table?" my mother asked over
the top of the booth.

"That's just me," I replied as I scrambled across the cushioned bench to a standing position. "I'm going to use up some of these tokens. Anyone want to help use these?"

No takers at their table. Raphael, however, spoke up. "I'll take some."

He was really pushing it. I poured tokens into his hand, waited at least ten seconds to put distance between us, then proceeded to the play area. I found Eric on a motorcycle racing driving game and issued a challenge.

"I'm about to beast on you, Momma!" Eric chanted. "Beast, beast, beast!"

We straddled our simulated bikes and revved our engines. When the green light flashed, we both took off, swerving left and right to avoid obstacles in the roadway. Eric popped a few wheelies, sending his bike in a slight tilt. I crashed into a light pole and felt the violent vibrations of the seat. This game was tight!

Maybe it's wrong to beat your own child on a video game, but the competitor in me came out and I digitally zipped across the finish line in first place. Whew! That felt good. I raised my arms in triumph. "Who's the beast now?"

I growled at Eric and clawed at him. His face revealed he was approaching embarrassment (my baby hates to lose). I let up on him. "It's okay, Eric. One of these days you'll beat me."

A quick poke in my side caused me to jerk slightly. Raphael entered the picture. "I can beat you now."

"Yes! Daddy's gonna beat you, Momma." Eric danced around the game platform, taunting me with the promise of Raphael's victory. Sure enough, Raphael opened up a can of whip-tail on me. All I could do was slink off the motorcycle when the game was over.

"I told you," Eric gloated as he gave his father a high five. "Daddy, I got another game we can play." He tugged at Raphael's arm. I was amazed—all these friends Eric had to play with, and he chose to hang with his father.

Raphael winked at me while being dragged away. "Hey, every boy needs a hero."

At the expense of his mother? I doubted.

The tokens were burning in my pocket now. I shot hoops for a while, collecting more tickets to donate to Eric's parting prize fund. Skee-Ball followed. Then I met up with Raphael again and we played a few flirt-full games of air hockey.

Half an hour later, Jordan approached me at the game table. "Ma'am, um, we have to get ready for the next party. So would you like to pay with cash or credit?" A sweet way of putting it, I suppose.

Jordan must have said something to the rest of our crew, because when I got back to my purse, I found the adults gathering their belongings and boxing up the cake. "Next crew is coming in," my mother said to me.

I said my good-byes to Eric's friends' mothers and thanked them for coming, then headed to the front counter to pay the tab while LaShondra consolidated Eric's gifts. As usual, the bill was more than expected. The bill is always higher than the quoted amount at events like this—extra cups, another pizza for the adults, a tip for the hostess. Those little financial surprises never bothered me until now.

The need for sleep almost caused Eric to whine when I told him it was time to leave. Raphael reminded Eric that he was nine now, and nine-year-olds didn't cry like two-year-olds throwing tantrums.

Raphael and I said our temporary good-byes in the parking lot. The plan was for him to come to my place later that evening. Probably watch movies. Definitely end up in bed considering my mother practically begged to have Eric spend the night at her house so he could go to church with her Sunday morning. She got no objections from me. So far so good.

But for as much as we'd tried to keep our whatever-you-wanna-call-it semirelationship under wraps, LaShondra wasn't fooled. As soon as I'd packed the last gift in the trunk and slammed it shut, she was on me like white on rice. "You know, you and Raphael were mighty friendly tonight. What's going on between you two?"

"Nothing." I walked to the driver's door of my car. "See you later, girl."

"See me later my foot. You're lying. You're seeing him again, aren't you?"

I felt like one of those silly damsels in a horror movie. The hunter was on my tail and I couldn't find the keys to open my door.

She slammed her hand on the hood. "Answer me, Peaches."

"Go easy on my ride, okay? Anyway, what if I *am* seeing him again? Then what?" The supposedly hypothetical questions were enough to confirm her suspicions.

Her mouth gaped open for a moment, then she whispered, "I cannot believe you dumped Quinn for Raphael."

"Let's get it right. I did *not* dump Quinn for him."

"So you are dating Raphael again?"

"I didn't say that."

She crossed her arms and gave me the superholy smug grins. "What are you saying?"

"Nothing! Absolutely nothing, since you think you've got everything all figured out already, Little Miss Perfect Life."

"You know what? I've had about enough of this hatin' from you, but I'm going to let it slide right now because we're talking about *you*—not me." She ended with her index finger poking into her own chest.

A wildly sadistic laugh overcame me. "No, let's not talk about LaShondra—and God forbid Stelson should be anything less than perfect. Bow down, my sister, bow down."

"Peaches, you are so far out of line. What has gotten into you? You kicked a wonderful man to the curb for someone who's—wait a minute. Isn't Raphael engaged to somebody?"

"They're breaking it off."

"When?"

"As soon as he moves out of their house."

She threw her hands into the air. "Oh, my God—and I am *not* using His name in vain. I need Him here right now because this cannot be happening to one of His daughters."

A surge of anger throbbed through my veins. "I'm sick of you and everyone else trying to run my life."

"Well, by the looks of things, you could use some help in the life-running category. You're dating Ra-pha-el"—she clapped out the syllables of his name—"while he's living with another woman. Life doesn't get much worse.

"Am I missing something here 'cause a man doesn't go from being a dog one week to a prince the next without some divine intervention. What has he done to change your opinion of his character?"

"For your information, he *has* changed. *I* changed him."

"You and I both know we don't have the power to change people—least of all men. The best we can do is pick one that looks and acts right and pray he *stays* right. And here you are picking the same bad apple *twice*. This is just stupid, Peaches. Pure dee stupid."

I know the truth hurts, but she really stabbed me with that one. I was already feeling pretty stupid about my job and about not knowing my son had a reading problem. Being in financial distress wasn't helping, and being called stupid by my best friend certainly didn't dim the neon "L" sign I suspected was glowing on my forehead lately.

"Yeah, well . . ." *Don't say it, Peaches. Don't say it.* "At least I picked one I could actually *reproduce* with." I said it.

LaShondra's eyes moistened. I wanted to bust out in tears and tell her I was sorry. Problem was, I didn't *feel* sorry. I was hurting and I wanted her to hurt, too. I wanted to hurt her so much she would leave me alone so I could hurt all by myself, if that makes any sense.

She straightened her back, wiped her eyes. "Peaches, you

deserve a better man than Raphael, and I deserve a better friend than this person you've become."

Quietly, she walked back toward her car. I watched her get inside and start the engine even as families schlepped baby carriers and oversized gifts through the parking lot. Across several vehicles, we got locked in a gaze.

Part of me wanted LaShondra to throw me a line—get back out of the car and just come hug me, tell me she loved me despite myself, because the truth was I needed *somebody* to love me, even if I didn't.

My plan to hurt her must have worked. She took off without another word to me. I saw her bring the cell phone to her face as she turned onto the side road. I'd bet anything she was calling Stelson to let him know what happened.

The list of people against me was growing longer each day.

When I finally crawled into my car, I tried to make myself cry, but there was no gush of emotion springing forth. *Why am I so heartless?*

I wished Quinn was there. He always knew what to say to me when I'd messed up. Can't count how many times he calmed me with, "Peaches, don't worry. Everything's going to work out just fine." His favorite verse was Romans 8:28 ". . . all things work together for the good of them that love the Lord . . ."

Of course, those words weren't Quinn's. They came from our Father. And, more than anything, I wished He was there, because I was afraid of how much more damage I might do if He didn't step in pretty soon.

Chapter 25

I got my first pastel-colored bill exactly four weeks after I was fired from Northcomp. *So, this is what it's like to be flat broke.* I hadn't been broke since my undergraduate days, but even then I always knew my student loan check was on the way, and it would cover everything plus leave me with several hundred dollars to spare. But this high yellow cell phone disconnect notice was another issue. Maybe in some other people's worlds, this made sense. Not mine. How does a full-grown woman with an MBA get a cut-off notice for a bill totalling less than two hundred dollars?

The two hundred dollars was certainly available, sitting in my checking account. I knew I had to pay the bill. The problem was I didn't like seeing my zeroes disappear. At the same time my zeroes dropped at the bank, the numbers on my bathroom scale rose. I was closer to 200 than 150 now, and anyone with a pair of eyes could see the difference. At five foot six, I could get away with five or ten pounds lost or gained without of a change in appearance. Nineteen pounds, however, can't be hidden.

I'd even started wondering if perhaps my weight was standing in the way of my career, because none of my job interviews had resulted in employment offers. I got called back only once for a second interview, and I was promptly notified they had chosen someone else for the position. There had to be some type of discrimination going on, because I know I was well qualified for every one of the positions I'd applied for. *I'm smart. Experienced. Good work history, good credit. What's the problem?* There had to be something wrong with the rest of the world, because the problem could not be me.

Though I had filed for unemployment, I knew my severance pay would negate when and what I was eligible for. Too bad I couldn't show them how much I'd paid for my new air conditioner or how much Eric's tutoring cost every week.

Truth be told, I had even begun to seriously consider working in LaShondra's school district. She said they were always desperate for teachers, and there was some sort of alternative certification plan through which I could learn a little something about being an educator while earning the check at the same time. I'd be taking a pay cut, of course, but I'd have vacations off with Eric. Plus, in the process of becoming a teacher, I might actually learn how to help him work through dyslexia and save myself the extra couple of hundred dollars I was shelling out every month for tutoring.

And I did say *I* was paying Frierson. Raphael was whining about being on his own now and having to pay all his bills by himself. Said he needed a little time to regroup and get settled into his new way of life.

Must be nice to have time to regroup.

Now that Raphael had officially dumped Cheryl, Wednesday nights were family night for Raphael, Eric, and me. After Eric's tutoring session, we usually parked Raphael's truck at my place and then headed for dinner. Raphael did, at least, agree to pay for family night. I won't lie, sometimes I held off my appetite until dinner so I could chow down on his money. I guess Raphael had gotten hip to my game, because the last few Wednesdays, he suggested all-you-can-eat buffets and insisted on us all drinking water.

The first time he made the water demand, I couldn't help but laugh, because Raphael sounded just like my father. I remember one time when were driving back from a visit to my grandfather's church. I got so thirsty I cried out for a soda from McDonald's. "Drink your spit—it's free!" he yelled. I cried the rest of the way home and promised myself I would never tell my child to drink his or her own hot, nasty spit if they were dying of thirst. Right about now, however, free spit sounded good to me, too.

Raphael also insisted on parking quite a distance from the doors to avoid acquiring dings in my panel. After spending so much annually to keep my ride in tip-top shape, I should have been practicing this skill all along to make sure my car looked good. Not to mention I could have used every bit of exercise I got.

I helped Eric fill his plate with various meats and vegetables from the food bar while Raphael secured a table for us. We had only been seated for a few minutes when Cheryl's ringtone blasted through Raphael's phone loud and clear. I really don't think he knew I had figured out her ringtone, because he lied, "Oh, I gotta take this call. Business."

Men just don't know how to cheat well. I mean, come on. Haven't they learned anything from Tiger Woods? Bill Clinton? Kobe Bryant? Ridiculous.

Even more ridiculous was the fact that I waited at the table while my man walked all the way to the other side of the restaurant and talked to his ex-girlfriend privately. This whole situation was straight-up Jerry Springer. In my normal state of mind, Raphael wouldn't have had the chance to cheat on me, because he wouldn't have had a chance to be with me in the first place. My life was far from normal, though. It was off track. So far off track I was actually in a ditch. And as I sat there mindlessly inhaling roasted chicken and a loaded baked potato, I realized the only person I could be angry with was myself.

I was morphing into a fool right before my very eyes, and I really didn't know what to do about it. Especially not without a job and a way to support myself. If push came to shove—and there sure was a lot of elbowing between my checking and savings accounts—we could always move in with Raphael. He'd given the option more than once.

"If you and Eric move in with me, it'll cut down on the amount of money we're both spending. Plus we won't have to do all this creeping. We can both have our cake and eat it, too." A poor analogy, I thought. Especially since the reason we were "creeping," as he called it, was to protect my son from my indiscretions. The cake would be totally dry if we moved in together.

Thinking of cake, of course, prompted me to get a slice. "Stay right there, and watch my purse," I instructed Eric as I stood and pulled my shirt down over my abdomen and behind. A classic big-girl move, almost automatic now.

Raphael was chowing on his food by the time I returned to our table.

"Who were you talking to on the phone?" This was, of course, a total setup.

"Somebody from work," he said, looking down at his food.

I threw my fork down on my plate. "Okay, let's get something straight. We cannot carry on in this relationship with all the lying."

"Who says I'm lying?"

"I know Cheryl's ringtone, Raphael. I'm not stupid."

He sat there with this silly, dumbfounded look on his face. He could have been the picture of "busted" in the dictionary.

"Let's not have this conversation in front of Eric." He tried to switch modes and busy himself with cutting Eric's steak.

"Let's not have this conversation at all," I fumed.

"Okay, okay." He nodded. His eyes darted to and fro. "You want me to embarrass myself in front of our son? Okay. I lied, all right? I lied because I didn't want to upset you."

"No. You lied because you're—"

Something behind me grabbed Raphael's attention. His eyes filled with alarm. I quickly turned to look over my right shoulder. Before I could figure out what the problem was, Raphael had gotten up from the table and was running toward the emergency exit door.

The door's siren blared, but not nearly as loudly as Raphael's voice rambling off a list of expletives. Through the windows, I watched him chase a sky blue PT Cruiser as it raced dangerously through the parking lot.

"What's happening?" Eric asked, his voice trembling with fear.

"Baby, I don't know."

A soft mumble of confusion swept through the restaurant. The standard "mall cop" security guard closed the exit door, silencing the alarm. Raphael was no longer in view.

"Where did my daddy go?"

I couldn't answer Eric's questions, of course, because I was just as puzzled as everyone else—wondering if I should run outside to investigate or take cover under the table. On second thought, I supposed if the security guard had enough sense to stay inside, I should probably do the same.

Raphael walked back into view. He tried, unsuccessfully, to enter through the same door he'd used to leave the building. When beating on the door didn't help, he walked the perimeter of the building back to the main entrance. Almost every set of eyes was fixed on him.

Security must have met him at the front door and refused him entrance because my phone's screen lit up with a text message from him. *Problem. Can't come in. Come outside.*

"You finished?" I asked Eric.

He didn't have much of a choice, seeing as I was already

wiping his mouth and throwing my bag over my shoulder. "Yes, ma'am."

I grabbed my son's hand and rushed outside to meet Raphael.

"Baby, I'm sorry." He put both hands on my shoulder. "I'm sorry."

"Sorry for what?"

He clamped his lips shut and breathed out of his nostrils. "She . . . she messed up your car."

"Who messed up my car?"

"Cheryl."

A string of bleep words flowed through my head. I stomped off in the direction of my car. *Was that really my car?*

"Ooh-wee, Momma! Look at your car!"

"Oh, my God!" The first thing I noticed was the gaping hole in the front windshield. This hole was followed by two more on the passenger's side. The B-word was keyed into my hood, and three of my tires were completely flat.

"Oh, my God!" I repeated, scanning the parking lot for any sign of Cheryl's car. Seriously, I would have beat her down. She didn't know who she was messing with.

"Call 9-1-1," I screamed to Raphael.

He held up the time-out sign. "Peaches, just calm down."

"Calm down? My car just got vandalized by your ex-girlfriend, and you want *me* to calm down?"

"Look, I'll help you take care of it—"

"I'm not taking care of it. *She's* taking care of it." I stomped the ground in vain.

"Just . . . you don't have to call the police."

"Yes, I do. A crime has been committed. Unless you want me to resolve this the old-fashioned way. Tit for tat."

Eric stood between us with his eyes lobbing back and forth to make sense of our conversation. Let me tell you, here's one good thing about having kids—they give you a reason to stay out of jail. I flipped my phone to dial for help.

Raphael snatched the device from my hand. He put an arm to my shoulder. "Let me talk to Cheryl first."

"Man, you betta give me back my phone."

"Hold on a minute."

I saw his lips moving, but I was not hearing him. I demanded Eric's phone and pushed the red emergency icon.

When the police finally arrived, they took pictures of my car. They tried to obtain voluntary statements from people who were sitting nearest the window where I was parked. Those patrons claimed they hadn't noticed anything while they were eating. Raphael was the only one who could definitively say he'd actually seen the person with the motive in the parking lot. But when it came time for him to fess up, he got all foggy on a sistah.

"I . . . I saw a car that *resembled* Cheryl's vehicle," he stuttered.

The officer, a female who had obviously smoked a pack of cigarettes a day once upon a time, asked in a raspy voice, "So what are you saying? Did you see—what's her name—Cheryl's face or not?"

He dug his hands into his pockets, and I dug into him. "Raphael, you said yourself Cheryl did it. You said so only ten minutes ago!"

"Maybe it wasn't her. I mean, she was here, but maybe she didn't do all this damage. I mean, there is a *lot* of damage. She'd have to be pretty quick." He gestured toward my car.

I crossed my arms and looked him upside the head. *I cannot believe this!* "Are you crazy? Dozens of cars are parked here and my car just *happens* to get vandalized while your ex-girlfriend is strolling through the lot?"

The policewoman flipped to a blank page in her notes. "What's the suspect's name?"

"Cheryl," I readily replied.

"Cheryl what?"

For this information, we both turned to Raphael. He shrugged again. "Mmmm . . . I'm not sure. Smith. Jones."

"You have her address?"

I knew how to get to the place Raphael had shared with Cheryl, but I didn't have the exact house number and street on me. Again, we deferred to Raphael.

"No. We don't live together anymore."

The only thing stopping me from clawing out Raphael's eyeballs was the fact that we were in the company of a peace officer who would surely arrest me in front of my son, who was sitting in the backseat of my busted-up vehicle as the interviews took place. I called Eric to me.

A longtime fan of law enforcement, he quickly bounded to me. "Yes, ma'am?"

"Tell the officer what your daddy's address is."

Raphael laughed nervously. "I just moved."

"Not his current address"—I spoke to Eric but wagged my head in Raphael's face—"the address I had you memorize in case of an emergency."

"Oh." Eric eagerly rattled off the address, and the officer jotted it down.

"Thanks, good buddy," she said. She paused to present Eric with a pin-on silver star.

We don't have time for this! "Officer, are you going to pay Cheryl a visit any time soon?"

"We'll question her. In the meanwhile, here's your copy of the report." She ripped off a carbon copy and gave it to me. "You can call the station in the next few days and get an update on the case."

"When are you going to arrest her?"

"We don't arrest people on suspicions. Without a witness, strong evidence, or a confession, there's not much we can do."

"So, that's it?"

Her lip corners dipped. "Yeah. Pretty much."

"What am I supposed to do about my car?"

"Call your insurance company. They can lead you from here," was her only advice before she walked away.

Between the anger brewing in my heart and the jumble of facts in my head, words got caught in my throat. I pointed toward my car and looked down at Eric, who quickly read my body language. He returned to the vehicle.

"Momma, can I just climb through the hole in the window instead?"

Rage ran through my veins and gave me a voice again. "This is no time for an adventure, Eric!"

Raphael's hand on my arm was enough to push me over the edge. I jerked my arm from him and aimed my words at the real target of my frustration. "And what's wrong with your memory today? Why are you protecting Cheryl?"

" 'Cause I . . . I don't want her in jail right now."

"Look at my car! It looks like it's been in a demolition, Raphael. And you want to sit here and tell me you just don't want to see her in jail right now. I don't want to see my car lookin' like this, but I don't have a choice!"

He rubbed his hand across his head a few times. Always a bad sign. "She's four months pregnant, okay? *That's* why I don't want her in jail."

"She should have thought about that before she damaged my car." *Lightbulb.* "Wait a minute. Did you just say Cheryl is pregnant?"

He nodded slowly, eyes downcast.

"And you left her while she was pregnant?"

"I left her for *you.* So we could be together."

A burst of laugher barreled up through my belly. In my mind, I was doing the math. Four months ago, she probably told Raphael she was pregnant. Shortly thereafter, I told him I was getting married. He jumped at the opportunity to reconcile with me as a means of getting out of his obligations to Cheryl and, if history repeated itself, their unborn child. "So, you left her. Just like you left me—pregnant and alone."

"It was different with you. I was scared back then. Afraid I couldn't be the man you needed me to be."

"And you were right. The man *I* needed you to be then is the same man I wish you could be now—unselfish. Faithful. Truthful, honest, right. *Not* triflin' enough to leave a woman who's carrying his child so he can be with somebody else."

His defenses sprang forth. "Say, I don't know what to tell you. It is what it is. I can't help who I fall in love with and when it happens."

"If you had any kind of integrity, you wouldn't be on the market to hook up with somebody else and leave your own flesh and blood to be raised without a father. You have to know that walking out on your baby's momma while she's pregnant is going to make it all but impossible to have a good relationship with your child for the next eighteen years. I mean, come on!" I slapped my forehead with my palm.

He jogged his head in a sarcastic rhythm. "Oh, okay. I get it. You want me to *fake* it until she has the baby, right?"

"No. You know what, you're right. You can't fake integrity."

"Look, I'm sorry I can't be all the stuff on your little church-girl list. Can't be all perfect Mr. Love and Happiness like, what's his name, Quinn?"

I hung my head for a moment and laughed at myself again. "Those are, like, the truest words I have *ever* heard come out of your mouth."

"Oh, what? You wanna get back with old boy now?" he huffed.

"Go away from me, Raphael. Just leave."

"I'm not leaving my son's life."

"Which one?"

Next, I heard a set of footsteps from behind. The same security guard who'd locked Raphael out of the building approached us now. "Folks, I'm going to have to ask you to leave the property. Customers inside are gettin' pretty nervous with all the commotion going on out here."

"Sir, look at my car." I motioned toward my broke-down Benz. "Does it look like we can leave right now?"

He followed my hand gesture and winced slightly when he glimpsed the destruction. "Yeah, I see your problem. Would you like for me to call a towing company?"

Somehow, his kind offer settled me enough to take a deep breath and clear my head for a moment. "No, thank you. I'll call my insurance company. I'm sure they've already got something arranged with a local tower."

"Alrighty then. I'll give ya a little longer to vacate the premises." The guard slowly took his post at the restaurant's entrance, letting us know in no uncertain terms he was watching us.

Raphael entered, "You want me to—"

"Nope."

"I'm trying to—"

"No. Step away from me."

I flipped open my cell phone and dialed the 800 number for my insurance company. Lord knows everyone in the entire DFW metroplex had heard the jingle enough on television to know it by heart. With Raphael's eyes still fixed on mine, I began to explain my dilemma to the agent. "Yes. My *ex*-boyfriend's *ex*-girlfriend just vandalized my car. . . . Yes, I have a police report."

Raphael tore out of the lot on foot. I watched him walk away from the scene of our last breakup. Reminded me of those movies where the bad guy walks away scot-free as the credits start to roll.

It probably wouldn't take Raphael long to find his next conquest. He was tall, dark, handsome, and employed. *Watch out, sisters.* He's on the loose again.

Chapter 26

Only an experienced tire slasher like Cheryl would know that some insurance companies won't pay if all four tires aren't slashed. Had I been up on my psycho game, I would have slashed the last one myself. Replacing the tires was on me. My deductible for the rest of the damage was a thousand dollars, and I got the feeling I was now in the "drama queen" category of insurants, because my new monthly payment was fit for a king. Good thing I finally had a seriously promising interview set up for next Monday.

The police department wasn't any help. Without evidence, they couldn't charge Cheryl with anything so I had no recourse for getting reimbursed. "Ma'am, if the person in your party didn't see her do it, you have nothing," I was advised by someone downtown.

I thought about going on *Judge Mathis* or *Judge Judy*, but after consecutive weeks of watching the shows—thanks to my continued unemployment—I realized they would probably say the same thing. No witness, no evidence, no justice.

Raphael was calling like crazy trying to apologize. I pretended to accept his apology a couple of times out of pure lust. He caught my drift quickly after a while and we decided to dismiss the pretense. Anything outside of a conversation about Eric boiled down to a bootie call, because at that point, there was only one thing Raphael could do for me. Mind you, he did it well. I just had no other use for him.

Another week of moping around convinced me I should find someone else. Start over fresh. Start something new, go clubbing again. I was certain Deniessa would go with me. Then again, I was sure we'd look like two old ladies trying to hang on the club scene.

I remember when LaShondra and I used to try to club. (I say try because we always felt like fish out of water.) Any time we saw someone who looked over thirty years old, we'd wonder why such an "old" person was so pathetic as to be single and desperately seeking the company of twenty-year-olds. It never occurred to either of us we might still be flying solo when *we* turned thirty.

Deniessa answered her phone in the usual negative tone, her voice dragging every word to the ground. "Heyyyyyy, girl. Whatchu doin'?"

"Tired of being cooped up in my place. Thinking about getting out tonight. You game?"

"Might as well. Ain't nothin' goin' on here but the rent. Where to?"

"Anywhere's fine with me. Eric's at my mom's so I've got no curfew."

Club clothes were not a part of my regular wardrobe. Since I recommitted myself to Christ (an event that now seemed like centuries ago) I hadn't bought too many see-through shirts or rump-hugging jeans. As it turns out, though, my butt was so big at this point, every pair of pants in my closet fit like skinny jeans. I tugged and pulled at a deep blue indigo pair until they screeched into place. Buttoning required major inhaling. When I finally got the jeans on, a flap of fat settled over the rim. *Oh, well.* If memory served me correctly, clubs are full of people who haven't figured out that just because you can zip it up doesn't mean it fits. My muffin top wouldn't be too out of place.

An hour later, Deniessa rang my bell and we were off to some club she said was owned by one of Jamal's relatives who actually had two brain cells to rub together. Since ladies got in free before ten, she got no objections from me. I would have much rather gone to a jazz club or someplace with an open mic night, but Deniessa promised we'd be given V.I.P. treatment thanks to her husband's connections.

"He ain't got no job. He's got to be good for something," she muttered as we took off in her car. "And I done already told him—if he won't get a job and be a real man to me, I ain't wearin' my wedding band." I don't know what kind of sense she made. Then again, few things made sense in their relationship.

She drove while I filled her in on all the drama in my life. Deniessa's advice to me: just stay single so you can live your life the way you want to live it. She gave such a speech that we ended up singing the chorus line (the only line we knew) to Frank Sinatra's "My Way."

Cigarette smoke was the first thing I noticed upon entering Club Zeno. I don't know why it surprised me. I supposed since I hadn't been in a club or any other place permitting smoking for years, I had forgotten all about the odor. Judging by the density, my eyes could probably take an hour of this place before I'd have to leave.

Though the lights were dimmed to mask all physical imperfections, I could still see the red booths lining the side two walls. The bar took up a third wall, and the DJ stage took up the fourth.

Deniessa introduced me to Phillip, Jamal's cousin, after we found a seat at a table already semioccupied by two other women in their mid to late thirties who had no more busi-

ness in a club full of half-naked twenty-somethings than Deniessa and I did.

"This seat okay for you, boo?" Phillip asked Deniessa.

She flashed all thirty-two. "Perfect."

I wondered what grown man in his right mind called
anybody *boo*, but hey—stranger things have happened.

One of the ladies at our table yelled over the music to introduce herself as Margie. She asked if Deniessa and I came
there often.

"Yeah," Deniessa yelled back while I shook my head ve-
hemently *no*.

Deniessa slapped my knee with her own. I supposed she
was trying to tell me to be quiet, but I couldn't imagine why
I should lie to these women. She explained to Margie, "We
don't come to *this* club every week, but we get out quite a
bit."

"Y'all together?" the other woman asked.

This time I nodded and Deniessa shook her head. Another slap on the knee followed. "Would you hold our seats?
We'll be right back."

Deniessa grabbed my hand and pulled me to the ladies'
room. When we got inside, she visually searched the tiny
two-stall enclosure. Empty. "Peaches, those two women are
lesbians. And one or both of them is trying to hit on one or
both of us. Just follow my lead so they don't get any ideas,
okay?"

I smacked my lips and exhaled. "How do you know they're
gay?"

" 'Cause I just know. Turn on your *gay*-dar, Peaches."

"I don't *have* a gay-dar."

She laughed. "You sure better get one if you plan on dating in the real world these days."

Arms crossed, I responded, "I've been dating. I mean, before Quinn I went out a few times, you know, with some
guys from church."

Deniessa raised an eyebrow. "That's what I'm saying. You've been in church-world, Christian-world, LaShondra-and-Stelson-perfect-world." We both laughed. "But you're in the *real* world now with the rest of us. You have to be aware. Got it?"

"Got it. I'm just going to stick with you tonight."

"And watch yourself."

"Okay."

Easier said than done. Once Deniessa got a few drinks in her system, she let loose like a wild bird flying out of a cage. Dancing all nasty with strange men, singing the lewd lyrics in the music blasting through the speakers surrounding the hardwood dance floor. I knew Deniessa had a rowdy side, but I didn't know she could be straight-up hoochie. I mean, this girl was backin' it up, flippin' it, and droppin' it like she was auditioning for a Luke video.

I tried, in vain, to hang with her. But when she dern near did the splits, I had to bow out. My feet had begun to throb and my eyes entered phase one of stinging shutdown. It was past time to go for me, and I think our waitress would have agreed, since all I ordered was Coke. No big tip for that drink.

Margie's friend sat alone now at our table, bobbing her head to the music. I sat across from her and looked off into la-la land, hoping she wouldn't try anything. No such luck.

"What's your name?" she began.

"Tianna." *Ha!* I was proud of myself for having my old club name ready on my lips. It was all coming back to me now.

She leaned in and I got a whiff of her body odor. Don't make no sense for no grown woman to be going around smelling like boiled onions. "I'm Bridget."

What am I supposed to do with that information? I flattened my lips together and gave a sterile half smile without looking at her directly. Having returned to the sitting area, I noticed that the smoke was more concentrated now and my eyes were transitioning into phase two. I shut them tight for a second or two, combating the tears.

"You all right?" Bridget asked.

"Yeah. The smoke just makes my eyes sting."

"Mine used to do the same thing. You'll get used to it after a while."

I had no intention of getting used to it. I closed my eyes for a few more seconds, knowing full well that when I opened them, the sting would only be worse. Kind of like when you get soap in your eyes. You know you have to open your lids eventually, but as long as you keep them closed, there is momentary peace.

Honestly, I wished I could keep my eyes closed the rest of the night. Then maybe my whole life wouldn't be happening to me. Maybe all the problems would magically disappear and I could go back to three months ago, when Quinn told me he had been offered a job in Philadelphia. I wasn't quite sure what I would do differently, but if I had known then what I knew now, I certainly wouldn't be sitting up in a nightclub with my eyes burning while Deniessa was out on the floor looking like a *Solid Gold* dancer on steroids.

I was down to squinting at this point, just enough to get the outline of things around me. The Coke I had was getting watery, so I drank it quickly to keep from feeling like I was squandering the last of my savings.

I guessed the sudden rush of sugar in the soda gave me a new burst of energy. Before I knew it, I was on the floor doing the bump to an old-school jam with Deniessa on one side and Bridget on the other. Then Phillip somehow appeared and began grinding to a slower song with Deniessa.

What felt like ten minutes later, I was sweating so hard my shirt stuck to my back. Deniessa was nowhere in sight. Heat swirled around me, and the music's beat seemed faster and slower at the same time. The vibration from the speakers whooshed through my body quickly, but somehow my ears were delayed. Like when you're at a football stadium and the drum's beat doesn't quite line up with the sound.

Suddenly, I felt dizzy. My eyes were on fire, too, so I made the mistake of closing them. I must have lost my balance because the next thing I remember is Bridget helping me back to our table. I heard myself saying to her, "I need to lie down. I need to lie down."

Need to button up my shirt. Someone is trying to take off my pants. Who? Why? "Sssssstop."
"You're so pretty, Tianna. So beautiful. I want to love you."
"Sssssstop." Slap her. Kick her.

"Why you back here with this tramp? I'm sick of you cheating on me!"

"Peaches, are you okay? Say something!" Deniessa. Can't see her face.
"Baby, she's probably drunk."
"No. There's something wrong with her, Phillip."
"Happens every night. Let her sleep it off."
Help me.

Chapter 27

My next vivid memory was hearing the violent trajectory of foul-tasting liquid splash at the bottom of a plastic trash can. I rolled onto my back. Someone patted my head with a damp cloth and I nearly jumped out of my skin.

"It's me," Deniessa said in a whispery tone.

I took a moment to survey my surroundings. Daylight. Low ceilings, cheap lighting, and a rigid sofa. I was definitely in Deniessa's living room, lying on her couch. "What's going on?"

"Girl, things got kinda wild last night."

Slowly, I tried to sit up. The movement caused another surge of vomit. Deniessa responded in record time, placing the wastebasket beneath my mouth. "This reminds me of my college days," she giggled slightly as she guided my head back to the couch cushion.

I hoped whatever transpired was petty enough to laugh about. "What happened?"

Deniessa sat on the arm of the sofa and spoke down to me. At this angle, her face looked ten pounds heavier. Distorted, almost. "Well, apparently, Miss Bridget had a little crush on you."

You are so pretty, Tianna.

"We *think* she may have drugged you, although I really don't think so because I know you were sitting there with your drink the whole time." She pointed an index finger at me. "I told you to watch out, right?"

"Who's *we?*"

She lowered her voice again. "Me and Phillip."

"And then . . ." I prompted her to continue even as a sense of the previous night's helplessness crept into my memory bank.

Sssssstop.

"Anyway, you and Bridget went into a back room in the club. You two were . . . alone, I guess. Margie found y'all together. She confronted Bridget, and they got into a fight. The bouncers kicked them both out of the club. Phillip told me to come get my girl, and here we are."

I couldn't believe what she was telling me. I had to read her facial expressions right side up. She had to know more than she was telling me, because I was not going to be able to live with this sketchy outline.

Deniessa helped me to a sitting position, then plopped herself down on the pillow next to me. "So that's what happened, girlfriend."

I saw it in her face now. The nervousness twitch in her cheek.

"So you and Phillip didn't ask any questions?"

"I mean, what's there to ask? I . . . figured maybe you'd ordered a real drink while I was dancing . . . and you'd decided to, you know, take a walk on the wild side."

I wanted to yell, but I didn't have the energy. "I don't have a wild side."

She laughed slightly. "You could have fooled me. All the drama you told me on the way to the club, and the way you were dancing after you sat over there talking to Bridget. Hey—I thought maybe you were just gettin' your freak on in a different way." She held up her hands and sank back. "Who am I to judge?"

"Deniessa, you know I'm not gay. And you know I don't drink alcohol anymore."

"But you know how to watch a drink, right?"

"I *couldn't* watch my drink. My eyes were stinging. I had to close them for a little while."

"It don't take but a second to slip a pill in somebody's drink, Peaches, everybody knows that." Her pitch held a hint of accusation.

"Wait a minute. Are you blaming me?"

She paused. Dipped the corners of her lips. "No. Bridget was wrong. You were maybe a little bit wrong for not paying attention. I just know Phillip's not wrong and . . . sometimes these kinds of things happen. You live and learn, you know?"

I had a few more questions to ask before I went completely off on her. "Was I wearing my clothes when you walked in the room?"

"Your shirt was undone, and it looked like she was trying to take off your pants, but I guess they were too tight or something." She tried to change the subject. "It's kinda crazy when you think about it. You grow up learning how to watch out for men. Now we gotta watch out for women, too. Ain't that somethin'!"

She babbled on, "I guess we should at least be thankful it wasn't a man who tried to get at you. I'd rather be taken advantage of by a woman than a man any day."

Is she serious? My brain reeled as the bits and pieces were starting to come together. "Why didn't you call the police on Bridget? Or an ambulance for me?"

"I wasn't sure exactly what was happening. You might have been sleeping, for all I knew."

No. There's something wrong with her, Phillip.

"Yes, you did know there was something wrong. You said so to Phillip."

She shrugged. "Maybe I should have. I don't know. All's well that ends well, though."

"Naw, it ain't well. And it ain't over." I numbered off my complaints with fingers. "If you thought I had alcohol poisoning, you should have called. If you thought I had been drugged, you should have called. If you thought someone had assaulted me, you should have called. In any of these three scenarios, I needed help."

"You can't just call the police out to a club every time someone passes out or has a fight. It makes your club look bad. Then the cops start trying to find reasons to shut you down.

"Besides, I gave you help. I've been up with you all night." She held up the trash can in one hand and a wet towel the other. "Jeez, some people don't appreciate anything."

Baby, she's probably drunk. A bell went off in my head. *Baby?*

"So you didn't call for help because of . . . Phillip?"

She lied through clenched teeth. "This has nothing to do with Phillip."

This seat okay for you, boo?

"It has everything to do with Phillip. *He's* the reason you didn't call for help."

"Peaches, that's stupid."

"No, it makes perfect sense to me now." I managed to stand as the puzzle parts flew into place. Every second brought a little more wit. "You've got something going on with him. That's why you're trying to protect his club."

Stress lines formed in her forehead. "You need to quit trippin'."

"Tell me I'm lying, then. Tell me there's another reason you practically vanished while all of this was happening to me. And another reason why Phillip calls you 'boo' and 'baby.' "

"Shut up. Jamal's right over there." She pointed toward their bedroom.

She shouldn't have told me that. With the tiny bit of anger-inspired gusto reserved within me, I hollered, "I don't give a rat's behind if Jamal finds out that you're cheating on him with his cousin! I could have been dying last night for all you knew!"

Deniessa flew off the couch and lunged at me. We both tumbled to the ground as she tried to cover my mouth with her hand. She clamped down on both my mouth and my nose. I couldn't breathe. Survival mode kicked in and I bit her hand to get her off me.

She howled, "Ooooow!"

On hands and knees, I crawled toward the front door. I grabbed my purse handle from on top of the couch, a fortunate move that allowed me to see a spherical object being hurled in my direction. I ducked. The ball continued on its path and broke through a window.

By this time, Jamal had come barreling out of their bedroom. "What the—"

"Shut up!" She yelled at me again as she resumed the beating.

I was in no position to repeat my accusation. I tried to push Deniessa off me, but I suppose a night of throwing up tends to zap the energy out of a person. All I could do was curl up into the fetal position while she wailed on me. The fight happened in slow motion, like I was on the outside looking in. Hazy is probably the best word to describe the action. I wasn't sure whether to blame the adrenaline or the drugging.

Jamal managed to pull her off me, then she started in on him. "I hate you! You're nothing but a sorry excuse for a black man!" Deniessa punched him dead in the nose.

Blood spurted out of his nostrils. He took a quick moment to verify what had happened to him. When he saw the red on his hands, something must have snapped. He struck her in the face once.

She went down screaming, "Oh, my God! You coward! Phillip is going to kill you for hurting me!" He pulled her up by the hair and threw her against a wall. Deniessa kicked him in the shin, a move affording her a few seconds to get back on her feet and pick up a lamp. She hit him upside the head with it. Jamal was stunned for a moment, but he came back even stronger with two quick blows to her stomach.

All the while, they fussed and cussed. And from what I could gather, Jamal must have had some suspicions about Deniessa and Phillip all along.

My work there was done. Common sense told me to get out of this hot mess while those two were going at it, but Jamal was whippin' the snot out of Deniessa. Her tiny frame was no match for his muscular build. I had never seen a man hit a woman before. I can tell you this, though, it has got to be one of the scariest sights you could ever see.

"Leave her alone!" I weakly ordered. If he heard me, he wasn't paying any attention. Didn't even look my way.

Deniessa's screams were quieter now, her breathing labored as Jamal loomed over her, kicking as he cursed her a few more times for good measure. The last time he kicked her, I heard a loud crack. Deniessa let out a bloodcurdling shriek that propelled me to instinctive action. I ran to the kitchen and grabbed the biggest butcher knife from the wooden box displayed on the counter.

"I said leave her alone!" I yelled at him again. This time, he turned toward me. *Oh, Lord.* I was staring a mad man in the eyes, watching his rage transfer from his broken victim to me. *Help me, Jesus.* I hadn't given much thought to what to actually *do* with the knife.

Something in me said, *Raise up the knife,* so I did. By the shock on his face, it was clear he could see my weapon now.

I warned him. "I don't want to stab you, Jamal, but I will."

"Kill him, girl!" Deniessa squealed. "It's self-defense."

He swiped the blood from his nose with the back of his

sleeve. Stretched his neck on both sides and made a popping sound. Our eyes were still locked. My right hand started to shake, so I covered it with my left. He took a few steps toward me but stopped cold when he heard the door's chime.

This was the best sound I could have hoped for. "Dallas Police. Open up."

I dropped the knife and ran for the door while Jamal darted toward the restroom.

"Ma'am, we got a call about a domestic disturbance."

I nodded, opened the door wider. The police quickly ascertained something had gone down, but between Jamal's and Deniessa's lying, they couldn't determine which one of us was the aggressor. So guess what? We all got escorted to the police station. According to the "detaining" officer, there's some kind of law saying any time there's a call about domestic violence, somebody's goin' down.

So there I was, a thirty-four-year-old, single, nearly raped mother, sitting in the back of a police cruiser, wearing handcuffs. Three months ago, you couldn't have told me I'd be in this position. Shoot, three hours ago I couldn't have imagined it.

The interrogation room was confining. A claustrophobic person might give up all kinds of information in that setting. White walls, a chalkboard, a single brown table, and two chairs. Just like the crime shows, actually.

As I waited for an officer to come in and question me, I got my first inclination that this fight was more violent than I realized. I became aware of my tongue protruding beyond my front teeth. *Oh, my gosh.* A quick check with my index finger confirmed my suspicions. One of my front teeth was chipped. I don't remember Deniessa hitting me head-on, so I'm guessing I must have caught her ring as I bore down with my teeth on her hand.

Oh, great. This will look nice and professional when I go on my interviews next week.

I waited for almost another two hours before an officer finally got around to questioning me. By this time, they must have gathered from their interviews with Deniessa and Jamal I was a near-innocent bystander caught up in their mess.

"Ma'am, I have only two questions for you. Did Mr. Rutherford ever strike you?"

"No."

"And do you want to press assault charges against Mrs. Rutherford?"

I didn't even have to think about my answer. "Most definitely."

The paperwork took another ninety minutes. A female station clerk told me that I would receive information about a court date in the mail within a few weeks. She issued my belongings to me and asked, "Any other questions?"

"No, thank you."

"So . . . would you like to call someone to come and pick you up?"

Her question was another punch in the gut. *Who can I call?* You can't call just any old person in your phone book to come pick you up from the jailhouse.

I didn't want my mother bringing Eric up to the station. LaShondra—out. Raphael—out. The only other person I might have called in a situation like this was the reason I was downtown in the first place.

The clerk was waiting.

"Could you give me the bus schedule?"

Chapter 28

All I could think about the whole way home was the need to take a hot shower. I wanted to wash away any place Bridget might have touched, the smoke from the club, the welts on my face from the fight. I also had a busted lip in need of attention. The tooth was a different situation altogether. I'd need a dentist and some extra money to handle that one.

No one sat next to me on the rail or on the bus. Good thing, too. Next to a shower, the only other thing I craved was to be left alone. My cell phone battery was dead and I had no intention of charging it any time soon. No one desired to speak to me anyway. I didn't even want to speak to me right about then.

It's your own fault.

My conscience wasn't telling me anything I didn't already know. Yes, I had systematically burned all my bridges with everyone who gave two cents about me. Now I was stuck on the bad side of the river with no way back and nobody canoeing my way.

After the last bus stop, I still had to walk another quarter mile home. My club shoes were killing me. I took them off, letting my bare feet hit the nasty concrete below. I couldn't get any dirtier than I already was. *How did I get myself assaulted*

*two different ways by two different people within a twenty-four-hour
period? This is not normal.*

I dropped everything at the door and undressed on the way
to the bathroom. For as much as I longed for solitude, my mom
would be bringing Eric home sometime later that evening.

The face I caught staring back at me stopped me cold.
Oh, my gosh! My grill was a straight-up disaster zone. Missing
part of my tooth devalued my entire appearance. The left side
of my face was swollen, and I could see the faint trace of a
black eye. There was a small knot on my forehead, and my lip
was worse than I thought.

There was no way I could go to the interview Monday
looking like drama in heels. I know *I* wouldn't have hired me.
I'd have to call and try to reschedule, which wasn't likely.
Even if they did reschedule, they'd only be doing so out of
courtesy. Kiss that opportunity good-bye.

I stood under the hot stream crying, crying until there
was no hot water left. I hadn't been in a fight since junior
high school when Rosalind Young called me Peaches the Big
Fat Smeeches. I had no idea what a smeech was, still don't, but
I'd had my fill of being teased about my weight. Bad enough
when they called me names I *could* understand. This smeech
thing was the last straw. I found Rosalind that day after school
as we waited for our bus to arrive, and I must have taught that
toothpick-legged girl a thing or two about making fun of
people—especially people twice your own size.

Yet, when the fight was all over, I went home and cried.
Much like this incident with Deniessa, I honestly didn't remember the entire match. Just bits and pieces of it—feeling
Rosalind squirm beneath my blows, hearing her cry for help
from friends who were too astonished to jump in, watching
her cry all the way home on the bus. People actually congrat-
ulated me for kicking Rosalind's behind. "She got a big
mouth, anyway," they said. " 'Bout time somebody shut it
up." I wished somebody else had done it.

I wondered if Deniessa felt badly about what happened. There was no love lost between Rosalind and me, but I'd counted Deniessa as a friend. I had been in her wedding. She'd brought dinner over to my mother's house when my father passed away. She even helped me move when I found this townhouse, and everybody knows that only your true friends will help you move. Was I supposed to throw our friendship away?

My black eye said *yes*. Forget Deniessa's pain. I had my own to worry with.

Even with all the scrubbing, I still felt dirty. I wished I knew exactly what Bridget had done to me. *Did she kiss me?* The very thought made me gag, but after a night of throwing up at Deniessa's place, there was nothing left to regurgitate.

I stepped out of the shower and wiped the steam from the bathroom mirror, examining my face one more time. I couldn't let Eric see me like this.

A terry cloth robe would have to do while I rushed to my bedroom to call my mom.

"Hey. We were just getting ready to walk out the door. You ready for your son?"

"Not exactly. I think I've got a bug or something. Can you keep him for a few more days? I don't want Eric getting sick."

She clicked her teeth. "Peaches, are you all right?"

"Yes, Momma, I'm okay."

"I've been thinking. You might want to think about talking to a counselor or something. You've been through a lot lately—"

"You've been talking to LaShondra, huh?"

"Yes," she admitted. "And I've been talking to the Lord, too. You want me to set you up with someone in the counseling ministry at church?"

"Nope," I popped off.

"You don't have to be so ugly about it. We're only trying to help you, but I see you're not ready just yet."

Why is everybody picking on me? "I don't need help from anyone."

I could almost hear her eyes rolling as she spoke, "You may not be ready for help, but I'm not going to let Eric suffer on account of your bad choices. I . . . I've been thinking. What about giving me temporary custody until you can pull yourself together?"

My jaw dropped. "You're kidding, right?"

"No, honey. I'm dead serious."

"Bring Eric home. NOW."

She growled, "You watch your tone with me."

"And bring all of his clothes, because he won't be coming back over there for a long, long time." If my mom was shocked, I was double shocked. We both knew Eric lived to spend weekends with his granny.

Emotion flooded her voice. "I'm going to ignore what you just said, because I know you're not in your right mind. Something's wrong with you, Peaches, and you need to figure it out before you visit your problems on Eric.

"Now, I'm keeping him over here tonight. We can talk tomorrow or any time after you've had a chance to think straight. We have to work something out where I can keep an eye on both of y'all, 'cause I promise you, I'll call Child Protective Services on you *myself* before I let you harm my grandson, so help me God."

Was this my momma on the phone—the same woman who shied away from my father's reproach? The woman who let Pastor Eli impose upon her to make six sweet potato pies the night before Thanksgiving last year?

I slammed my phone on the receiver. *Who does she think she is?* She was taking the Momma card too far. Yet, there was nothing I could do to stop her. I didn't have a vehicle to go get my child. Didn't have anyone to ask for a ride. And if she did follow through with her threat to call CPS (which I now suspected she might actually be capable of doing), I certainly didn't want to talk to them any time before the swelling of my face went down.

Dang!

I caught another glimpse of my countenance in the mirror. *Man, I'm messed up.* I'd only seen faces like mine on court television shows, which reminded me, I needed to take pictures. I grabbed my digital camera from the closet and took a few shots of myself from different angles. Then, I printed them on the accompanying dock.

Deniessa is going down! I set the pictures inside my nightstand drawer and noticed the light on my ancient answering machine blinking the number 3. *Who would have called me on my landline?* I pressed the right arrow to listen. The first message was from the Visa folks wanting to know when I'd send in my next payment. They'd have to get in line behind everyone else.

Second, a Frierson representative wondered when I might be bringing Eric in again to "keep him on track toward life-long success." Her guess was as good as mine. I didn't know when or if I'd be able to afford tutoring again. Didn't she understand her phone call only brought on more stress and guilt?

I could feel my good credit rating slipping down the hard-times slide. Suddenly all those indulgent shopping sprees with LaShondra didn't seem like such a good idea. Should have been saving up for a rainy day, as the old people say. A rainy day, I had. I was not, however, prepared for a tsunami.

The third message nearly wiped me out. "Peaches, it's me. Quinn." My entire being sat up straight within me. "I really don't know why I'm calling you . . . or what to say. But I have to be obedient to the Spirit. You and Eric have been on my mind for the past couple of days. I've been praying for you. I heard you lost your job. . . . I'm sorry. Like I said, I don't really know what I'm supposed to say. Oh, I hope Eric enjoyed his birthday present. So . . . I hope things are well with you two. I'm sure they are. Things always work out. Bye."

Replay. Twice.

Hearing Quinn's voice broke me down. *Why were all these bad things happening to me? And why would God have Quinn call me to make me feel even more stupid?* Speaking of God, where had He been all this time, anyway? How could he let somebody darn near rape me? I screamed at the ceiling, "Where were You? Why are You making my life so difficult?"

I jammed the erase button on my machine, clearing all traces of Quinn's voice. How dare he call after leaving me high and dry. I was sure LaShondra had blabbed the news of me getting fired. Quinn must be calling me now to taunt me with his subtle "I told you so."

Everyone is against me. My mom, my friends, Raphael, the school system. Even God, probably. Or Karma put out a hit on me.

I didn't rest well that night. Minus the dulling effects of the drug, my mind was fully alert, busy cooking up demented scenarios involving me and Bridget. I didn't think she'd gotten my pants completely off, but how far did they actually come down? What if she'd touched me—down there? How long were we alone? Between conscious imagination and dozing in and out of dreams, worst-case scenarios played on my mental screen.

The day before, I'd thought maybe it was better that I didn't know exactly what happened. I mean, I've heard that sometimes the brain blocks out memories because revisiting them might cause a person more harm than good. Now I wanted to know everything so I could stop envisioning all the vile, repulsive possibilities.

Perhaps I should have been thankful that I wasn't . . . well . . . what? Totally raped? Hard to be thankful when you don't know what totally happened. *God, what am I supposed to do about this?* I waited for His answer, but it didn't come right away.

My mother didn't bring Eric home the next day, or the day after. We just stopped talking. She didn't call me and I didn't call her. My son did text me and ask if I could bring over some more underwear. It was as though he didn't even miss me. *Maybe I should add Eric to the list of people who have betrayed me. Perhaps he really is better off with my mother.*

Now that I was in possession of my vehicle again, I could fulfill Eric's request. I packed three more pairs of underwear, two shirts, and another pair of jeans. I had no idea how much longer he might be staying with my mother.

I wondered if this is how people came to live with their grandparents. One night turns into three. Five. Then weeks at a time while the mother runs the streets doing whatever. Granny's health and/or mind starts slipping away, and the child begins to get into trouble at school because he knows his sweet little granny can't do anything to stop him. Next thing you know he's joining a gang. Getting somebody pregnant. Hanging out with the wrong crowd, dropping out of school. A few years later, he's in prison for whatever reason, angry with his mother for not being there. Then she takes her turn raising *his* kids while he's serving time.

Whew! It was too much to think about. I promised myself I wouldn't let Eric fall into the trap, and I had every intention of keeping my promise. But I really couldn't trust myself. In recent months, I had done a lot of things I said I'd never do, things I ridiculed other people about because I wasn't in their shoes. I had no control over my own life, let alone Eric's.

After I dropped off his things uneventfully, I drove back to my townhome and took solace in a frozen Oreo pie. Now that the effects of the drugs had worn off, my appetite kicked into overdrive. I consumed the entire family-size dessert and lay on the couch for an hour, stuffed as a tick.

When I woke up, I figured the least I could do was get on the Internet and rev up my job search. Unemployment checks would start soon, but they'd barely cover basic expenses. Raphael was already up to his old tricks again, late on the child support payment. I was well versed in taking care of me and mine, because if I couldn't do anything else right, I could work.

Problem was, I needed somebody to hire me. I checked every job search Web site I could think of for open positions. Made a few calls to my good ole HR contacts. "Everybody's in a freeze right now," one staffing agency told me, "waiting to see the next quarter's projections." Code term for *we're in the red and can't afford to hire anybody else.* Another one said, "Our biggest client just made huge cuts. Sorry, Ms. Miller, we're all scrambling to keep our jobs right now."

Time to pull up the spreadsheet and crunch numbers. My unemployment check was projected at approximately two-thirds of my normal take-home pay. I needed to make some cuts of my own. I needed to make a decision soon about COBRA insurance. The premium was ridiculous. My only hope for keeping both myself and my son insured was to see if Raphael would put Eric on his plan, then maybe I could do COBRA for me. Better yet, maybe I could get an individual policy with another company.

I spent the next hour online checking out individual health and dental policies. When I entered my current height and weight, I noticed that my premiums were significantly higher than the advertised preferred rates. *Ain't this something! Bad enough we're fat—we have to pay more, too?* Scrap that. Four months ago, I was twenty pounds lighter. I wasn't about to pay extra because of a few cheeseburgers. I reversed the screen and entered my old weight, yielding a lower rate. I justified my actions by reasoning I could easily get back down into the normal range in just a few months. None would be the wiser.

Besides, it just wasn't fair, and I wasn't about to let one more person—or system—take advantage of my bad luck.

Now to call Raphael and have this discussion. I hadn't actually held a full-length conversation with him since the vandalism incident. His phone barely rang before it switched

over to voice mail. *This fool done blocked me on his phone!*
"Raphael, I need you to call me. Eric's child support is late,
and I am severely unemployed. This is not the time for you to
be slacking up. I also need to talk to you about an arrangement for Eric's health insurance since I don't have a job anymore. Call me."

Not even a minute later, Raphael's name and number
popped up on my screen.

"I see you got my message."

"Yes, *we* got your message," a female voice responded.

"Who is this?"

"This is Cheryl. And I'm gon' tell you straight up, woman-
to-woman. I would appreciate it if you would *not* contact my
man directly again. Anything you have to say to him needs to
go through me."

My heart was already beating a mile a minute. "I don't
think so."

"Oh, I know so, 'cause, see, *I* pay this cell phone bill. I'm
in charge of what goes on with *this* line. And I heard your little message. If you need any kind of support from Raphael,
you need to send him a certified letter. Go through the
courts or go through his momma 'cause I refuse to let you
steal him away from me again. You got that, Apple, Plum, or
whatever your name is."

Can you believe this woman? "Cheryl, in another nine
months, you and I will both be sitting in the attorney general's office trying to catch up with Raphael. He's a bum! A
deadbeat! He runs from his responsibilities like a dog runs
from the animal services unit."

Funny how, just a few weeks ago, nobody could tell me
what I was trying to tell Cheryl. I believe the word for this
inexplicable lack of comprehension is "whipped."

"I'm not going to sit up here and let you talk about my
man. He might have played you and your child, but he *loves*
me. He never loved you. He told me all about your high-paying

job and how you drive a Benz and got your college degrees. That's the only reason he ever dated you, 'cause you sure don't look better than me from what I saw at the restaurant the other day."

There! She'd all but admitted to vandalizing my car! Man, I wished it wasn't illegal to tape a conversation because I was sure I could extract a confession from this woman.

"Let me assure you I do not want Raphael in my life anymore. I've got enough problems without adding him to the mix."

"Whatever," she smacked. "Raphael and I are going to move on with our lives."

"Fine. What about my son?"

"What about him?"

She was really about to get cussed out. "He needs a relationship with his father. And I suppose it would be nice if he got to know his little brother or sister, too."

"Oh, that's not gonna happen. Like I said, we are moving on with our lives. I thought you and I were going to be able to get along, but not after what you did. Now me, Raphael, and our baby are going to move away from here and be a family. I don't want anybody messing us up."

I'd had enough of this craziness. "Look, heifer—"

"I got your heifer!"

The conversation went south from there. I had to give it to Cheryl, she could cuss with the best of 'em. I tried to keep up with her, but that girl rattled off blendings unheard since Richard Pryor's early stand-up comedy days—serious, down-home, nasty, perverted old man cussin'. If she had it in her to spit such filth at the drop of a dime, I could only imagine how she might treat my son now that she'd decided she didn't want him around anymore.

Cheryl got Mr. Click, too, and I buried my face in my hands. There went the last little piece of black male role modeling for my son. No more Daddy for Eric. My heart broke in two right over my laptop. I had to lean back to keep the tears from damaging the machine. I had thoroughly screwed up things for myself and my only child.

I certainly didn't want to hurt him anymore. Maybe I should let him live with my mother after all. If I was out of the picture, maybe Cheryl might let him see Raphael again.

And then I had a thought—a thought that hadn't entered my mind since my freshman year in college, when the teasing and taunting about my weight seemed to be at its highest. A boy who sat behind me in English 101 made a comment about my behind sticking out beyond the chair's railing. It was then I realized—people would never stop messing with me. Never stop trying to make me feel like an outcast. Like nothing I'd ever done before mattered, because nothing would ever truly get better for any substantial length of time.

That's exactly how I felt again. And that's when the thought reoccurred.

Maybe I should just leave the picture altogether.

I'd like to think I would never seriously consider suicide. I mean, it's not like my problems were life-or-death issues. But the reality of this singular thought actually crossing my mind was depressing in itself. Maybe people didn't have huge life-or-death issues pushing them to cross the line. Maybe it was just a matter of a bunch of smaller things quickly piling up one on top of the other that forced them overboard.

The enemy brought me a vision of myself creeping on hands and knees with tons of bricks on my back. Bricks labeled losing Quinn, losing my job, losing my independence and my dignity to a sick Bridget. There were still parts of my body that felt dirty since the night at the club. And sometimes I could still smell Bridget's scent on my skin. Made me want to throw up again just thinking about it.

Chapter 29

The phone company turned off my Internet service as a warning of sorts. Ten more days and I'd be without a landline altogether. When I thought about it, I really didn't need a landline. The only people who called me on my house phone were collection agents. The Internet was my potential job source, however, so I had to cough up money to catch up the phone bill plus have my network reconnected. I swear, companies must have whole departments full of people who sit around making up ways to collect extra fees.

My first unemployment check was even less than estimated. After two weeks of moping around, stuffing my face, crying about something I really couldn't even put my finger on anymore, the dismal payment was fitting. Nothing in my life was going as planned—why should the check be any different?

By now, my answering machine was filled to capacity with requests for payments. The phone rang and rang all day. Visa, my car financing company, a few retailers. Frierson had given up on me. I kept on top of my student loans and my mortgage. Those two bills I had to pay for sure every month. Nothing messes up an employment opportunity like a student loan in default, and the housing industry was so jacked, they were probably chomping at the bit for the opportunity to snatch up the equity in my house. But everybody else was going to have to get paid on a final-notice basis. I'd have to straighten out my credit later.

Come to think of it, I had a lot of things I'd have to straighten out later. My life. My weight. Even my hair was in dire want of a perm. I considered making this my big opportunity to convert to a natural style, but even the transition would require funds in order to keep my hair from looking like I was half-permed, half-nappy—braids, kinky twists, pressing, or something. A five-dollar box of relaxer would have to do for now. Whenever I got around to it.

My new best friends were Judge Mathis, Judge Milian, and Judge Judy. I took comfort in knowing there were a few people out there in the world who worse off than me. People whose parents were on crack and whose uncles owed them five hundred dollars for bailing them out of jail. "I wouldn't have bailed his butt out of jail," I spoke to the plaintiffs. "He'll be right back in next week for the same thing."

Of course, they never listened to me.

It had become my routine to call my mother's house to talk to Eric as soon as the episode of *Judge Judy* concluded. He always sounded happy to hear my voice. "Hey, Momma!"

"Hi, baby. How was your day at school?"

His days were always "good," especially when he got to see his father. So long as Raphael communicated with Eric via my mother, Cheryl stayed in her place.

My mother enrolled Eric in the free reading improvement tutoring program at her church. Although it was actually intended for older members, they agreed to let Eric participate given his diagnosis. He actually got to work one-on-one with a lady who taught special education in the Dallas Independent School District. As my mother explained it, she was working on her M.Ed., and she said Eric was the perfect case for her research.

"Ain't it good how God works things out? She says Eric's going to do well on the test."

I agreed to the tutoring, with some reservations. "Will there be someone there with Eric and this lady? Watching them?"

"I suppose there's other folks around," my mother asked with a questioning tone.

"Just because she's a woman doesn't mean she won't try anything with Eric."

"Peaches, you're paranoid." My mother downplayed the warning. "Act like everybody's out to get you."

They are. I couldn't tell my mother these things, though. She wouldn't understand. No one seemed to understand me, actually, which is why I felt it best to stay inside. Safe from all scrutiny and danger. No need for combing my hair or changing clothes regularly so long as I kept the shades closed and stayed away from mirrors. I didn't even have the desire to clean up much since Eric wasn't around. Really, who cares if there's a pile of clothes on the floor in my bedroom? To quote King Solomon, "This too is meaningless."

I probably would have stayed in my house forever were it not for my stomach's cravings. Cinnamon rolls, chocolate chip cookies, apple turnovers. Hey, at least the turnovers had fruit in them. Seems my life had become centered around the "least." Any time I sat down too long thinking about how lame things had become, I would say to myself, "At least I'm still paying my mortgage" or "At least I'm not as pitiful as that lady on *Judge Judy.*" When it came to Eric, I even thought, "At least I'm not some prostitute who left him with my pimp."

A weekly trip to the grocery store was my only outing. This week, I wore a pair of dingy gray sweatpants; a too-little, pink T-shirt; and black flats. One look at my ashy heels told the story. I really didn't care how I looked. Maybe if I looked ugly enough, people like Bridget wouldn't try anything with me.

"Peaches Miller? Is that you?" A vaguely familiar voice addressed me while I was loading my basket with cookie dough.

I turned and gasped. "Natasha Jackson!"

"Hey, girl!"

We hugged like we hadn't seen each other in a million years. Actually it was more like sixteen years. The last time I saw her was the day of our high school graduation. Natasha and I were never superclose. We just had a lot of the same classes and the same friends. Back then, she was probably fifty pounds lighter, and had long hair that LaShondra and I determined was actually real. I'd heard Natasha went off to Southern University, majoring in premed. From the looks of her shabby windbreaker and tired weave, she didn't finish.

Then again, who was I to talk?

"Girl, what have you been up to?"

"Nothing," I replied. "Just tryin' to make it."

She gave a weary sigh. "I hear you, girl. Me too."

"What you doin' back in Dallas? I thought for sure you'd moved to Louisiana."

"I came back after Hurricane Katrina—me and my ex-husband. We were living in Addison until he decided I wasn't enough for him and started spreading himself around."

"No, he didn't."

"With a white girl, too." She tipped her head. "I could have handled it if he'd cheated with a sistah. Not a white girl? I mean, I knew he liked Eminem, but dang!"

Natasha's humor was a welcome relief. I covered my broken tooth with a hand and laughed heartily. Honestly, I couldn't have recalled the last time I smiled before I saw Natasha in the grocery store that day.

We must have stood there in the refrigerator aisle for at least twenty minutes catching up with each other. I learned that Natasha's mother passed away suddenly during Natasha's senior year in college, an event that threw her off track for nearly a decade. She'd married in 2005 just before the hurricane hit. She and her ex-husband lost a baby due to some unfortunate accident she really didn't go into. Divorced three years later. Next to Natasha's life, my problems seemed significantly smaller.

"So now I'm back here starting over. Living with my dad, and he works my nerves something fierce," she snarled.

We fussed about our parents for another five minutes and even joked about hooking them up. "My mom is a handful," I warned Natasha.

"My dad is a *barrel* full," she topped me. We both laughed, grabbing on to each other's arms. I was careful to direct my grin at the ground so it wouldn't be all up in Natasha's face looking all snaggletoothed.

"So, whatever happened to your best friend? What was her name? Shanna?"

"LaShondra," I corrected her. "She's fine. Girl, she's the one with real jungle fever. She married a white man."

"No way!"

I added, "He's good to her, though. They live in North Dallas."

"I ain't mad at her. I might fool around and get me a white man if these brothers keep trippin'."

"You ain't said nothin' but a word," I agreed, holding my hand up like a church lady sitting on the front pew. This, of course, led to my story about none other than the triflin' Raphael, which took another five minutes. The unabridged version would have taken three hours. "So it is what it is. If my son stays put at my mother's house, he gets to see his daddy. If he comes home to live with me, he loses all contact."

The whole arrangement sounded better when I threw in the Daddy situation. Less shameful on my part. Perhaps if I replayed it enough times in my head, I might actually feel a little better.

"Looks like we're both in some tough spots right now," Natasha concluded. "Let me get your number, girl, so we can keep in touch. My pastor was just saying last Sunday how black people need to start helping each other more, you know?"

Natasha and I exchanged numbers through a call from my cell to hers, then she invited me to her church. "I go to Colby Tabernacle. We only have one service—at eleven-thirty. My pastor don't believe in having all those different worship times. He says either you're coming to church or you ain't."

"I guess he's got a point."

"Girl, Pastor is just *real*. He talks, you know, so we can understand him. And he's doesn't try to, you know, make it all holy and make you feel bad. He keeps it *real*."

The whole concept of me going to church without being made to feel bad was actually quite appealing, seeing as I was too ashamed to set foot in my mother's church. My home church would have been even worse. Since Quinn and I were no longer an item there, I figured I'd feel out of place. Not to mention sad.

I had no idea how real *real* was until I visited Natasha's church the following Sunday. The church was a small store-front venue, located in a shopping strip. The congregation was working toward the perpetual building fund, as evidenced by the thermometer poster on the wall directly behind the makeshift choir stand. There were probably about seventy-five people in attendance, and they were more than ready for Pastor Colby to bring a word after the women's choir sang a questionably adapted rendition of R. Kelly's "I Believe I Can Fly."

I'd never heard a preacher curse from the pulpit, but Pastor Colby slipped in a few PG-13 words sending the crowd into a frenzy of commentary. "Go 'head, Pastor!" "You know you right about that!"

He wiped the sweat from his brow with a handkerchief. "See I got to tell the truth and shame the devil."

"Yeah!" from the congregation.

"And I got to talk to y'all in terms y'all can understand," he whooped between the organ's hits.

The room roared in agreement. I thought for sure we were all going to hell.

Natasha stood and cheered the pastor on during this sermon he titled, "You Can't Live Right Until You Get Tight." Seriously, I thought the whole message sounded like a Dr. Seuss book. To this day, I cannot tell you what that man preached about. I would have counted myself among the last people on earth who could judge anybody right then, but I had enough to sense to know he wasn't delivering a word from the Lord because he never even opened his Bible.

After church, Natasha wanted to know if I'd enjoyed myself as we walked back toward her car. "It was . . . interesting."

She smiled. "I know, girl. I felt the same way when I started coming—like what the heck is going on here? But if you keep coming, you'll get it."

I didn't *want* it. "Hmmm."

She treated me to lunch at the South Dallas Café, and I stuffed myself like nobody's business. Neither Natasha nor I was counting calories. My heart warmed at the chance to be myself—the *new* myself—without being judged. To my relief, Natasha wasn't even staring at the jagged gap in my mouth, which, by the way, caused me slight difficulty with my eating. It's amazing how one little change can mess up a process I'd been doing since I was a baby.

"Ooh, I've got to get this tooth fixed," I said between bites.

"Girl, I can't talk. I've been walking around with a temporary filling for almost eighteen months now," she admitted. "Dental work is so expensive these days!"

"I know, huh?"

"What you ought to do," she suggested, "is go to the

Bazaar and get a gold cover for your tooth until you can get it fixed. They size 'em up and put 'em on right there in the store."

I thought she was joking, but her face was set on serious. "Costs a whole lot less than going to a dentist. Until you can get on your feet."

"I can't wear go around wearing a gold tooth."

"Pastor got a gold tooth," she argued her case.

This girl was serious about Pastor Colby. "It's not for me."

"All right. Suit yourself, then. I was just trying to help." She resumed her face stuffing, and I made a mental note to avoid any comment contradicting her shepherd.

Chapter 30

Natasha and I started hanging out together. Movies, restaurants, nicer clubs, and of course Colby Tabernacle, because I had nothing better to do on Sunday mornings. I suppose I could have gone to another church or sought out a different friend, but it just seemed easier to go backward than forward.

After a few more Sundays, Natasha's words rang true for me. I got used to Pastor Colby's preaching. A lot of what he said made common sense, when I thought about it. His messages still rhymed—*Try in order to Fly; You'll Come Back, So Don't Be Wack;* and an antifornication sermon titled "No Ding-Ding Without a Ring-Ring." I guessed with so many single women in his congregation, he had to tailor to his audience.

Above all, the members were extremely cordial to me. Unconditional hugs and cheek kisses abounded in Colby Tabernacle. I suspected a few of the men were a bit too touchy-feely, but there were so few of them, it didn't bother me too much. The women always complimented me on my too-tight clothes, my home-permed hair. I gathered they didn't get out much.

The third Sunday I visited was actually their monthly Friends and Family service. To my surprise, Natasha introduced me as a high school friend who was going through a tough time right now and had found their congregation a safe haven.

Ohhh-key-dokey. I did my parade-float wave at the members. After church, they fawned over me a bit and told Natasha I seemed like "the right type." Then Natasha invited me to get "on the bus." I'd heard this term thrown around the church for weeks, but I thought they were using it metaphorically. You know—the glory-bound train? For the first time, I understood they were referencing a physical bus.

"Pastor said you can come visit the center."

"What center?"

"It's where he and a lot of the church members live. I'm moving there next month."

Another *Ohhh-key-dokey* rushed through my brain. "That's okay. Can you take me home first?"

"What? You don't like my pastor?"

"He's okay. I just don't feel like going to the compound."

"The *center,*" she corrected me sternly. "Pastor really wants you to come. We'll be back at around six, when Sunday evening service starts. If you don't want to stay for the late worship, I'll take you back home then."

I couldn't afford to make the only friend I had left on earth angry with me. "Well, all right."

The vehicle was actually an old school bus painted blue and white, the church's colors. Natasha and I were scrunched together on our tiny bench throughout the twenty-minute ride. The members' hymn-singing didn't help by any means.

Since the church was already on the outskirts of town, little time passed before our surroundings began to resemble a prairie. I took out my cell phone a few times to check the time and noticed my signal fading in and out. A long stretch down any Farm to Market Road in Texas could lead to countless desolate destinations.

Colby Tabernacle Center was basically a tired trailer park

built alongside a lightly traveled dirt road. I did not want to get off said bus, and I suppose my consternation voiced my objections.

Before we came to a complete stop, Natasha turned to me and said, "Peaches, I want you to keep an open mind about this, okay?"

"About what?"

"Promise me. An open mind."

I shrugged. "Okay . . ." What else could I do?

We ventured off the bus and into the first trailer with Sister Orlene Gingerson, who asked us to excuse her mess. "My son, Chuck, keeps this place looking like a pig sty." Orlene was probably in her mid-fifties, old enough to have a child close to my age. I hoped she was talking about a godchild or maybe even a grandchild, not some thirty-something-year-old man still living at home with his mother.

Still, I didn't see anything out of place, but Natasha agreed with the lady of the trailer. "I know what you mean."

Two other church members followed us. One was male, the other female. They said their cordial hellos and moseyed on down the narrow hallway to their separate rooms. Stark contrast to the bubbly sanctuary greetings.

"Don't mind them." Orlene fanned in their direction. "I've got two sleepyheads for roommates. Have a seat."

Natasha and I placed ourselves on Orlene's slip-covered sofa. I had been inside only one other trailer home before then. The mobile park inhabited by several students at my undergraduate school was actually on and poppin' back then. No dorm monitors, no curfew. A bunch of twenty-year-olds surviving on ramen noodles, barbecued hot dogs, and beer.

"Y'all want something to drink?"

"No, I'm good," I declined. "Thank you, anyway."

"I'll take a Coke."

"Sister Natasha, I ain't got no Coke." Orlene snickered.

"Remember, Pastor told us to stop poisonin' ourselves with so much sugar last month. I've got some iced tea."

Orlene took three steps to the kitchen and drew a pitcher from the refrigerator. Her trailer seemed like such a small place for three adults and a child. The doorway to the last room down the hall wasn't more than twelve feet from where I sat on the couch. You know my mind, I wondered who in the house wasn't pulling their weight because three grown, reasonably intelligent, able-bodied people ought to be able to afford something a little more spacious than this. Then I remembered: This is the *center*. They must all be living here because they want to be near Pastor Colby and each other.

"So, what do you all do at the center?" I asked, hoping she would tell me they performed some kind of community service work so I could shelve this whole situation favorably in my brain.

Orlene's eyes met Natasha's for an instant. Natasha stumbled through an explanation. "We care for the sick and elderly. Nurse them. Back."

"Oh, that's good."

My cell phone vibrated in my pocket. I flipped it open to an unexpected text from LaShondra: Happy Mother's Day to all the moms I know. You are blessed beyond measure! Must have been one of those mass messages. My heart ached for her, knowing how much she wanted to be on the receiving end of Mother's Day wishes.

"Is it Mother's Day already?" I asked with a hint of sarcasm, trying to offset the emotion coursing through me.

Natasha's curled her lips inward.

"Oh, girl, I'm sorry. I wasn't thinking." Leave it to me to say something insensitive.

"It's okay."

"Yeah, it's Mother's Day," Orlene confirmed as she gave Natasha the glass of tea.

I remarked, "I'm surprised church wasn't packed today."

Orlene shook her head. "Oh, no, honey. Pastor don't allow folks to pop up in church when they get good and ready. You got to be *invited* to our church, escorted in by one of the members."

I twisted my face in disbelief. "Invited? All churches belong to God. They're our Father's house."

Natasha elbowed me in the side.

"People need to have more respect for their pastors than to just come when they get good and ready. Puttin' all that hard money in the collection plate." Orlene's double chin shook as she spoke. Anger splashed across her face. She softened after a deep breath.

So how could I tell Natasha I was "ret-2-go" without spoiling their attitudes? Aside from their peculiar passion for Pastor Colby, an inexplicable hunch deep in my gut said something wasn't quite right. I was out in the middle of nowhere with a bunch of people who lived right next door to their pastor, for goodness' sake. I'm all for fellowship, but this seemed a bit much, in my opinion.

Orlene's house phone rang and she shuffled to the kitchen to answer it. "Yes, sir. They're here. Okay." Then she announced, "Pastor is ready to see y'all now."

I had no idea we were on his waiting list.

Natasha stood. I followed her lead and walked toward Orlene's front door. The two ladies embraced. "I hope you get to hear from her today," Orlene said.

Natasha, now tearful, replied, "I hope so. And I hope you hear from Chuck, too."

"See who? Where's Chuck?"

Orlene whispered to Natasha, as though I wasn't standing right there, "You haven't told her yet?"

"Told me what?"

My friend flaunted a fake smile. "Don't worry, Peaches. It'll be okay. Come." Natasha grabbed my elbow and pulled me across the dirt road. We stopped, approaching the home with a star bearing Pastor Colby's name hung from a rusty nail in the trailer's splintered door.

Natasha started to knock. She stopped, turned her eyes from the door, and squeezed my hand. "Remember. An open mind."

"Natasha, I know he's your pastor. But he's just a man."

"Shhhh!" She cupped my mouth with her hand. I wanted to push her hand away, but the whites of her eyes stopped me. "He's not just a man or a pastor. He has a special gift. You'll see."

Chapter 31

"Hello, Sister Peaches—oh, may I call you Peaches?" Pastor Colby wanted to know.

"Yes, sir." He could have called me anything and I wouldn't have paid any attention. The way his trailer looked on the inside took me completely off guard. Flat screens, wood flooring, lavish heirloom-quality furnishings. And could somebody please tell me how he tacked up some crown molding in a manufactured home? If I hadn't just stepped off the front porch, I wouldn't have dreamed we were inside a trailer.

First Lady Colby appeared at his side. "Sister Peaches, Sister Natasha, please come in."

"You have a lovely home," I complimented her.

"Thank you. Pastor and I always say—it's not *where* you live, it's *how* you live."

They were definitely living it up in there.

First Lady motioned for Natasha and me to rest on the love seat. The plush leather puffed up all around my behind and made me want to snuggle up with a throw blanket. These folks knew how to pick out some furniture.

Pastor and First Lady sat directly across from us wearing anxious expressions. Again, my stomach quavered. I tried to think of what I might have eaten to make me sick. Nothing came to mind.

Pastor began, "Sister Peaches, our church is, uh, very different. As you might have guessed."

Natasha nodded, looked at me. I followed her lead and nodded, too.

"When I first opened the doors of Colby Tabernacle, I had no idea how God was going to use me for His service. He commanded me to start a church and I obeyed."

Sounded easy enough.

"And before long, I realized He had a special assignment for me. You see, the Lord, sends me . . . special members."

The business major in me wanted to prod him along—out with it already. Pastor Colby positioned his hands in a steeple gesture, fingertip to fingertip. I supposed he had to take his time.

"The members He leads to my church have experienced a great deal of hardship."

That's me.

"Shame. Guilt. Most important, loss."

Me, me, definitely me.

"And it's my job to connect them with . . . their lost loved ones."

You got the wrong sister now. My body tensed as the trouble in my stomach rose to my chest.

"Natasha brought you to our church because she thought you might need some guidance. Some closure."

I jerked my face around to study hers. "What is this all about?"

"Just listen," she pleaded. "I know it sounds crazy, but he's helped me get in touch with my mother and my daughter." Natasha focused her attention toward the opposite couch now. "Is Jayden's spirit here tonight, Pastor? Is my daughter here?"

"Patience, Natasha. Perhaps our guest would like to get in touch with someone first."

"I'm not tryin' to talk to no dead people." Proper English notwithstanding.

He tilted his head and stared at me for a moment. "Someone is here to talk to you." His index fingers pointed squarely at me.

I glanced to my left. Right. Over Natasha's shoulder and into the kitchen, then back at him.

"A male figure. Older," Pastor continued with his séance. "Do you feel him?"

"Nope." I did feel a nervous energy flowing through my body, but I'd been feeling that since I was in Orlene's living area.

"Do want to hear what he has to say?"

"No, I surely do not." My throat tightened.

Pastor closed his eyes. Then he laughed and informed to me, "He's says he's not going to leave until you pay heed."

I rocked myself off the couch. "Well, then *I'll* leave."

"No," First Lady countered. She took hold of my arms and tried to force me back down. "You will hear the message through the mand of God."

"You need to take your hands off me." Suddenly, the trembling in my stomach intensified. Bile traveled up, splashed out all over First Lady and her priceless coffee table. Already, I could see the vomit seeping into the tiny crevices between the beveled glass pieces on top.

First Lady stepped back, her arms spread wide, like Carrie after they dumped the blood all over her. "You! You!" She looked daggers at Natasha. "She's not ready yet, you idiot! Get her out!"

You ain't said nothin' but a word. I was out of there so fast, I twisted my ankle trying to scurry between Natasha and a solid oak end table. Beyond the front door, I had no idea where to go, but that didn't stop me from running down those steps.

Natasha was right behind me. "Peaches, wait! He can help you talk to your father again!"

I yelled, "This is crazy!"

"No! Wait a minute!" She caught up to me, put both hands on my shoulders, forcing me to a halt. "People underestimate what God can do. God is using Pastor Colby to help people. Don't you see?" Her eyes bounced quickly as she searched mine.

To this day, I don't know how I knew what to say to her. I guess all those dreaded but mandatory Sunday school lessons must have come to the surface, because when I needed the truth, it was there for me. "Girl, talking to dead people is *not* one of the gifts God promised His people. Have you ever seen anywhere in the Bible where God wanted someone to bring messages from beyond the grave?"

"Pastor talks about it all the time," she said, still trying to catch her breath. "He's like Jesus."

"Natasha, Pastor Colby is not Jesus."

"He's . . . he's not?" Her eyes darted wildly from side to side.

Just as I perceived this little spark of revelation registering in Natasha's brain, Pastor Colby appeared on his front deck. "Natasha! She's here! Jayden is here!"

Her attention seized, she cried, "My baby?"

"Yes!" from First Lady Colby.

Natasha took a step toward their trailer. I grabbed her arm. "Listen to me. That man is *not* hearing Jayden. And if he is, he's not supposed to be, because Jayden is with the Lord now. Let her go."

Emotion spilled from her lids. "I can't. I left the pool gate open and . . . I want her to know I'm sorry." She tore away from me and rushed back toward the Colbys' trailer.

I chased after her. "Natasha!"

She ran even faster.

"Get off our property now, or we'll call the police!" Pastor Colby hurled a warning at me and slammed his door shut.

Breathless, I stopped. Whooo! Lord knows I was too big for all this running and carrying on. I bent over for a second to get my wind back and gather my thoughts. I wanted off the property as much as they wanted me off, but I thought it pretty safe to say the church bus wouldn't be transporting me.

If memory served me correctly, the road leading into the trailer park was at least three miles long; it was another two or three miles beyond that to a main thoroughfare. All pride aside, I needed somebody to come rescue me.

I flicked my phone open and dialed the first person who came to mind. "LaShondra, it's me."

"Yeah," she came back in a flat tone.

My ego crumpled at the sound of her voice. "I'm sorry." Great sobs overtook me as I tried to express how completely wrong I was, not that she hadn't already figured it out. "I don't know what's wrong with me. Everything, my whole life, it's just . . . I can't even begin to tell you how wrong it is."

She sighed heavily. "I know, girl, I know."

"Can you come get me?"

"Tell me where you are." I didn't deserve her compassion, which made her loving response all the more precious.

Chapter 32

My ankle, which was quickly swelling, throbbed so much I had to take a seat on the hard, damp earth while I waited. I used to think that the worst day of my life was when Raphael left me. But even then, there was a bright side to the dilemma. I did have a cute, cuddly baby to look forward to. This situation, however, set a new record low. Sitting outside with a chipped tooth, a puffy ankle, and an empty heart. Not to mention broke and nearly sonless. My life was akin to the old lady who swallowed a fly, one bad remedy after another, each one more bizarre than the one before.

Eric and I used to sing that song when he got restless in the car.

I missed my son fiercely. Yet there was no need in him coming back to me. I was busy fighting grown women and running from mediums. I couldn't even afford to give him the proper tutoring he needed.

Tears trickled down my face one at a time. I longed to have one of those deep, heaving wails, but how could I? When other people did me wrong, pity parties came easily. This was different. Nobody had done me wrong except me. Stupidity didn't deserve sympathy, in my book. A swift kick in the behind, yes, but not sympathy.

After a semieternity, LaShondra's Honda Accord groaned up the dirt road, followed by Stelson's Range Rover. I should have known she'd bring him. Why they were in two separate cars was anyone's guess. I didn't care, though. She could have brought a whole caravan so long as they got me out of there.

My only regret was leaving Natasha to the Colby Tabernacle crew. I wished I could save her. Maybe I could, if I got myself together first.

LaShondra made a U-turn and stopped a few feet in front of me. I looked up at Stelson. He waved to me, wearing a goofy smile on his face. *Why is he always so happy?*

I couldn't put any weight on my ankle so I had to roll over on my side and try to push myself onto my knees. In an instant, I felt Stelson's support under my arms. He helped me to my feet and up to LaShondra's car door.

"Thank you," I whispered.

"Glad to help."

LaShondra helped him get me into her car, gently lifting my ankle and carefully placing it on the floorboard. "You need to go to the emergency room?" she asked.

The truth was probably *yes,* but without health insurance, whatever was wrong with me would have to wait for regular clinic hours. "No. I just want to go home."

She secured me in the vehicle and then walked back to the driver's side. She was barely in the car before she offered an apology. "I hope you don't mind Stelson being here. He refused to let me drive out to the boonies by myself. I told him you might want to talk privately, so he drove his own—"

I held up my hand to stop her. "I understand. Hmph, that's what a real man ought to do, anyway."

For all the talking we didn't do, Stelson probably could have ridden with us. I sat with my heavy skull leaning against the headrest, rocking with every turn. LaShondra fiddled with her CDs a bit. She didn't ask me any questions; I didn't offer any explanations. I wondered if she was still angry with me, but her behavior didn't fit the mold. LaShondra wasn't the silent-treatment type. If she had a bone to pick with me, she would have fussed the whole way home.

Against the backdrop of inspirational music, our silence actually comforted me. In the past few months, I'd forgotten what it was like to just be with someone who knew you. The only nuisance was my pulsating leg.

When we got back to my townhouse, LaShondra put the car in park. She turned off the music, a sure sign that she wanted to talk. I looked through the sideview mirror and realized Stelson must have veered away somewhere on the highway, because he was no longer behind us.

She clasped my left hand and I reciprocated the gesture. "Peaches, I'm sorry—"

"For what?" I interrupted her. I'd heard of killing folks with kindness, but she was taking things too far.

"Let me finish," she said. "I'm sorry for trying to play Jesus in your life. Trying to make you do what I wanted you to do.

"The last time I was at your house, you told me you had a right to be in a funk and I disagreed with you. You were correct. You have a right to go through trials and tribulations to grow your faith. My job as your best friend and your sister in Christ is not to pull you *out* of them or try to shame you *away* from them but to pray you *through* them. So, I'm sorry," she repeated.

"Girl," I sang, "what I needed was a straight-up whippin' for making stupid choices and actions. I know you were just trying to help, LaShondra. I thank you for praying for me, even though I can't really say I'm right with God."

She looked straight ahead in a trancelike state, eyeing my garage door. "There's a verse the Holy Spirit brought to mind the other day as I was praying for you. Luke chapter twenty-two, verses thirty-one and thirty-two."

"What do the verses say?"

"I'm not going to tell you. I want you to read them for yourself, because I believe it's exactly where you are right now."

Okay, she was holding my hand and telling me all this religious stuff, but I still had no clue whether she was angry with me. An admission seemed appropriate. "Shondra, I'm really sorry for what I said about, you know, having a baby with someone. Would you please forgive me?"

She smacked, "Already done."

"I was completely out of line," I continued. "I don't think I'll ever be able to get your facial expression out of my mind."

For the first time since Eric's birthday party, LaShondra squared up with me and said, "Some things need to be forgotten. On purpose."

I reached across the console and gave the first real hug I'd given in a long time. "I love you, man."

She chuckled slightly and spoke into my spirit, "Love you, too, girlie."

I pulled away from her, all smiles.

"Oh, snap, girl, what happened to your tooth?" So much for silent observation. She immediately asked for forgiveness. "I didn't mean to call you out like that."

"Don't worry about it, I would have done the same thing to you. It's a long story. Me and Deniessa got into a fight. I've got an assault case pending against her in court."

"No way."

I nodded. "Yes way."

"No wonder she hasn't been returning my calls."

"Well, she's definitely the next one to add to your prayer list." I pressed the unlock button and let myself out of the car. Now that I had my best friend back, I could tend to my ankle, which was in dire need of elevation.

LaShondra rushed to aid me. Together, we hobbled up to the doorstep. I balanced myself on one foot and unlocked the door. No sooner had we glimpsed the surroundings than I wished I had left LaShondra at the car. My place was a mess. Clothes everywhere, shoes littering the floor, dishes in the sink. But LaShondra didn't say a mumbling word. She helped me to the couch and carefully propped up my leg on a few throw pillows. Then she asked if there was anything else I needed. When I declined, she offered, "I'll call Momma and see if she still has Daddy's old crutches from when he fell last year."

I saw her glancing around the place, checking out my nastiness, but she kept quiet. I'm sure her tongue must have had all kinds of teeth marks in it.

"Thank you. For everything."

"Remember—Luke twenty-two, thirty-one through thirty-two."

"Luke twenty-two," I repeated. "Got it."

LaShondra hurriedly let herself out. I didn't blame her. I hated being around filth, too. Worse, I couldn't clean up even if I wanted to.

I didn't have much choice about what to do for the rest of the day. My condition dictated bed rest. Self-diagnosis yielded a positive report. I could wiggle my toes and I could actually move my ankle to the left and right without waking up the neighborhood. I'd give it a few days before going into a doctor's office because, in my experience, they couldn't do much for sprains anyway.

A huge burst of laughter escaped my lungs as I listened carefully to my inner thoughts. If I wasn't Joe Miller's daughter! Daddy thought all doctors were crooks—especially general practitioners. "You tell 'em what's wrong with you, meanwhile they step out and go look up your symptoms in a big red book. Then they come back in and tell you there's three things could be wrong with you, so they're gonna put you on medication. Come back if you don't feel better, keep taking this medicine if you do. Tell you what, I'm gonna get me one of them big red books and take care of my own self!"

I suppose that's how the blocked arteries escaped him. The doctors said it was a miracle Daddy lived as long as he did. Over time, his body had actually created an alternate set of veins to flow around some of the blockages. I remember being amazed at the body's ability to set up these makeshift routes to keep the blood flowing. I wondered why God hadn't given him even more extra veins, thus more time to live. Time to connect with me. Change. I mean, if God had already given him an additional year or so, why couldn't He give him three more? Five more?

God's grace had never made any sense to me. Didn't seem fair. Some got more grace than others was all I knew. Somebody's father didn't live as long as mine did, and somebody else's did live long enough to walk her down the aisle. I guessed we were to be thankful for whatever grace we received. I just wished there was some kind of way to know how much of it He planned to allow, so we could get things under control before it was too late.

I wondered how much longer God was going to let the situation at Colby Tabernacle go on before He intervened. Poor Natasha, poor Orlene and all the others who were holding on to their pastor's every nonbiblical word. I hoped God would give them a little more grace, because they were hurting.

Lying up on the couch reviewing my recent past seemed to make my leg ache more. Maybe the Jacuzzi tub would do the trick. I hopped to my bathroom and started the water. While the water ran, I ambled around my bedroom collecting fresh undergarments and a long nightgown. I planned on settling into this tub for a while, so I decided to get a book as well.

I usually kept a supply of unread stories handy thanks to my automatic book club membership. Now that I was on their bad customer list, I was stuck with only two titles I'd been putting off for months. I grabbed the one on top and hoped for the best.

A ding of remembrance sounded in my head. There was something I was supposed to be reading, but I just couldn't remember what. Hate it when that happens.

The tub was calling, so I shuffled on back to the bathroom, undressed, and submerged myself in the pool of jetting water. Slowly, I lowered my ankle into the whirlpool. Those jets hit the spot. Right about then, I didn't care what else I lost in the economic slump, my Jacuzzi would be the very last thing to go. Take the house, the Internet, just leave the tub.

Thoughts of romance flooded my heart as I got caught up in the first few chapters of the novel. The hero, a handsome doctor from Sacramento, had just proposed to his equally brilliant partnering physician. She'd accepted and they'd begun planning the wedding, but she has some deep, dark secret (don't they always?) she's trying to keep under wraps until she gets him down the aisle. I was betting the secret had something to do with his brother's prison sentence. I wanted to yell at her: Just because he marries you doesn't mean he has to stay married to your sheisty behind!

I really didn't like those deep, dark secret characters. Being up front and honest was always my policy with every man. Hadn't gotten me down the aisle, mind you, but I still liked the idea. Quinn knew about Eric from the very beginning. At that time, Eric was the biggest "secret" I could have hidden.

These past few months had given me more than enough to want to sweep under the rug. I mean, let's say the entire sky fell and I somehow ended up talking to Quinn again. I'd have to tell him about what happened between me and Raphael during the interim. I know if I'd been chaste enough to wait on someone and then I found out they gave it up to somebody else a few weeks after I left, I would want to know so I could make an educated decision about whether to resume the relationship.

A quick nightmare reunion film played in my head. Quinn and I sitting on his couch talking. He says, "Peaches, I've missed you."

I say, "I've missed you, too, but there's something I have to tell you."

Dun-dun-dun. The piano tips him off. "What is it?"

"I slept with Raphael while we were broken up," I admit. "I'm so sorry."

Quinn stands, points me to the door. "Get out! You're not the woman I thought you were."

I run to the door like a poor little rich girl. "But Quinn—"

Violins screech.

"Out!"

Fade to black. Credits scroll. Role of the foolish woman played by Patricia Ann Miller.

The jet timer lapsed, slowing the whirlpool of water around me and bringing my horror film to an end. I don't think I could take Quinn's rejection. Wait a minute, why was I even pondering this scenario? Quinn was so far out of my life I'd never have to worry about him snubbing me.

I threw the novel toward the trash can but missed it completely. I'd toss it later because I already knew where this book was leading. The male doctor should have conducted a thorough background check before he popped the question. *Oh, well. That's life.*

Bath time was about to turn into nap time. I hoisted myself out of the tub, dried off, and staggered back to my bedroom. I said a quick prayer for Natasha, and that's when it hit me. I was supposed to be reading the Bible. Specifically, the scriptures LaShondra referenced.

My nightstand probably creaked, it had been so long since I looked at the Word. Truly, I felt guilty for being away from

God for so long. *How dare I come back to Him after the way I kicked Him out of my life?* If I started talking to Him under my present circumstances, wouldn't it seem like I was trying to use Him?

There was nothing less than a war going on in my mind. One part of me wanting, needing to hear what the Lord had to say. The other part condemning me for waiting so long, trying to convince me God was not interested in pulling me out of yet another Peaches-created jumble.

I wondered if I should ask for forgiveness first. Seemed so trivial, though, to just *ask* for pardon. I felt like I should *do* something, too—go wash somebody's feet or clothe a homeless person. The enemy bombarded me with tough questions: *Who's to say you won't go off the deep end again next year? Can you truly ask for forgiveness now that you have a glimpse of how much evil you're capable of? Did you ever really love God in the first place? If you did, how could you leave Him so easily? Did He ever really love you?*

The only question I could answer with complete confidence was the last one. Yes, He loved me. I doubted a lot of things about God sometimes—His advice, His timing, His planning, but never His love. When I was in the children's choir, we used to sing, "Yes, Jesus loves me for the Bible tells me so." And for many years, I figured He loved me because my mother, my pastor, and everybody else seemed to say so.

But when I used to get up every morning and spend time in His presence, I felt His love coming from the inside out. He was in me and around me all at the same time. We talked. We laughed. Sometimes I could feel Him waiting for me at the end of a hard day's work, ready to kick back and unwind with me. We'd review the day together and He'd point things out—things to remember, important lessons, His word in action.

We had the cutest little routine at night. Right after I

prayed, I used to pucker up, close my eyes, smack and say, "Good night, Jesus." Never told anyone about it, but that's how close we were.

Then I started dating Quinn and he fit right into the circle. Quinn had been a serious lover of the Word for more than a decade, so his insight put me on Godspeed for spiritual growth. I mean, he turned me on to books and tapes that added new dimensions to my understanding of God, Jesus, and the Holy Spirit. Amped up my prayer life, opened my eyes to the vision of holiness God has for His people.

Those were the good old days. Before Quinn and I broke up. As I turned my long lost Bible to Luke 22, I could almost hear Quinn's voice telling me to remember the context and read it as though Jesus were talking to me personally. My eyes scrolled down to the red lettering on the NIV side of my text. I read the verses substituting my name for Simon's: "Peaches, Peaches, Satan has asked to sift you as wheat. But I have prayed for you, Peaches, that your faith may not fail. And when you have turned back, strengthen your brothers."

Oh, I love the way He said my name. *Peaches, Peaches.*

I read the verses again, letting them sink into my spirit. "Satan has asked to sift you as wheat." Jesus must have been there when Bridget tried to rape me. He swatted the enemy's hand away, told her to get back because I was off limits. When Jamal turned his anger toward me, Jesus showed him the knife, for real.

"But I have prayed for you, Peaches . . ." I imagined Jesus pacing the floor, pleading my case before our Holy God, asking Him to give me another day, another week, another month. Hold off the full weight of judgment, have mercy on me.

I imagine God asked Jesus, "Why?"

And all Jesus could say was, "Because I love her," because there certainly wasn't any other good reason.

That your faith may not fail. I knew what I knew about the

Word before I went to Colby Tabernacle, and the faith I had established based on the Word lit my path out of there.

And when you have turned back . . . Jesus had enough faith to take it for granted that I *would* turn back. My spirit was flooded with verses I suddenly needed to see again. 1 Corinthians 13—the definition of love. Patient, kind . . . keeps no record of wrongs . . . always trusts, always hopes. Jesus always trusted and hoped I would get back on the right path, even when I had every intention of sleeping with Raphael again.

Hebrews 7:25 came to mind as well. The picture of Jesus still interceding for me was almost too overwhelming. I curled up into a ball on my bed and wept out loud. "I'm sorry, Jesus. Please forgive me." I didn't deserve to be loved like this, to have someone pulling harder for me than I was willing to pull for myself. I wondered if Jesus had cried for me. He must have been hurt by my betrayal, the Bible even says the Holy Spirit can grieve.

All the time I was doing my own thing, I knew I was messing things up for myself. But right now, that seemed irrelevant. Losing myself was not the end of the world. Losing the relationship with Jesus . . . mmm, mmm, mmm.

Yes, He loved me. And what I wanted more than anything else in the entire universe was *our* relationship restored, *our* everlasting fellowship reignited. Whatever else He restored on top of that was gravy.

"I'm sorry, Lord," I cried out from my innermost being. Lying on the bed didn't quite seem to express the depths of my remorse. I slid onto the floor and lay prostrate, my nose to the carpet as He began to bail huge buckets of guilt from my soul and throw them overboard along with my tears. Verses I had previously written on my heart through Bible study suddenly reappeared, and I recited as many as I could, refueling the power of the living Word, which had been dormant for months now. Psalm 51:10, 1 Corinthians 2:10.

I called on Jehovah M'Kaddesh, my sanctifier. Jehovah

Shalom, my peace and wholeness. El Shaddai, the All-Sufficient one. Every name and verse the Holy Spirit brought to my remembrance, I called. I have no idea how much time passed, I just knew I wasn't getting up from that floor until I knew beyond a shadow of a doubt that He heard me. And hear me He did.

My whole head felt as though it would explode from the mighty presence of the Lord. In my spirit, I heard Him welcoming me back. He reminded me of His love and forgiveness. *I can't stay mad at you, Peaches. I'm married to you. I have always loved you, and always will. Always.*

"Oh, Lord, I love you."

And then I praised Jehovah Shammah, God is here!

Chapter 33

My eyes flew open almost automatically. My digital clock shone 5:30 AM. Something had awakened me. Using only my eyeballs, I searched around the room and down the portion of my hallway I could see from my bed. If there was someone in my house, I wanted to act like I was asleep until I was forced to go wacko on him. I held my breath, listening for movement.

Nothing. I exhaled with relief and tried to drift off, but my lids popped open again at 5:35. 5:47. 5:55. Sleep was trippin'. What on earth was I doing up at that time of morning when I didn't have a job to go to? I flipped over onto my right side, and my cheek landed smack against my Bible. I pushed it ahead of me a few feet and tried again to fall asleep.

Before long, daylight started to creep in between the blinds. If I couldn't get some rest before the sun came up, my morning would be a bust. Thirty minutes later, I gave up on going back to sleep and decided maybe I was supposed to be up. Maybe something was wrong.

I called my mother's house to make sure she and Eric were okay. "We're fine, baby. Glad you called. You want to talk to Eric?"

My son's morning voice creaked through the phone. "Hi, Momma. Why you calling me so early?"

"Because I love you."

He yawned. "I love you, too, Momma."

"What do you think about coming home this weekend?" I suggested despite the fact I hadn't run this by my mother.

"Um, I gotta ask Granny."

I wondered for a moment if my mother had taken my place in Eric's life. Still, I couldn't put him in the middle of it. "Well, maybe we could all go someplace together."

"Yeah." He snickered. "Someplace with a motorcycle game."

Does he ever get enough of that place? "Okay. Maybe I can meet you there?"

"Yeah." He snickered. "I need to get you back on the motorcycle game."

"I hear you.

"You seen your daddy lately?"

"No," Eric answered. "Daddy is moving to San Antonio with Miss Cheryl."

"Oh." I attempted to mask my disappointment with short words. "I see."

"Don't worry. We'll be all right, Momma," Eric comforted me. "Here's Granny."

My mother confirmed the weekend excursion planned by her church for the youth. I agreed to meet them at Pizza Kingdom and asked permission to take my son home following the event. "We'll see."

Never mind the fact that Eric was my child, not hers. My mother, this weak woman who never stood up to my father, suddenly grew a backbone when it came to her grandchild. Had me practically begging for visitation. I didn't know she had it in her.

I spent the rest of my morning online searching for work. "Show me a job, Lord. The job You want me to have," I whispered as I scrolled through pages of results. I virtually applied for several openings, tweaking my résumé and cover letter to fit each job description. I was resigned to the idea that I would probably have to take a pay cut. Yet I felt certain I could work my way up quickly.

Being the one-woman HR show at Northcomp so long afforded me a great deal of in-depth expertise that few of my competitors, who were often skipping from one employer to another, could claim to possess. Since I'd stuck with North-comp for several years, they invested in me, sending me to conferences and seminars, providing thousands of dollars worth of training annually so I could be at the top of my game.

"Father, open the door for the job You have ordained for me," I continued to plead. I don't know exactly what I thought He'd do, but I was full of hope.

Since I was already up, I decided to don my kicks and go to the gym. I couldn't do any serious machinery because of my ankle, but the circuit was fair game. Ooh-wee, my body was so out of shape. I couldn't even do eight counts on the torso twister—with no extra weights added. An old lady who worked there tried to show me how to use the pins. "If you insert this yellow ball here, it'll add resistance."

"I know that," I nipped at her. Did I ask need this woman to humiliate me?

Immediately, the Holy Spirit checked me. *She's only trying to be helpful.*

I tacked on, "But thank you, anyway."

That's better.

The next morning was déjà vu. At 5:30 AM, an internal alarm sounded, causing me to awaken unexpectedly. I thought maybe somebody else in my complex had a clock set and the alarm's vibration was coming through my walls, 'cause *something* was happening to me. Or maybe there was some kind of high-frequency thing happening that I wasn't

supposed to be able to hear, like a weird dog whistle, only I
wasn't a dog. Crazy, I know, but so is waking up at 5:30 for no
apparent reason.

Again, my efforts to fall asleep were futile.

I sat up in bed and flipped on the television set. The final
wave of infomercials beckoned consumers to get fit, get
richer, get smarter. All I wanted to do was get snoozes.

Since I was up, I called my mother's again to say good
morning. "To what do we owe this pleasure, two days in a
row?" she asked.

"Well, aside from the fact that it's nice to hear Eric's
voice, I couldn't sleep. I've been waking up at five-thirty and
I don't know why."

My mother produced only a sly giggle.

"What's so funny?"

She finished her snickering and said, "Bless the name of
the Most High. I asked the Lord not to let your head rest well
on a pillow until you returned to Him. I see He's listening."

Oh, great. "Momma, you probably ought to let me know
when you're praying prayers against my *sleeping*. I mean, I'm
just saying."

"Listen, the next time He wakes you up at five-thirty, you
need to get up and see what He wants. Hear?"

"Yes, ma'am."

"We'll see you Friday. I love you, Peaches."

Wow. I don't think she'd told me that since my daddy
died. "Love you, too, Momma." Come to think of it, I probably hadn't told her the same in a while, either, but I did. I
loved her even more now, knowing how she'd probably been
up right alongside Jesus praying for me, even though I had
come within an inch of despising her outwardly passive tem-
perament.

I dedicated the day to getting my apartment in order.
Though the swelling in my ankle had decreased significantly,
I still needed frequent breaks. I wished somebody was there

to lay hands on it and pray for healing. The old saints at my mother's church were good for touching and agreeing on stuff. Matter of fact, if my job search went on much longer, I wasn't past taking my résumé up there and letting them pray over it, too.

A full day's cleaning and doing laundry had me feeling much better. A place for everything and everything in its place. I had even found a spot for all those boxes of Zingers and Star Crunches—the trash. My thrifty Daddy wouldn't have approved of chunking edible food, of course, but the way I saw it, the money was already spent. At this point, all those sugary calories could either sit in the garbage or on my hips. Either way, they'd be doing no good.

I took a good look around. This was more like it. For the first time, I was starting to feel like my old self again. No—better than my old self. Maybe tomorrow, God wouldn't feel the need to wake me up at such an incredibly wretched hour.

"God, I'm hearing you," I attempted to compromise as I tucked myself in bed later that evening. "I'm not a morning person, though. Five-thirty is early. Old folks early. Can we please talk at, like eight or nine? And then when I get a job, we can change the time, okay? Amen."

I gave Jesus his kiss good night and tucked the covers under my chin.

You know what happened next. At 5:30 on the dot, I was looking at that clock. "Okay, God, okay." My lips were moving, but my body wasn't. Took me another fifteen minutes before I raised up enough to lean my back against the headboard. I grabbed my Bible. Dozed off for a minute. Woke back up and flipped to the concordance. I had to find some kind of biblical precedent to let God know there was no need in me waking up at five-thirty just because *He* never sleeps or slumbers.

Most of the references to prayer time and prayer closets took me to Psalms. I could have bopped David on the head for the King James translation of chapter 63 verse 1: "O God, thou art my God; early will I seek thee: my soul thirsteth for thee, my flesh longeth for thee in a dry and thirsty land, where no water is."

What kind of mess? Then Solomon came behind him in Proverbs 8:17 with, "I love them that love me; and those that seek me early shall find me."

I couldn't do anything but laugh. Granted, maybe the Hebrew or Greek or seriously researched meaning might yield a different understanding. Maybe God wants us to come to Him early in life or at the very onset of a problem. But in my case, right now, I knew good and well God wanted me to get up before the sun rose and talk to Him.

Honestly, I had no problems talking to God before I went to bed at night. I mean, we could talk all night if He wanted to. There was no rush, no deadline. I used to cherish our time together at the end of the day, and I really couldn't understand why He wanted to change things up. Rather than fight Him, I gave in and read the chapters I'd already encountered. My prayer was another plea for Him to reconsider this five-thirty thing.

Eric took the liberty to call me this particular morning. "Hi, Momma."

"Top o' the morning to you. How's it going?"

"Granny said you'd be up."

I laughed. "Granny is funny."

"I called you 'cause guess what, Momma?"

"What, baby?"

"I passed the test!"

I cheered with my son for a good five minutes. We praised God, and he told me about how he'd used the strategies the lady at church taught him, including prayer. I can't tell you how proud I was of my baby.

My mother interrupted our conversation. "He's got to get ready now."

"Okay. Give him a kiss for me."

"Chile, he don't want me kissing on him. He's so smart now, I think he's got a girlfriend."

"What?!"

I heard Eric yell in the background, "No, I don't, Momma."

My mother laughed and told him to go on and brush his teeth. "I see you've been summoned again this morning."

"But why does it have to be so early?" I whined.

Momma's tone switched to serious. "God's asking you to make a sacrifice. Askin' you to get up and meet Him just like He met you where you were. You got to give up some part of yourself, in a godly way, in just about every relationship. Give up your right to have everything your way. First Lady even said sometimes you got to let go of your right to be in a bad mood when you're in a good relationship—if you want it to last, that is. So if you wanna see God's presence and blessing in your life, maybe it's about time you showed God you'd rather be *a*-nointed than *a*-sleep, hear?"

Chapter 34

I wish I could say that I readily jumped up from that morning forward in joyful anticipation of my time alone with the Lord. I have to tell the truth, though. It took me a while to adapt to the sacrifice of waking up earlier than I felt I needed to, especially since I had nowhere to go. But the Holy Spirit poked and prodded me until I finally surrendered and became a bonafide member of the five-thirty club.

I didn't have much to say during our daybreak discussions. For one thing, it was too early to be moving my lips. God did most of the talking through His Word, showing me how much He loved me and reassuring me He hadn't given up on the plan for my life. He revisited several scriptures on righteousness that I printed on index cards and taped all over my house. And when I was out and about, He reminded me of His faithfulness through the verses on the WordWatch LaShondra gave me. For weeks, I couldn't eat a bowl of cereal or wash my hands without seeing a word from the Lord. Once the first round of verses were written on my heart, I replaced them with more scriptures, confessing them out loud to the negative suggestions that the enemy brought to me.

Every morning at around six-thirty, I'd begin listening to

a gospel television station while I started my morning routine in the restroom.

One particular morning, the preacher was making a comparison between God's guidance and the modern-day global positioning devices. "Even though you might veer off the chosen path for your life," he hollered, "just like one of those G-P-S machines, God will reconfigure your route. Y'all don't feel me!"

I rushed back to my bedroom and stood directly in front of the screen like a two-year-old watching his favorite commercial. "At whatever point you decide to give it over to God, He will direct you back to His original destination for you! See, that destination ain't gon' change no matter what you do. Those coordinates were preprogrammed before you were ever born!"

His words registered in my spirit. I threw my face towel at the screen. "You betta preach!"

"The moment you turn back to Him, He orchestrates the route for your return! Angels, go here and open this lane for her. Satan, you gon' have to take down your barricades because *I* said so! I know I allowed you to block it off before, but things have *changed* and you *have* to flee!"

Those people who started shouting in the audience didn't have anything on me. Despite my sore ankle, I danced around my bedroom like it was my first day in heaven. I blessed God for His grace, for Jesus, and for remembering my destiny even when I was acting a plum fool.

After my worshipfest, I made my usual call to Eric. My mother and I had reached a mutual agreement regarding his residence. He'd finish the school year staying with her during the week and with me on weekends. The arrangement was easier considering his ongoing tutoring at church. Plus my mother wasn't fully convinced I had all my marbles back yet, because I still wasn't attending anybody's Sunday morning services.

I checked my e-mail. Most of the messages were junk. A few were notifications from job Web sites about new openings. Still soaked with praise, I clicked the application links and sent my résumés accordingly.

Something *had* to give soon, because I was restless after my prayer time every day. I wanted to tackle the world—tell somebody about God and what He was doing for me. I wanted to go find all the Natashas in the world and say, "Hey! You don't have to suffer! Ask God to pull you out and He will!"

I called LaShondra and witnessed to her for as long as she could stay on the phone. She praised God with me and thanked me for sharing what I'd learned on television, but I could hear a little twang of sadness in her voice.

"What's wrong, girl?"

"I got my monthly visitor today." She sighed. "We're going to go ahead and set up an appointment."

"Shondra, there's no shame in getting help."

She busted out laughing.

"What?"

"Is this Peaches Miller on the other end of my line?"

"Uh, yes. And?"

"The same Peaches who only asks for help when she's stranded at religious compounds?"

"Whatever." I smacked my lips. "I told you, God is changing me, okay? I'm back on course."

She apologized. "I'm gonna leave you alone about the compound, after a while. You know I gotta wear it out first."

A soft beep interrupted our chat. I stared down at my phone to check the caller ID. I didn't recognize the number, but with so many job applications floating around, I couldn't afford to miss one call. "I have to take this other call. Check you later."

"Hello?"

"Miss Miller, this is Michael Yancey, from the Yancey group. We worked together at Northcomp," he began.

Why is incompetent Michael calling me on my cell phone? "Yes, Michael. How are you?"

"I'm well. Glad you remembered me."

I didn't want to give him reason to feel at ease, so I kept silent.

"I guess I'll cut to the chase. I was very impressed with your professionalism and knowledge base during the time we worked together at Northcomp."

I could feel the Spirit smiling within me. *Oh my You, God!*

Yancey continued, "By contract, I had to wait ninety days before contacting you to avoid a conflict of interest. So here we are. Ninety days later. I'd like to offer you a director's position with the Yancey Group."

What I meant to say was, *Can I start yesterday?* but instead, I stuttered, "I . . . I'm—"

"I know, I know." He cut me off. "You're probably within the probationary period at your new job. Your employment record shows you're not a job hopper, so this is not a light decision. I've taken all that into consideration. We're offering a ten percent raise over what you made at Northcomp. And given what I've seen of your work ethic, we'll allow you to telecommute as much as possible. The way I see it, with an Internet connection *you* could pretty much conduct this job's functions any time, from anywhere in the world."

Still speechless, I was scarcely able to ask Michael to hold on for a second while I ran to my room, jumped on my bed, and whisper-hollered to the Lord, "Woooo-wooop! You go, God! It's Your Birthday!" Corny, I know, but I had to say *something* to let Him know He was the Man.

Backtrack to the phone. Didn't want to sound too desperate. "Michael, is it okay if I give you a call by the end of the week?"

"Perfect," he agreed.

After the nasty attitude I wore when we worked together, I needed to show the man at least a little gratitude for such a huge favor. "Michael, thank you for thinking of me. This really means a lot."

"You're welcome. I look forward to hearing from you by Friday."

Nothing but praise came from my lips the rest of the morning.

A detective from the Dallas County Police Department called me to follow up on the case with Deniessa. "Ms. Miller, I understand you're pressing charges against Deniessa Rutherford. Normally, you would have received a letter in the mail from us by now, but there was some delay due to computer error." Next, she rattled off a message that she must have been reading from a script. "Our system has set a court date for August thirteenth at two-thirty. If you have any witnesses to call forth, please make sure they are present in court with you. If your witnesses are unable to attend, you may submit a sworn affidavit of their testimony. Do you understand?"

"Yes."

"Should you decide to drop the charges, you must notify the court no later than thirty days before the proceedings. Do you understand?"

"Yes."

She disconnected our call without a salutation. Poor woman, she must have called a hundred people already that morning. I grabbed a pen from my kitchen's junk drawer, flipped the calendar to August, and wrote "court—2:30" in the appropriate box. I couldn't wait to show the judge pictures of my jacked-up tooth so he could throw the book at her. I was hoping to pull in some background information about Phillip and the club, too. They want the *whole* truth, right? I would have my testimony ready *tight*.

LaShondra and I were getting back into the habit of going to the track, thanks to her upcoming summer break.

We rejoiced over the job offer, skipping arm-in-arm around a corner of the track like Charlie when he found the last of Willy Wonka's golden tickets.

"Whoo." I slowed down. "Girl, I'm out of breath. I've gotta get myself back together."

"Why you tellin'?" She panted, too.

We took the rest of our laps considerably slower, chatting as we had done in times past. Stelson was, of course, her topic of the day. He always traveled heavily during the summer months. "I'm going to have to come out of my newlywed bubble and get me a life when he's gone."

I couldn't have agreed more. "It's about time."

"Anyway." She rolled her eyes. "I'm taking a cake decorating class Saturday morning. You should stop by after twelve or so and see my first creation."

"You know I don't turn down cake. I will be there front and center, even if I have to drink a ton of water first so I won't overeat."

LaShondra inched her phone out of her front pocket and glanced down. Quickly, she shoved it back in.

"Who was that?"

"Nosy!" She shoved my arm.

"Please. Ain't nobody but Stelson."

"Actually"—she hesitated—"it was Deniessa."

"Mmmm." I stared straight ahead at the track before me, arms swinging in stride. "I hope she plans to be in court on August thirteenth."

"Well, actually . . . she was hoping you might drop the charges?" LaShondra queried.

"Is she crazy?"

LaShondra moaned, "I don't know."

"Look at my toof!" I opened wide and pointed at my jagged enamel. "I had to cancel a job interview and everything because of her."

"Yeah, but God had an even better job for you."

"Irrelevant." I dismissed her observation. "She can't just go around hitting people. That's wrong." I changed pace, pumping my arms faster.

LaShondra tagged along. "Peaches, you and I both know Deniessa is not a threat to society."

"She's got a mean right hook."

LaShondra snatched my arm, twirling me around to a dead stop. "Look, I really didn't want to have to tell you all her business, but you leave me no choice. Jamal left her. They've already repo'd her car, she's about to lose the house, and I know she's lost what little self-esteem she was renting. It would be really . . . gracious and merciful of you to drop the case right now."

"Am I supposed to feel sorry for her?"

"I hope you feel as sorry for her as everybody else, including God Himself, felt for you." That girl could turn a table in a heartbeat. "Deniessa probably deserves to get a fine or a record or whatever they give people for assault, but I'm begging you, as her friend and yours. Please don't give her what she deserves this time."

The moment those words left her lips, conviction hit me in the stomach and I heard the Holy Spirit whisper Hebrews 7:25 in my soul. . . . "he always lives to intercede . . ." La-Shondra's act mirrored what Christ does for me twenty-four seven, standing in the gap between me and judgment.

I took off walking again. Before long, I heard LaShondra's feet pounding. She was right and I knew it. Still, anger tugged at my tongue. Even if I did drop the charges, I wanted to wait until the last minute so Deniessa could sweat it out.

"So what are you going to do?" LaShondra asked from behind me.

"Not sure yet."

That was a lie. I couldn't deny the Holy Spirit's prompting.

LaShondra called me on it. "Yes, you are. I know you. You can't go through with this. Not after all God's done for you."

"So what if I am going to drop the charges. You don't have to go leak the news to Deniessa just yet."

"Why wouldn't I?"

I stopped and pivoted toward my friend. "Deniessa needs to learn a lesson."

LaShondra shook her head. "I can't believe this. Haven't *you* learned *your* lesson in all of this?"

"What are you talking about?"

"This whole disaster started because you knew what to do when Quinn was moving to Philadelphia, but you let your stubborn attitude keep you from acting on the right decision immediately. What's with these pride delays? All you're doing is creating unnecessary stress and strife. You ought to be sick of yourself by now."

She put both hands on her hips. I did the same. We faced off for a good ten seconds before I gave up. I smothered my best friend in a hug, thanking her for being just that—a friend who puts me in check when I need it. "Girl, you know can't nobody talk to me like that except you."

"I'm sure glad," she gasped. "The way you looked at me just now, I thought you and I were about to squab."

We both laughed and continued our course around the track.

"Don't worry. I don't fight people with glasses," I assured her.

"You'd have to catch me to fight me," she challenged.

"I'm too big to catch you, anyway." I acted like I wasn't game, but as soon as I was a step ahead of her, I dashed down the track.

"No, you didn't!" She laughed, chasing me down the path.

Chapter 35

Michael didn't have to wait until Friday. I called him back Thursday and accepted the offer.

"Great," he cheered. "You can start Monday."

Great didn't begin to describe this miracle. Seriously, how do you get fired by somebody and then get rehired by that same person, in the middle of a terrible economy, with a 10 percent raise only three months after they led you to the slaughterhouse? This marvel had G-O-D written all over it.

Michael gave me a few directives about my first day. I carefully wrote them down and then ended our call. *Thank You, Lord!* For safekeeping, I decided to keep the notes right next to me in my nightstand. When I opened the drawer, the ugly pictures of my banged-up face stared at me. This part of my life was over. My next call was to the Dallas County Police Department to drop the charges against Deniessa. Turns out it's not so simple to drop cases these days. I'd have to go into the station and fill out an affidavit, but that was okay. I was riding too high on God's mercy to question my resolve.

I picked up my mother so she could come celebrate big-time Friday night with Eric and me. I figured it was as good a time as any to get the third degree from her about the tooth and my weight. Maybe now that I had a job, I could take it.

She entered my car, took one good look at me, and re-marked, "Peaches, it's time for you to draw the line on those hips of yours." This advice from a woman whom I've never known to pass up an extra helping of mashed potatoes.

Might as well beat her to the punch on the next issue. I raised my top lip with my index finger. "Look. I've got a chipped tooth, too."

"Hush your mouth! You sure do. Lord, it's a good thing you got this job sight unseen. What happened to you?"

"It's a long story."

She shooed my words away with her hand. "Something tells me I don't even want to know what happened."

Thank God!

I decided we should graduate to GameEvent, a combina-tion arcade, bowling alley, and restaurant. Loud music and pins clashing on the wooden floors filled the atmosphere. When I looked around at the patrons, it was clear that Eric fit in more with this group than the crowd at Pizza Kingdom. My baby was growing up.

Laser tag, one of the main attractions, found Eric and me on opposite teams. Eric's team whipped up on mine. He even had more points than me at the end of the match.

"Now I got you!" he bragged all the way back to our table.

I sat down and caught my breath. "Next time, son, next time."

He grabbed a hand full of tokens from the plastic cup my mother was guarding and ran off to play more games, leaving her and me alone at our booth.

She smiled at me, searching my face for a reaction.

"Yes?"

"Eric sure misses you."

"I miss him, too. And I thank you for stepping in to help with him." I tiptoed around my desire to resume the full-time job of parenting my son. "I'm sure ready for school to end. I think I'll have lots of flexibility with this new job, so Eric and I should be able to spend lots of time together. LaShondra gave me some reading tips—"

"When you gonna start coming back to church?" she poked.

I shook my head. "I don't know. I guess whenever I'm ready."

"Ready for what?"

"I don't want to hear people's mouths. 'Where you been, little sister Miller?' 'Sure been missing you.' "

"Aw, girl, please." She waved me off. "Folks ain't studyin' you. That's a trick of the enemy." She pushed a stray hair behind her ear and turned to watch a random bowling game.

I watched her face go from passive to pensive. She wanted to say more, I was sure, but she wouldn't. Just like she used to do with Daddy. She'd sit there and say absolutely nothing while Daddy ranted about a cup that wasn't washed properly or scratchy sheets. He'd go off over little stuff and she'd sit there biting her tongue.

"I hate it when you do this." Try as I might, I couldn't hide the resentment in my voice.

Slowly, she faced me. Her brow arched and rounded. "When I do what?"

"When you refuse to speak up for yourself."

"I speak up for myself plenty fine, thank you very much."

"No, you don't. You never stood up for yourself when Daddy was alive." I struggled to keep a lid on the rage piping within me. "And when he died, he left you clueless about how to handle things."

My mother looked me up and down a few times. "Is that what's been bothering you?"

"Yes. It bothers me."

"Peaches, I'ma tell you like this. I had my part, your daddy had his part. I didn't know how to pay bills on the computer, he didn't know how to separate laundry. We were a team, like married folks ought to be. So he died and now I have to learn things and ask for help. I'm okay with it. Unlike you, I wasn't tryin' to be every woman," she spat out. Then she added for good measure, "That's why you're single now."

I knew it was coming and, of course, I had a reply ready on my lips. "And I'll stay single if it means I can't express my feelings."

"You're right about that," she agreed sarcastically. "You will most definitely continue to be by yourself until you understand how to pick your battles with a man. Everything ain't worth arguing over, and some things ain't gon' change whether you spend two days fussing at him or not. By the time me and your daddy had you, I'd figured that out already."

"So . . . you had given up on letting Daddy know how you felt about things?" I surmised.

"The other part of picking battles is knowing when and where to fight them. Just 'cause I didn't buck up to your daddy in front of you don't mean I didn't have my say. Your daddy could be downright stubborn and prideful, just like somebody I know." She winked at me. "But believe me when I tell you, I had his ear."

My last Saturday before starting my new job, Eric and I spent the whole day together. He seemed perfectly content to follow me around the house like a puppy. While I laced my shoes, he sat on my bed harmlessly tinkering with the trinkets on my nightstand. A twang of guilt stung me as I wondered if he was trying to refamiliarize himself with our home.

"Thank You for your redemption, Holy Spirit," I whispered under my breath.

"Momma, who gave you a black eye?" Eric held the pictures of my battered face in his hands.

I snatched the evidence from him, ripped the pictures to pieces, and tossed them into the trash. "Stay out of my stuff, son."

He followed me to my bathroom. Eric's little face appeared at the bottom of the mirror. "Who did it, Momma? Tell me so I can go bust 'em up."

"You will not be bustin' up anything except a book, okay?" I shooed him away. "Go make sure your room is clean."

"Did you have to go to the hospital?" he persisted, worry hovering between his brows.

There was no escaping this line of questioning. Plus I supposed he deserved some kind of explanation after having encountered disturbing photos of my injuries. "I had a disagreement with someone. That person hit me—"

He slapped his right fist into his left palm. "Did you hit 'em back?"

"No, I did not hit that person back. I protected my head until someone else came and pulled the person off me."

Eric jumped to his feet, kicking wildly. "Man, I wish I would have been there. I would have came out like Kung Fu Panda and done a super-dropkick on 'em, then I would have—"

"That's enough, Eric. The police arrested the person. It's over now, okay? And don't go tellin' your granny I had a black eye."

With the issue settled, we headed out for a healthy breakfast of fruit smoothies. Then I logged a few miles at the track while Eric played on the playground. Coincidentally, the same little red-haired boy was there again with his mother. I remembered the last time we were all there. I was just about to embark on that stupid replay of a relationship with Raphael. In retrospect, I have to admit that I knew it wouldn't work all along. He hadn't changed.

Raphael wasn't thinking about changing, and it was stupid of me to try to "wish" him right. Leopards don't change their spots, because they can't change their own spots. Any time a leopard wants his spots changed, he has to go back to the Creator and ask for new skin. Christ being that skin, of course.

Even though Raphael wasn't right for me, I still held out hope that, someday, he would be right for Eric and this other child who was on the way. I resolved to pray earnestly for Raphael forever. Well, at least until my son was eighteen years old. Somebody needed to pray for that man.

After my jog, we came home and cleaned up a bit before going to LaShondra's house to get a look at her debut cake. She displayed it proudly in a covered glass dish. Eric said it was pretty except for the pink roses, which leaned to the right a bit.

"My teacher said I relied too much on sight rather than instinct. I have to become one with the icing," she sang, and dipped in a traditional Chinese bow.

"Girl, if you don't get a knife and cut this thing."

Eric ate enough for both of us. "This is good, Auntie Shon." My poor child was a little piglet! I thought about scolding him, but the Holy Spirit checked me, told me to wait until we got home to talk with him about acting so greedy.

My lips clamped shut as he munched away. I sensed the Spirit smiling inside me. I sat there thinking, "It's a beautiful thing when the Holy Spirit speaks and I actually listen." He agreed, reminding me of 1 Thessalonians 5:19. "Do not quench the Spirit."

Although the extent of LaShondra's involvement with the cake was decorating, she gladly accepted Eric's voracity as a compliment. "Maybe I'll make you a cake for your birthday next year."

Eric swallowed quickly. "When you have a son, he's gonna really like this cake for his birthday."

LaShondra smiled and rubbed a hand across Eric's hand. "I receive that word, Eric, in the name of Jesus."

A trip to the movies rounded out the rest of our day. Since this was the first weekend my mother had been without Eric, I don't think she knew what to do with herself. She called us twice during the show to see if we planned to drop by her house later.

"Momma, I'm pooped. I think we're gonna go on home," I whispered so I wouldn't disturb the other viewers.

"Well . . . I was just wondering. He left so many clothes over here, he probably ain't got enough socks to make it through the week at home."

No doubt, the light from my phone was probably annoying the people above me. I had to satisfy her or this was going to be a long conversation. "We'll come by on our way home."

I should have known my mother would be waiting with a church trap. After she smothered Eric with hugs and kisses, she loaded my car with three grocery bags full of his clothes. Collecting his belongings was a sweet reminder that Eric lived with me again, where he belonged.

"Thanks again, Momma, for everything."

She straightened up, squared off with me while Eric buckled himself into his seat. "When you coming back to church, Peaches?"

The million-dollar question. "Soon." I put one foot inside my car.

She breathed heavily. Bit her bottom lip. "If you won't go for yourself, at least go for Eric. There's too much happening on out here in the world. He can't afford to be without knowledge of the Word of God, 'cause the enemy is startin' early on these kids today. He ain't waitin' like he used to."

That night, I watched the news and saw my mother's

warning illustrated. A local thirteen-year-old girl was found dead after sneaking out of the house to meet her online boyfriend. Her friends said she thought he was fourteen. He turned out to be twenty-four and a pedophile. The mother's face twisted in anguish as she displayed pictures of her daughter taken just a few months earlier. Beautiful, sweet little girl. "He tricked our daughter," was all the girl's mother could say before grief seized her ability to speak.

I remembered how gullible I was at thirteen. Shoot, I was fooled by the enemy at age thirty-four. It's like you think you have to look out for one thing, but the enemy attacks you from a whole different direction. The least I could do was gird Eric up with the Word, have him write the scriptures on his heart, and get some more saints praying for him on a regular basis.

He had prayer warriors covering him at my mother's church because my mother was a long-standing member of New Zion. The members at *our* home church, however, knew Eric by name because of his involvement with Sunday school. When Quinn and I were an item, he saw to it Eric was one of the first students in class every week. He helped my son memorize verses to make sure he was ready for class. Come to think of it, maybe that's how Eric had slipped under the reading radar. Quinn worked with him so much, it was hard to tell Eric had a problem.

My mother was right about the whole church thing. I was planning to get back to church soon, but to be honest, I rather enjoyed the growth I was experience in the five-thirty club. Felt like I had Jesus all to myself. A honeymoon phase of sorts. Alas, there's the rest of the world to deal with.

I turned off the television, kissed Jesus good night, and told him I was coming to His house tomorrow. I do believe He kissed me back.

Chapter 36

Eric used the alarm clock my mother had given him to beat me getting up for church Sunday morning. He'd dressed himself in a navy blue shirt with black slacks. The brown belt and shoes didn't quite match, in my opinion, but he was decent. One thing Quinn had taught me about raising a son was to resist questioning his every move.

I wondered what else Quinn might be able to tell me about raising Eric, but it appeared I was on my own now. Before Quinn came along, my oldest brother, Cedrick, filled the role of father for my son. I knew early on that I'd need outside help with Eric, because that boy had only two speeds—on and off—when he was a toddler. I saw firsthand the power of a male presence. Cedrick could say "stop," and that would put an end to Eric's mischief. I, on the other hand, had to sometimes physically work at securing Eric's obedience.

And I sure couldn't teach him how to go to the restroom.

Unfortunately for Eric, Cedrick's work in the banking field sent him and his family globetrotting every five or six years. When they packed up and moved to California, I wondered who would fill that void in Eric's life, because Raphael certainly wasn't up to the challenge.

Right about then, I met Quinn.

"Stop," I said to myself in the dresser mirror. Although our relationship blossomed at Dallas Christian Fellowship Church, I had to be able to set foot inside again without beating myself up over Quinn. I gave myself a pep talk. "Quinn doesn't even attend DCF anymore. He's got a new life and a new church family in Philadelphia. He'll always be the one that got away. Get over it."

Granted, if I had it to do all over again, I probably would have been in Philadelphia at the moment. Too bad we can't push a big "rewind" button on life. Not that I wanted to. Despite all the drama in recent months, the outcome was worth every moment. I was closer to God than I had ever been before. I knew Him not just with my head or because I knew a verse or because I'd been to church all my life. Christ revealed Himself to me in my circumstances. I knew Him as my personal redeemer who's up at 5:30 AM filling me with His presence and wisdom.

I'm not saying God caused those bad things to happen to me. I think we both know—if I had listened to the Holy Spirit in the first place, He could have been just as faithful *keeping* me as He was with *rescuing* me. God can reveal Himself to us the easy way or the hard way. I chose the hard way this time, but with the help of the Holy Spirit, never again! I didn't want any more reconfigured paths. Point A to point B would be just fine for me.

Point B this stormy morning was my church. I escorted Eric to his class, where he was greeted like a celebrity. Sister Evans gave Eric a gold star to stick on the attendance chart. My poor baby had a big row of starless boxes due to his consecutive absences. But when he put the star on this Sunday's box, Sister Evans announced, "Alrighty, Eric, you've got your next star! You only need three more to earn another Bible buck." He picked up right where he left off, despite the delay.

During the congregational worship portion of service in the main sanctuary, I thanked God for protecting my son through my detour. Then, when the women's praise team came forth, I seriously broke down as the songstresses sang The Clark Sisters' "Blessed & Highly Favored." I held my hands toward the sky and poured out my heart in gratitude. *It could have been, should have been, and would have been me if it wasn't for the blood.*

I was nothing but mush afterward. Every time somebody so much as said "amen" I melted in humility.

Though our church was high-tech with big screens and digital announcements, we still collected offering the old-fashioned way. The choir sang softly as we filed around the offeratory table. Several rows ahead of me, I peeped a tall male figure. Reminded me of Quinn, from behind.

Still high in the Spirit, I turned my attention back to the words of the familiar tune in progress. "This is the day, this is the day that the Lord hath made," I mouthed slightly as the ushers guided the first person on each row toward the baskets. Giving to the ministry made my heart even lighter. I couldn't wait to start tithing again when I got my first paycheck.

Pastor preached a word on digging ditches, referring to 2 Kings chapter 3 verses 14 to 20. "Some of you need to start digging ditches," he ordered. "You've been in a dry place for a while and God's getting ready to do something mighty. He's about to bring water in a way that you couldn't have imagined, and He's going to fill whatever space you have carved out for Him—starting with you."

He charged us all to add ten minutes to our daily prayer for the next thirty days. Following his message, Pastor extended the invitation, and members of the Discipleship team prayed with four people who had come forward to accept Christ. I prayed from my seat that God would create a hunger and thirst for the Word within them and never let them stray from His shadow.

Deacon Williams dismissed service and the usual hum of conversation followed. Brother Johnson, the singles Bible Study leader whom I'd spent many hours with in study, approached me in the foyer. "Sister Miller, so good to see you. We've missed you in class."

"I've missed your teachings, too." Seriously, Brother Johnson could cut the Word up and sew it back together again.

Brother Johnson and I pressed in closer so we could talk and keep in step with the crowd flowing outdoors.

"Did you see . . . Brother Robertson?" he fished.

I threw in my rod, too. "Wh . . . what?"

"Yes, Brother Quinn was in service today. I thought maybe you two were . . . friends again."

That *was* Quinn! "No. I haven't talked to him in a while."

"I know. Prayed with Brother Quinn many a night about the breakup. I was only wondering if you two had made peace with each other. It's always best to get closure when you can."

"Thank you, Brother Johnson. I'll be in class again on Tuesday."

"Mighty fine."

Perspiration built under my pits. My entire body buzzed. Where was Quinn? I just knew the moment I saw him my knees would buckle. He must have seen me—I went around the offering table in full view. Then it occurred to me: Maybe he did see me, he just didn't have anything to say to me. Maybe he was already gone, headed back to the airport even. A negative murmur nagged in my mind, "He probably got a look at your big butt and thanked God he got out before you blew up."

My throat tightened and tears pooled in my eyes. I tried to blink them back before I got to Eric's class. My head whispered to my heart: *Life goes on.* My heart wasn't listening. I had to stop and collect myself in the restroom. Standing in the stall, I called on the Holy Spirit to help me through this heartbreaking episode. I could understand my reaction if this had been a few months ago, but now? "God, this is crazy."

Toilet tissue in hand, I finally emerged from the restroom and rushed to get Eric. Signing him out was my last task at the church, thankfully. Sunshine greeted me us as we walked outside the church doors. Everything shined like brand new, given the morning's rain. While my head was down, searching my purse for keys, Eric took off running through the parking lot. "Eric!" He knew better.

I glanced ahead to see what had caused him to lose his ever-loving mind. When I saw the prize, I almost lost mine, too. Quinn stood next to my car, his arms ready for Eric's embrace. My son rushed into Quinn.

"Hey, Buddy." Quinn squealed almost as loudly as Eric. Their reunion was ecstatic, YouTube worthy. I wished I could run up on a brother, too. All that chocolate hotness I threw away. Shame on me.

I approached cautiously. Positioned my lip to cover the chipped tooth. "Hi."

"Hi."

"Oh! I forgot my Bible," Eric announced. "Don't leave, Mr. Quinn. I'll be right back."

"Slow down, Eric."

He obeyed me slightly.

"It's good to see you," Quinn started.

"Same here. How have you been?"

A tentative smile graced his face. "Okay. Getting adjusted. What have you been up to?"

I wanted to spew my soul out to him and tell him how miserable things had been since he left, but that's not how the game is played. If I told him the truth, he might . . . *listen?* I'd already lost everything I could lose with Quinn. The worst thing he could say is, "I told you so," and I'd already said that to myself a million times. What difference would it make coming from him?

Still waiting patiently for my response, Quinn's smile faded.

I laughed slightly and gave a quick, truthful summary. "My life fell apart. But God restored me. I'm good."

"LaShondra told me about your job. Are . . . are you and Eric okay?"

I nodded quickly. "Oh, yes. I'm starting a new job tomorrow. And I get to telecommute, too."

"Really?" His face lit up.

"Yeah. It'll give me a lot more time with Eric. And with God. He's totally revamping me. It's amazing." Hope sprang up as I begin to think about God's work in me and how far he'd brought me. "I am sooo not the woman I used to be, thanks to God."

Quinn concurred, "I've learned a lot, too."

My flirty eyes raked over his. "And I know you were keeping tabs on me through LaShondra, thank you very much."

He laughed. "Aw, you caught me."

I focused on my feet again, still trying to hide the tooth, among other things. "No, I really *do* mean thank you very much for praying for me."

"Always."

My ears probably stood up like a dog's. *Did he just say always?* I looked into my long-lost baby's eyes and read the love. One of us needed to just come out and say it. If I was going down, let me go down swinging the truth. "I still love you, Quinn. And I'm sorry about everything. I mean, I still don't agree with everything you did, but we should have worked through—"

He hushed my blabbering with a kiss.

I forgot about the tooth and everything else that was

wrong with me and focused on what was right. God. Quinn.
Me.

I settled back down on my heels. "Quinn, so much has
happened. I—"

"I really don't care what's happened since the last time I
saw you. My life hasn't been so great, either. Let's just write it
all off like a bad debt and start over."

I looked into his face and cheesed big time.

Quinn's facial muscles twitched and his eyes, probably instinctively, focused on my chops.

To relieve him of potential embarrassment for gawking, I
blubbered, "I know, baby. I'ma get that fixed."

He shook his head. "I love you."

"I love you, too."

Epilogue

Six Months Later

Philadelphia is beautiful in the winter. Some of Pennsylvania's oldest buildings strike postcard-perfect poses in the snow. No outdoor workouts for me. I invested in a few workout videos, and Eric, of course, can't get enough of this winter wonderland. He and Quinn made a full snowman family—mom, dad, and child draped in old hats and scarves—in front of the house we're renting until my credit score climbs back within a decent range.

God might have forgiven me instantly, but FICO didn't. Neither did Deniessa. According to LaShondra, Deniessa blames me for her impending divorce. LaShondra won't tell me much more except to say the friendship between the two of them is going through major changes.

"One thing I learned through this drama with you," she recalled during one of our cross-country girlfriend chats, "is when people aren't ready to change, I need to step back, pray, and let them fall directly into the hands of God."

I can't say whether I want to befriend Deniessa again. Might be kind of hard to break bread with somebody who cost me hundreds of dollars in dental work. Our friendship will only be rekindled under the express direction of the Holy Spirit. Otherwise, I'm closing that chapter in my life.

The chapter I'd like to reopen is the one with Natasha. I wrote her a few letters. She responded with short notes I imagine she scribbled when her newly acquired roommate (none other than Orlene) wasn't looking. Still, Natasha is responding to my outreach, and I continue to be thankful for the door God leaves open to her heart. I suppose I'll have to take LaShondra's words to heart—step back, pray, and let God do His thing in His time, trusting that His grace is sufficient.

Work is awesome—70 percent of the time. The other 30 percent, I'm flying back to Dallas handling business that can't be conducted remotely. As much as possible, I try to take Eric back with me so he can spend time with my mother. She communicates with Cheryl to organize meetings with Raphael and Eric's new little sister, Aisha. The baby was born several weeks early and had to remain in the hospital for quite some time. I think Cheryl and my mother formed a bond in praying for baby Aisha, which has made their interactions quite friendly and productive, according to Momma. Sometimes it's almost weird how God works things out.

"Ain't nothin' wrong with Cheryl except Raphael," Momma told me once. "But I'm still prayin' for him, too, so he can be a good daddy to Eric and Aisha."

And, speaking of babies, I've got to get busy making arrangements during my next trip to Dallas. LaShondra and Stelson are expecting my godson, and I'm in charge of the shower, which, if LaShondra has her way, will be nothing short of a praise party. And I'll just stand there right next to her and say, "Go on, girl. Praise Him!"

LAST TEMPTATION

Michelle Stimpson

ABOUT THIS GUIDE

The suggested questions that follow
are included to enhance your group's
reading of this book.

DISCUSSION QUESTIONS

1. In the beginning of the book, Peaches is excited about getting married. But then she begins to reconsider after Quinn brings up Philadelphia. Do you think Peaches had good reason to reconsider? What would you have done in her situation?

2 At work, Peaches wears a stone-faced mask, but at home, she melts down (Chapter 3) from the pressure. Do you wear different masks in different settings? How is it working out for you?

3. Peaches says she doesn't want to pray because she doesn't think she will like what God tells her to do. Have you ever felt that way? Share what happened.

4. By Chapter 4, Peaches has begun to take out some of her frustrations on Michael Yancey. Have you ever mistreated someone out of frustration? How did that turn out?

5. At one point, Peaches feels as though everyone is trying to run her life. Do you agree with her? Have you ever felt that way? How did you respond?

6. One of Peaches's biggest fears is losing herself after she gets married. She doesn't want to be like her mother—dependent upon a man. Can a woman be *too* independent? Does independence interfere with interdependence in marriage? Is Peaches being too hard on her mother, given the generation gap?

7. Throughout the novel, Peaches struggles with thoughts about her ever-expanding waistline. Could you relate to her struggle? How was this struggle connected to what was happening in her life?

8. Peaches feels guilty for not recognizing her son's learning disability, which leads to some bad decisions about her relationship with Raphael. If you are a parent, could you relate to Peaches's guilt? How do guilt and shame propel bad decisions?

9. Quinn decided he had to move on without Peaches. Do you think his decision was harsh, or was he perfectly justified? Have you ever had to move on without someone you loved?

10. Raphael says he realizes that Peaches was the best thing that happened to him. Do you think Raphael meant what he said? Are people more attractive when they're off-limits?

11. Do you think Peaches needed to go through that last temptation with Raphael to get him out of her system for good? Why or why not?

12. At some level, Peaches always doubted the rekindled relationship with Raphael. Have you ever gone through with something even though you knew from the beginning it wasn't the right thing to do?

13. Peaches says, "The bad thing about a good friend is, they won't give up on you." Do you agree? Did LaShondra overstep her boundaries when she showed up unannounced at Peaches's home? Have your friends ever done an intervention on you?

14. While Peaches is busy running from the Lord, she attends a church that she believes will not challenge her spiritually. Are you spiritually challenged at your church? How can one recognize a cult?

15. Peaches feels, "Everyone is against me. My mom, my friends, Raphael, the school system. Even God, probably. Or Karma put out a hit on me." Does this agree with God's Word? Have you ever felt this way? In retrospect, were your feelings true?

16. When Peaches finally returns to God, she lays out before the Lord and puts her "nose to the carpet" in repentance. What finally brought her to that point? Do you think some people have to be laid out flat before they can look up to see God? How did this scene affect you?

17. Despite Peaches's initial attitude problem, Michael Yancey still wants Peaches on his team and graciously offers her a contract. Have you ever been given an opportunity you didn't deserve? How did you respond?

18. Peaches wants to keep in touch with Natasha, but not with Deniessa. Do you agree with her decision? Is it okay to make a conscious decision to keep some friendships and not others? Have you ever ended a friendship? Under what circumstances?

19. What do you think Peaches and Quinn learned during their time apart? How can God use these lessons to strengthen their marriage?

A CONVERSATION WITH THE AUTHOR

How did the idea for Last Temptation *come to you?*

This book was kind of different for me because usually I write from my own firsthand experience. But what happened with *Last Temptation* was that in about an eighteen-month time frame, I had two friends who just dropped off the radar. They stopped returning calls, e-mails, texts—and I thought I had done something wrong! But then I started talking to other mutual friends and discovered that the MIAs weren't contacting anyone, not just me. As time went on and my two friends eventually came around, I was fascinated by what they shared with me—the isolation and embarrassment they felt, and how much they wanted to reach out but felt they couldn't. The situations also caused me to rethink how to intercede for a friend who is going through a rough time.

Rumor has been circling through the grapevine that you didn't want to write another book with LaShondra and Stelson. What happened to change your mind?

LOL! When I finished *Boaz Brown,* I was so tired of LaShondra and Stelson I didn't think I could write anything else about them. But over the years, I started to miss them—and I especially missed Peaches. *Last Temptation* was my way of winking at LaShondra and Stelson again while hooking up again with a character, Peaches, whom I really wanted to know more about.

It has been said that writing a full-length novel in first person is extremely difficult. Do you agree?

I don't find it difficult because I've been keeping a diary for decades, so writing in first person is actually my default mode. Plus, when I really connect with a character, it's hard for me to stay out of first person.

So you connect with Peaches?

Peaches is me on a bad day. Thankfully, I don't have many bad days. I've been trying to get the term "go off on somebody" out of my vocabulary, but every now and then . . .

What's up with the WordWatches?

In 2006, I started looking for ways to keep the Word of God literally on my hands so that I could meditate on what God says versus what the enemy says. Over the years I crafted several prototypes and finally came up with something that was durable and visible enough to fit on my wrist. This practice literally changed my life. Then I started making them for friends who needed encouragement in the Word (because, really, God's Word is all we really have for sure). Then, in early 2010, I launched WordWatch.net (based on Deuteronomy 11:18, *"Fix these words of mine in your hearts and minds; tie them as symbols on your hands . . ."*) to share the power of keeping scriptures and godly affirmations at hand.

What are you working on now?

I think the better question would be, what am I *not* working on now? Of course I'm working on my next book (yet to be titled). I'm also working on getting my kids out of the house and wondering what I'm going to do with this crazy dog when my son leaves for college.

Don't miss Vanessa Davis Griggs's
newest novel of faith and resilience:

RAY OF HOPE

In stores January 2011

Here's an excerpt from *Ray of Hope*. . . .

Chapter 1

There shall not any man be able to stand before thee all the days of thy life: as I was with Moses, so I will be with thee: I will not fail thee, nor forsake thee.

—Joshua 1:5

Rayna "Ma Ray" Towers had fallen asleep on the couch in the den. She'd called herself staying up to watch *The Tonight Show,* but in the end, it appeared some other show—muted—was watching her. Still, at age seventy-five, Ma Ray's senses were keen. That's why she heard sounds of someone breaking in. A few folks she personally knew had had their homes broken into just this year alone. Her granddaughters, Sahara and Crystal Nichols, were staying with her for the summer. Ma Ray quickly got up and went to the hall closet, where she kept a twelve-gauge, double-barrel shotgun. She quietly loaded it.

A man who appeared to be around eighteen years old, dressed in washed-out blue jeans and a black Sean John shirt, started up the stairs. She pointed the barrel, then pulled back the hammer of the gun, causing it to make a metallic clicking sound. "Freeze," she said. "Don't take another step. Put your hands up or I promise I'll blow you away!"

Six steps up, the young man stopped and raised his hands.

"Lady, please don't shoot." He glanced back, looking like a deer caught in headlights. "Please put that down."

Ma Ray glanced out of the side of her eyes toward the table with the telephone on it. She needed to call the police at this point while making sure he didn't somehow manage to escape. "Turn around . . . slowly," she said, repeating what most people associate with a good law-and-order type show.

Standing at five foot five in her stocking bare feet, a blue flowered cotton nightgown, and a baby blue satin scarf wrapped around her roller-filled head, Ma Ray raised the twelve-gauge shotgun even higher, aiming it squarely at the young man's scrawny chest. A woman who had shot her share of snakes, Ma Ray wanted to be sure that, should she have a need to pull the trigger, she wouldn't miss this target, either.

The young man raised his trembling hands higher. "Lady, are you crazy?" he said. "Look," he said, sweating so hard Ma Ray could now see clear beads forming on his forehead before a few drops began to slowly make their way down his face. "If you'll just put that thing down"—he nodded toward the gun—"I'm sure we can straighten all of this out in no time. I know we can."

"Ma Ray, don't hurt him," seventeen-year-old Sahara said as she ran and stood at the top of the stairs dressed in light blue skinny jeans and a see-through, black laced shirt. "Please, don't hurt him."

"See, lady," the young man said. "I'm not here to hurt nobody. Listen to Sahara. Listen to your granddaughter"—he began to stutter—"sh-sh-she'll vouch for me." He glanced up at Sahara as though he were now mentally pleading for her to fully back him up. "Sahara was the one who told me to come here like this. Tell her, Sahara."

"Ma Ray, please . . . just put the gun down." Sahara walked toward the intruder.

"Yeah, Ma Ray. *Please* put the gun down." The young

man pleaded with his hands still in the air. "This is all just one big misunderstanding. You'll see."

Ma Ray motioned with the barrel of the gun for him to step down to the floor; he obeyed. Lowering the barrel of the gun, she pointed it at the floor. Cautiously, he lowered his hands. Sahara made her way to the bottom step, looked at Ma Ray, and stopped.

"What's your name?" Ma Ray asked him.

His voice squeaked when he spoke. "B-Man." Then again, but stronger. "B-Man."

Ma Ray lifted the gun back up slightly, pointing at his shoes.

"Bradley," he said hastily—his eyes fixed on the long, steel barrel of the shotgun. "But everybody calls me B-Man."

Ma Ray lowered the gun again. "Bradley, huh? And did you happen to come with a last name?"

"It's Crenshaw . . . Bradley Crenshaw."

"I take it you're not from around these parts," Ma Ray said.

"No."

"*No?*" she said, clearly indicating she had a problem with this answer.

"No, ma'am," Sahara hurriedly added, looking at her friend to clearly let him know he didn't need to do anything more at this point to provoke her grandmother.

"I'm talking to him," Ma Ray said, nodding at Bradley.

"No, ma'am," he said. "I live more in the city."

"You said that like you have a problem with the country or something." Ma Ray tapped the gun several times with her trigger finger.

"No. I mean, no, ma'am. I was just saying that I live more in the city, that's all, ma'am. That's all I was saying." His voice sounded like he was on the verge of tears.

"So why are you so far from home this time of night?" Ma Ray asked him.

"I-I-I was bringing something to Sahara."

"Is that right?"

"Yes, ma'am."

"Something that couldn't wait for a decent hour? It must be good, then. So you can give me what you came to give Sahara." Ma Ray took a step toward him.

His eyes widened. "Ma'am?"

"I said you can give *me* what you came here to give Sahara." She glanced down, peering over her wire-rimmed glasses. "And will you *please* pull your pants up! Walking around with your pants hanging down like that. I tell you that just don't make no sense, no sense at all," Ma Ray said.

He quickly grabbed his pants by the waistband and pulled them up.

Ma Ray nodded as she watched him hold up his pants to keep them from falling down again. "You need on a belt. Or maybe you should buy pants the right size to begin with. Okay, Mister Man . . . now give me what you came to give my granddaughter."

"But-but—"

"But-but nothing." She raised the shotgun once again, pointing its barrel at the hardwood floor in front of him instead of directly *at* him.

He quickly looked down at the gun, then back into her face. "Ma'am, I'm sorry for having come up in your house like this. I promise you I am."

"The correct terminology is breaking and entering. And honestly, by right, were I to have felt me or my family's life were in danger whatsoever, I would have been well within my legal rights to have shot you on sight, no questions asked, with my actions most certainly to be ruled as justified."

"Yes, ma'am. And I really am sorry, Ms. . . . Ma Ray . . . ma'am. Now if you don't mind, may I go? I really need to be getting home. All of a sudden, I don't feel so well." The look on his face said it all.

"It depends"—Ma Ray lowered the gun and softly put the hammer back in place, taking it off ready—"on whether you intend to do anything like this again."

"Ms. Ray . . . Ma Ray, ma'am, I promise you: After I leave here, you won't *ever* have to worry about seeing my face in your house without your permission again. *Ever.*"

Ma Ray nodded. "Then I suppose you can go." She went to the front door, opened it, and escorted him out. "Let me give you some advice. You need to do something more constructive with your life. You got off this time. But the next time, you might not be so lucky. And I'm not talking about with just me. Bradley, folks don't play now and days. And ending up dead is nothing to play with. It's not like the movies or those video games y'all play where you press a *replay* button and start all over as though nothing has happened. Now, you chew on what almost happened and on what I just said."

"Yes, ma'am. And thank you, ma'am." Bradley stumbled off the wraparound wooden porch, stopping and throwing up in Ma Ray's beautiful flower garden. Holding up his pants, he jogged down the road where he'd left his car without once looking back.

Ma Ray walked into the house, unloaded the shells from the shotgun, and safely put it back in the closet. Fifteen-year-old Crystal now stood in the den next to her sister.

"Ma Ray—" Sahara said as she stood as still as a framed scene on pause.

"You and I will talk in the morning," Ma Ray said as she started to her bedroom.

"But, Ma Ray—"

Ma Ray stopped without turning around. "I said, we'll talk in the daylight."

Chapter 2

Only be thou strong and very courageous, that thou mayest observe to do according to all the law, which Moses my servant commanded thee: turn not from it to the right hand or to the left, that thou mayest prosper withersoever thou goest.

—Joshua 1:7

"Ma, Sahara called me a little after two o'clock this morning crying, saying that you pulled a gun . . . a gun on one of her little friends," thirty-eight-year-old Lenora Nichols Stanford said to Ma Ray as soon as her mother answered. "I started to call you after I hung up with her, but it was so late that I didn't want to wake you. Ma, you know you can't go around pulling guns on people like that. You can't."

"And a top of the morning to you, too, daughter," Ma Ray said.

"I'm sorry. Good morning, Ma. But did you hear what I said?"

"Oh, I heard you just fine. And for the record: When you're an old woman who lives in the country alone, it's perfectly okay to pull a shotgun on someone when that someone happens to be illegally breaking into your house."

"*What?*"

"Oh, I guess Sahara left that little part out. And you didn't happen to put two and two together—the fact that she called you after two in the morning," Ma Ray said. "Well, that little 'friend' of hers broke into my house. But then again, in my defense, when I saw him sneaking up the stairs like some cat burglar, I didn't know he was Sahara's friend. I just knew someone had come into my house, uninvited, and whoever that person was, as far as *I* was concerned, they were a threat. And since I'd specifically told both Sahara and Crystal when they got here that there would be none of that sneaking out or anyone in while they were staying here, I could only *assume* we were in danger from an intruder. I mentioned to you some months back we've had a few break-ins around here."

"I don't know, Ma. Maybe I made the wrong decision to let them come and stay with you for the summer," Lenora said. "Perhaps I should come and get them and see if their having been with you this week hasn't shown them that I'm serious about them straightening up and acting right."

"Lenora, who was the one that called here hollering and crying about how out of control Sahara and Crystal are? I believe your exact words were, 'Ma, I can't take this anymore! I'm about two seconds away from either strangling them or shipping them off to a boot camp somewhere.' That *was* you, was it not?"

"Yes, it was me. I admit that when I called I was having a really bad day, a *really* bad day."

"And I told you then, and I'm telling you now: I believe I can handle a seventeen-year-old and a fifteen-year-old just fine. I raised you and your brother all right, didn't I?"

"But let's be real: You were younger then. And Daddy was there to help you. Children are different these days. Some of the things they do are totally unexplainable. After I told Sahara and Crystal they would be going to your house to stay for a little while, I overheard Sahara asking Crystal what you could do that someone half your age couldn't." Lenora purposely left out the part Sahara had said about Lenora having a college degree, where their grandmother did not.

"I'll tell you what. For the time being, you worry about taking care of Kyle and Nia and leave your other two children to me, at least for the rest of the summer. We'll be fine. Between me and God, we're going to work this out. And you know how much I love Sahara and Crystal."

"And they love you, too, Ma. They love you a lot. But I keep telling you that teenagers are different now. They're not as respectful as we were back in our day. There's a lot more peer pressure on them. Sure, there were things I had to deal with when I was growing up, but it's nowhere near the level that these kids deal with these days," Lenora said.

"Yeah, well. I'll give them that much. They do have things neither you nor I had to deal with when we were coming up. At least, not in the exact same vein. But you know what I always say."

"Yeah, Ma, I know. 'There's nothing new under the sun.' I know. But I feel bad that I can't control my own children any better than I've been able to." Lenora began to cry a little. "Let's face it: I'm an awful mother."

"You're not an awful mother."

"Okay, then. I'm a terrible daughter. I mean, what kind of a daughter pushes her delinquent-acting children off on their senior citizen mother?"

"You're not an awful mother and you're not a terrible daughter. And I was the one who insisted that you bring Sahara and Crystal here for the summer. They used to love coming here to visit and spending time with me," Ma Ray said.

"Yeah, but that was when they were young. Now they don't seem to want to have anything to do with any of us, let alone hang around us for any extended period of time. I suppose we're too old-fogey for them. We're not fun anymore. Ma, you know how teenagers are."

"Yeah, I know. You went through the exact same phase. You didn't want to be around me or your father. Every chance you got, you were off somewhere with your friends. There were times when you thought you were grown and you got a little too big for your britches. But we made it through all of that."

"We did. One might conclude that I'm reaping some of what I've sown. Talking back to you, staying out past the time you told me to be home. It's all coming back on me, big time. But in truth, I was nothing compared to Sahara and Crystal. Nothing. And they won't admit it to me, but I'm pretty sure they're having sex. Granted, I did have sex when I was in high school, going totally against everything you told me, I might add. But at least it was only with Quinton, my boyfriend, and not with God-only-knows who or how many guys. And yes, I admit there were times when I did just what I wanted regardless of the consequences." Lenora let out a sigh.

"I also believe Sahara and Crystal are experimenting with drugs even though I've spoken with them about this until I was blue in the face," Lenora said. "I've explained the dangers of sex before marriage as well as illegal drugs. Sahara just throws the hypocrisy of me taking prescription drugs for my depression back in my face. I just don't know, Ma. Where did I go wrong?

"Lenora, will you please stop beating yourself up. However we find ourselves now, the fact remains that we're here. And God is going to help us through this."

"But sex can be deadly in this day and age. When I was being rebellious, the worst I had to worry about was an unplanned pregnancy or contracting a venereal disease—VD. Now that AIDS is on the scene, people hardly ever mention VD anymore. People now get things that can kill them." Lenora sniffling began to subside. "Kill them."

"Well, every generation has something. My generation dealt with shame, being an outcast . . . sometimes ostracized—"

"And Sahara's report card this past school year contained nothing but Ds and Fs," Lenora said, quickly moving to a different topic. "She barely passed the eleventh grade, only because her Ds outweighed her Fs. I just knew she was going to have to go to summer school. Edmond and I told her she's never going to get into college with those grades. But she doesn't miss an opportunity to remind Edmond that he's merely her stepfather and she could care less what he has to say about anything. She doesn't care about her grades since she wants to drop out of school anyway. All she talks about is becoming a model. She thinks school is just a waste of her time. I don't know."

Ma Ray let out a slight chuckle. "Since she was knee-high to a grasshopper, Sahara has been playing dress up. That child would get into my closet and find my Sunday's best and my high heels. Oh, that child loves herself some shoes even more than I do. And at what . . . five-eleven, she's certainly tall enough and pretty enough to be a model. Got those high cheekbones from the Choctaw blood running in our family. But regardless, Sahara needs schooling."

"I know this. The problem is getting Sahara to see it. And Crystal, who has always been a bit envious and intrigued by her big sister, is being influenced by Sahara's bad actions. So, of course, whatever Sahara is doing, Crystal wants to do it, too. I blame a lot of this on Quinton. He has been such a deadbeat father pretty much all of their lives. He hasn't helped either one of them with their self-esteem *or* their daddy issues."

"For sure, Quinton hasn't been the best father. I get that he has his own issues, many of his own making. I've told him that very thing myself. But that's still no excuse for Sahara and Crystal to act out the way they have lately."

"Well, my poor Edmond has been doing all he can. He was the one who found that boot camp set-up for out-of-control teenagers. He strongly suggested that we think seriously about sending them to it or something like it."

"Oh, those girls don't need to be put in a boot camp. They're going to be okay. And just how *is* my son-in-law?" Ma Ray asked.

"He's fine. We'll be celebrating our tenth anniversary on the tenth of July. And of course, Nia has him completely wrapped around her little finger. I don't know how a two-year-old can wield so much power over a forty-year-old grown man. Edmond and Kyle are going fishing this Saturday and Nia keeps asking why she can't go with them. It's hard to explain to a toddler that her seven-year-old brother is not as much trouble as a two-year-old. Or that the boys need boy time together. Truthfully, Edmond has a hard time trying to take care of them when he takes them fishing at the same time. So he alternates between them."

"Then why don't you go so she can go with them?"

"Ma, you know I don't like to fish. I don't care to sit in that little canoe Edmond calls a boat, in the hot sun I might add, casting a line into the water just so I can further sit and watch absolutely nothing happen. Fishing is just not my thing."

"But it's something Edmond likes to do. And it's something the whole family can do together. I think you should go with them and make it a family affair."

"Well, I've told Edmond that I'm not interested, so that won't be happening. He and Kyle can go and have a great time. Nia will be all right. Maybe she and I will go shopping or something. We'll find something fun to do while they're gone."

"All right, daughter. Listen, I'm going to get off the phone now. I need to finish cooking breakfast. Then Sahara and I are going to have a nice little chat."

"Ma, look. I appreciate you wanting to help me and the girls and everything. But if this is too much on you—"

"Honey, no matter the weight of a thing, love can hold up anything. So don't you worry your pretty little head about me or these daughters of yours. Somehow or other, we'll find a breakthrough through all of this."

"Well, if you need me to come and get them, just let me know. I'm feeling better, now that I've gotten a little break. It was just getting too much, and I guess I broke down. But should they get too much out of hand with you, call me and I'll come and get them."

"Lenora, all I need for you to do now is to pray. One thing that I know for sure is that nothing is too hard for our God. Nothing. I've told you we're going to get through this together." Ma Ray suddenly stopped talking. "Good morning, Crystal . . . Morning, Sahara," Ma Ray said in a pleasant voice.

"Sahara's is there?" Lenora asked.

"Yes," Ma Ray said in an even tone.

"Well, put her on the phone. I want her to know that I don't appreciate that little stunt she just pulled. I don't appreciate it at all."

"Not a good idea," Ma Ray said, continuing to speak in a codelike manner.

"But Ma, she called me in the middle of the night . . . two o'clock in the morning, to be exact, telling me that you're pulling guns on folks while conveniently leaving out her devilment in all of it. Sahara needs to know things like this are not acceptable and they won't be tolerated." Lenora's phone beeped to indicate another call was coming in.

"And that will most certainly happen," Ma Ray said. "Sounds like someone is trying to get you."

Lenora looked at her caller ID. "It's your favorite son," she said.

"Okay. I'm going to get off now. Say hello to Beau for me."

"But, Ma—"

"I'll talk with you later, dear." Ma Ray hung up before Lenora could protest further.